# CHINA SEA

# CHINA SEA

STANTON SWAFFORD

KING HARBOR PRESS
REDONDO BEACH, CA

Published 2015
King Harbor Press
Redondo Beach, CA

ISBN: 978-0-9964028-0-4

Book design by Stacey Aaronson

Printed in the United States of America

*For my three sons,*
*Allan, Stanton & Louis*

*History does not repeat itself, but it rhymes.*

—MARK TWAIN

# 1

---

APRIL 1973

I FIRST MET THE SELF-TAUGHT RUSSIAN JAZZ PIANIST, Sasha Popov, in that dark, funky Manila bar on New Year's Eve 1974. I have at times wondered about Sasha and Flora, his lovely Filipina mistress. He'd needed to get out of the Philippines in a hurry, and I assisted him with his escape. I've also speculated on what became of Sasha's stunning Russian wife, who remained behind. So many lives left in the wake. One thing I do know: the Palestinian is dead. A Mossad double-agent gave the notorious sweet-tooth a birthday gift, a box of Belgian chocolates that contained a slow-acting poison. It took him several months to die.

But the saga had begun several months before that fateful December night in Manila.

I was living contentedly in San Francisco. The very idea of operating as an "illegal," under deep cover in Asia, was the furthest thing from my mind. Occasionally, and following a second or third cup of coffee at around ten o'clock in the morning, I would jump on the Hyde Street cable car outside my apartment building on Russian Hill and run down to the seamen's hall at the Embarcadero. I'd check the bulletin board to see if there were any interesting openings for a radioman on a cargo ship. Scores of American freighters in those days departed beneath the Golden Gate Bridge. I figured it would be only a matter of time before I signed on to one of them and, as a lark, sailed off into the sunset.

Invariably I'd leave that union hall the same as I entered it: jobless. I was never particularly unhappy about that outcome. Life, all in all, was good in the city.

It was around noon when I left the seamen's hall on a clear day in early April 1973, the day that altered the course of my life. I'd decided to linger over lunch at a favorite Italian restaurant in North Beach. I took a window table that overlooked Washington Square and the sundry action nearby. As I sometimes did those afternoons, I began to thumb through the help wanted ads in the *San Francisco Chronicle* over a second glass of Pinot Noir. And there it was. The classified ad from heaven!

```
We are a large shipping company headquartered
on the U.S. east coast, and we seek an
executive to manage our new office in East
Asia. Prior experience in Asia and fluency in
an Asian language would be a distinct
advantage. Send your resume to Monarch
Executive Staffing (with a post office box in
Baltimore) if you believe you might qualify
for this challenging position.
```

The irony wasn't lost. I had spent the morning perusing the openings in the seamen's hall for a gig on a freighter, and now here was this ad in the newspaper seeking an *executive*, no less, to run a shipping office somewhere in Asia. The portrayal of the successful candidate described me to a T—experience in Asia and fluent in an Asian language. I was fluent in two. My mood soared as I read and reread the ad.

I finished a double espresso, left a generous tip, and departed from the restaurant with a satisfied smile on my face. I took a stroll around the perimeter of the park and composed a brief resume in my mind. Later, for exercise, I walked up Union Street and back to the apartment. By the time I reached Hyde Street, I'd concocted a succinct resume and a pithy cover letter.

I typed up the letter and the resume that same afternoon in the apartment and slipped them into the mailbox before the last pickup.

LIFE IN THE CITY CONTINUED PLEASURABLY FOR THE NEXT few weeks. I was so content that spring that I discontinued those morning visits to the seamen's hall. The young woman I was dating and I took trips north—to Redwood country and canoeing on the Russian River. We drove to Napa for wine tasting and a jazz concert at Mondavi. Apropos of what was to follow, we would drive to Berkeley on a Sunday afternoon and have coffee at the original Peet's Coffee & Tea.

Then one day in May, six weeks after I had mailed that resume off to Baltimore and forgotten about the shipping job altogether, came the phone call.

"May I speak to Mr. Mancini, please?" the man asked, unsure who he was speaking with.

Damn. My credit card. I knew my payment was late again, and my check was not in the mail.

"Yeah. Speaking," I responded, annoyance in my tone.

"Hello, Roy. We received your resume a few weeks ago. And I do apologize for taking this long to get back to you," he said, now in a more conversational voice.

Relief.

That was the only time in my life I'd ever applied for a job so there was no doubt about the resume this fellow on the phone was referring to.

"Ah, yes. Monarch Staffing. Right?" a sudden enthusiasm in my tone.

"That's correct. My name is Brian Bradford." He sounded relieved that I had remembered the ad. He didn't have to go into a song and dance about who he was or which company he (supposedly) worked for. "The client has reviewed your resume. And on their behalf, I would like to meet with you." He paused for a second. "That is, if you're still interested in discussing the job."

My curiosity was piqued. "Sure. I'm interested. That's the position in Asia, right? Yes, let's meet. And did you mention a client? Who would that client be?"

"Well, as it happens, I'm in San Francisco for the day. Conducting some interviews out here. Can we meet later, before I leave town? Say, at two this afternoon?" He hesitated for a moment. "About the second question. Sorry, I can't reveal our client to you at this early stage. You understand."

We agreed on a place to meet. "Fine," I said. "I'll see you at two o'clock."

I was exultant. After I hung up the phone, I sat motionless for a minute, staring out the apartment's large bay window at a fleet of close-hauled sailboats as they beat out of Sausalito, and at a large outbound freighter as it sailed beneath the Golden Gate Bridge far below. "Yes!" I exclaimed, with a fist pump.

Brian Bradford and I met that afternoon in mid-May in the lobby of the Palace Hotel on Market Street. A perfectly nondescript location for a discreet meeting of this kind. It wasn't the Mark Hopkins or the Fairmont, where I might run into someone I knew, and where I'd have to make awkward introductions. I had arrived at the hotel early, at 1:30. I saw Brian stroll into the lobby at 1:58. He held on to a thin blue folder. He was about 5'10", a couple of inches shorter than I was. And he looked like a college professor with his tweed sports coat, knit tie, rimless glasses, longish hair, and droopy mustache. He did surprise me when he headed straight to where I was sitting. He had recognized me, as though he'd seen my photograph, which of course he had.

He ordered tea. I ordered an espresso. Brian stirred in milk and sugar, the way the English did it, as I recalled from an earlier life in colonial Singapore.

Brian explained that Monarch's client was a large ship owner which, by the way, owned more ships than any company in the world. He said that the client's headquarters was located somewhere on the U.S. east coast. He asked me if I would be willing to move back east in the event I was hired. "Sure," I replied, "I'd like that. I've never known the four seasons."

"Yes, the dogwood trees are beautiful this time of year." I didn't know what the devil a dogwood tree was, as a Californian who spent his childhood growing up in Singapore.

"So tell me, you have an interesting background, Roy. Spent your youth in Singapore I gather. How is it you speak Indonesian? You mentioned in your resume that you're fluent."

"My mother. And she still speaks to me in Indonesian, so I won't forget it."

"She's Indonesian?"

"That's right. From the Spice Islands, as they call them, the Moluccas. She's mixed Indonesian and Portuguese."

"I see. You grew up speaking Indonesian with your mother?"

"I grew up speaking the language with our nanny in Singapore, and with my mother. The only language I spoke as a child, with the nanny that is, was Indonesian. She didn't speak English. I'm told that the first words I ever spoke were in that language. Dad came home after a long business trip and I greeted him at the door in Indonesian."

"And your father—he's an American?"

"Yes. Native Californian. Grew up in San Luis Obispo, same place I did after we left Singapore."

"Oh? How old were you then? When you left."

"We moved when I was nine years old. There were riots in Singapore, and my father figured it was becoming too dangerous for us to live there. So we moved to California."

Brian sat back. And as he digested these personal details he looked at me.

"I can see, with your dark complexion and black hair, you could pass for any one of several nationalities. Overseas, no one would assume you were an American."

"I suppose that's true. That's been my experience anyway. People have mistaken me for Hawaiian, Brazilian, and Italian or Spanish."

"And you speak Chinese?"

"Yes, fluently. Mandarin. I studied it in Singapore as a kid and then at UH."

"The University of Hawaii?"

"Right."

The small talk continued for half an hour or so. Brian said

the client was impressed that I spoke those two Asian languages. They were also aware that six years earlier I had served as a radioman on a U.S. navy cargo ship. My master's degree in Chinese studies had been noted. I was young, in my mid-twenties. But he reckoned the client would overlook that, given my other assets. Brian appeared to be close to my own age, a few years older, same generation. We conversed comfortably, two young fellows discussing the prospect of a rather interesting overseas job. As the jargon goes in the trade, we established an easy rapport.

He eventually launched into some of the nitty gritty. The successful candidate, he said, would manage a new office somewhere in East Asia for the client, and from that location the manager would travel around the region, where he would check on various marketing opportunities and operational matters as the company's area representative. He continued, "You would be expected to transmit your strategic planning reports to company headquarters on a timely basis."

I was all ears, and on the edge of my seat. What more could I ask than getting hired, and paid, for the job of my dreams. Now, I'm a natural actor. A trait—little did I know— that would prove invaluable in my forthcoming career, a profession shrouded in mendacity. So I tempered my enthusiasm and queried Brian about mundane aspects of the job. I asked about the starting salary.

"I can't reveal that to you at this point," he said.

I asked when would I be expected to move to the east coast, and he replied that I'd begin work right away if I were selected for the position. All a little vague, but so what?

Abruptly Brian checked his watch and said he had a plane to catch. We'd been in the hotel lobby now for little over an hour and a half. He told me he'd be flying back to Baltimore that evening. He called for the bill and paid it in cash instead of signing. I suspected then that he hadn't been a guest at the hotel.

"Oh, by the way Roy, we'd like you to fill out this five-page form." He handed me the thin blue folder that had been lying in front of him during the entire meeting. "This will give our client a more comprehensive view of your background. Let's consider this your formal job application, shall we? Mail it to the post office box where you sent your resume. The Monarch address is listed here on the back."

THE LAST I SAW OF BRIAN THAT DAY WAS WHEN HE CLIMBED into a yellow cab on Market Street—no luggage, no briefcase, no notebook. He had conducted the entire interview without writing a single note. Of course the client had already done a preliminary background investigation by then. There had been no need for further note taking at that point in the game. And there was no office in Baltimore.

Wanderlust. It's in my DNA. After, say, sixty days I start to get an itch. I get restless. An itch to take off. To book a ticket to somewhere else. The idea of a job in Asia with a shipping company was appealing, to say the least.

I was twenty-six years old. The age, according to my theory, when a man experiences his greatest potency, a symmetry of his sexual and intellectual prowess. At nineteen, the young man is consumed during most of his waking hours with *sex*: fantasies and the real thing. By the age of fifty, that man has arrived at a mature state of emotional intelligence. But at twenty-six he's at that singular point in his life where those two curves, his virility and the intellectual, intersect. Think E=MC2. And that's where I was that year. On top of the world.

I realized now that I might have a consequential decision to make. Benign fate compelled me to pick up the newspaper that day in early April and skim through the classified ads. Then there had been the intriguing meeting with Brian Bradford. And I faced the probability that there would be a second interview. Brian had suggested as much. So I needed to decide. My choices: one, I would continue to express interest in the job in Asia, a ninety-degree turn in my life. Or, continue to live comfortably on Russian Hill—where I enjoyed a bracing life in my favorite city in the world. I had sufficient savings from my grandfather's will to keep me going for a while.

The phone call in mid-June came in the evening, before dinner, as I relaxed at home with a chilled glass of Napa Valley Chardonnay, taking in the view of headlights moving across the Golden Gate Bridge. Roberta Flack's new album, *Killing Me Softly*, played in the background. Another perfect evening in paradise.

Moments before the phone rang, I had been reflecting on my relationship with my father and the fact that we had not communicated with each other for the past two years. The last time we spoke he had expressed his utter disappointment in me because I had chosen not to go to work for him at his retail lumber yard. A case of my independent disposition clashing with his Taurean possessiveness. He would forever believe that it was a son's duty to follow in his father's footsteps. Especially so if the father was a small business owner and needed a son to perpetuate his legacy. I did try to explain to him that I had my own life to live, and I returned to Honolulu where I had been accepted for a master's program at the university.

"Hello, is this Roy Mancini?" said the buttoned-down voice. I knew it right away. The second interview.

I cleared my voice and asked with equal gravity, "Yes. Who is this?"

"My name is . . . (and for the life of me I can't remember his name). I'm a colleague of Mr. Bradford's. I understand the two of you met a little over a month ago." Part statement, part query. He needed to make sure he had the right person on the line before continuing the conversation. "You mailed us a job application."

"Ah, yes sir. That's right. I did meet Brian. He mentioned that someone might call."

"Good to catch you in, Roy. I'm in San Francisco today. Is this a convenient time for us to talk?"

"Sure is. What's up?"

"I'd like to meet with you tomorrow morning. I have a flight out of here later in the afternoon. I hope that works for you." A hint of duress from his end. Tomorrow morning. Take it or leave it.

"Tomorrow works fine. Where would you like to meet?"

He gave me the name of his hotel and the room number. I committed them to memory, and we agreed to meet at eleven o'clock the next morning. He told me to pass through the lobby and go right to his room and knock on the door.

The hotel was on Geary, about a block from Union Square. I wore my only suit, dark blue, a pinstriped dress shirt with buttons at the cuffs (never cufflinks), and a blue and white striped necktie. Blue is the best color to wear to a job interview. It keeps everything cool.

I passed through the lobby, and knocked on the door at eleven o'clock. The man opened the door after letting a few moments pass as he peeked through the fisheye, then he invited me in. He asked me to take a seat as he made an indifferent effort to crack a thin smile. His handshake was like iron, firmer than necessary. I never have cared for that pretentious code of *machismo*. He placed the Do Not Disturb sign on the door before he closed and locked it with the deadbolt.

As I said, I can't remember the man's name. Or much about him. I don't think we ever met again. He was in his late thirties, early forties. He wore a narrow, solid black tie, a starched white dress shirt, and a large class ring. His pants were dark and pleated. I also noticed his shoes. They were black and military. I should know. He had a cleanly shaved head, I guessed to disguise a premature hair loss, and a pale, cheerless face. I'd seen no-nonsense guys like this guarding U.S. embassies.

There wasn't any luggage in the room that I could see. No toiletries in the bathroom. He didn't appear to be staying at the hotel. His only personal item was a briefcase with brass locks.

"Roy," he began after thirty seconds of light conversation, "it appears you didn't go from high school right on to college."

"That's right."

"Just curious. Any particular reason?"

"My grades for the most part. I had so much fun in high school—I played trumpet in the jazz band, competed as the number one seed on the tennis team, raced a sailboat in regattas all over California, and surfed up and down the coast." I paused to think of anything else I could add. "I played in chess tournaments too. Something had to give. It was my grades. They sucked. That's what my father said." I recalled the stern lecture Dad gave me in my senior year. "He suggested I enlist. He was in the marine corps during the war."

"All right. That clears that up." He glanced at some notes in his hand.

Looking up and making eye contact he asked, "Tell me, Roy, about any regrets that you've had in life."

"Regrets?"

"Yes, you know, regrets. Everyone's had some regrets."

There was a long silence before I answered. "I can't think of any. Is having regrets in life a job qualification?"

He winced.

The interview was more like an interrogation. All business. No laughs. There was none of the quick rapport that I had established with Brian over a month earlier.

I became gradually more suspicious during this two-hour encounter. He dug deep into my personal life, asking intimate questions that could not have had much to do with a job in shipping. For example, he wanted to know how often I had consorted with prostitutes in the bars of Olongapo City when my ship docked in Subic Bay. By the end of this long, tedious session, I had reached the conclusion that this job was not as they had described it in the *Chronicle*. The underlying rigmarole was giving me pause. I smelled a rat. At last he stood up and told me to expect another call from someone, as he put it, "higher up the food chain."

"And we would like you to fill out this questionnaire." He handed me a twenty page file with the title Personal History Statement. "Complete this and return it to the Baltimore post office box ASAP. Been nice meeting you."

"And how long will that be?" I asked, before moving toward the door, "until the next interview?"

"Oh, we'll be in touch," he replied as he unlocked and opened the door for me. "Be sure to fill out and return the PHS. Have a nice day."

# 2

---

JULY 1973

THE THIRD INTERVIEW, THE ONE WITH PETE WRIGHT, took place a month later in a second-rate motel room in South San Francisco, near the airport. Through the slightly open window I could hear the roar of planes taking off and landing every five minutes or so.

The first thing I remember was that Pete was annoyed when he met me at the door. As he explained it, he had flown in from Tokyo that morning, and upon opening his suitcase he found that the two duty-free bottles he had packed had collided, shattered, and drenched the contents of the suitcase with scotch whiskey. In lieu of a fresh change of clothes, he appeared to wear the same rumpled dress shirt and loosened necktie he had worn on the long flight from Japan. He at last gathered his composure, greeted me politely, and asked me to take a seat. I saw a copy of my Personal History Statement laid out on a desk.

I would describe my first impression of Pete Wright as one

of intimidating self-assurance, like a light heavyweight prize fighter, or a district attorney. He had black, crew-cut hair and intense, chiseled facial features. He was one of those people who might be fifty but is mistaken for forty. His initial displeasure had made him appear rather fierce. You wanted him on your side. He was someone you did not want to tangle with.

"Have you wondered who we are, Roy?" This was his first comment to me as we took our seats. He held my Personal History Statement in one hand. I was speechless for a moment. Of course I had been curious about who they were ever since that bizarre second interview. I had a hunch by now they were not ship owners that wanted to hire some rookie to represent them in the Far East. I replied that I did have a sense things were not as they first appeared.

"That's the way we structure this series of interviews. By now, a smart guy is supposed to suspect that the whole thing is a ruse. If he hasn't been clever enough to figure that out by now, then we don't need him in the Institute."

Well, there wasn't much I could add to that. I knew now my gut feeling that the process had been a subterfuge had been right. With this out of the way, he asked me a few personal questions. He asked which *one* person had had the greatest influence on my life. I told him, without hesitation, that it had been my late grandfather, and I gave him the reasons. Papa, as we called Lorenzo Mancini, had trained me from an early age in the two sports in which I had excelled: sailboat racing and tennis. He'd encouraged my love of music, had given me my first trumpet, and introduced me to the music of Miles Davis. He'd stimulated my intellectual curiosity and love of reading. And, he had taught me how to play poker and a good game of chess. Wright seemed satisfied.

"Let me ask you," he continued, "do you have a living hero you can relate to?"

"Yes. That would be Sammy Davis Jr."

"Oh ... why?"

"His incredible talent." I spread my hands and shrugged in a gesture of amazement.

"Interesting. Let's move on," he said. "We're running a background investigation on you." He raised the questionnaire that he held. "It's almost complete. Some of your friends and family may inform you that the FBI interviewed them." I must have gaped at that. "I can tell you at this point, though, that you have provisional Top Secret clearance. What I'm about to tell you falls under that category. You are not to reveal this discussion to anyone—your family, your girlfriend, anyone at all."

"Yes, sir, I understand."

"That's good. Because if you don't agree, we can end this conversation right here and now. You can leave and we forget we ever met."

I nodded and remarked that I was here because I was intrigued. The notion of intelligence work, if that's what it was, appealed to me. I must have stammered in my eagerness to reassure him. He raised his hand somewhere in mid-sentence and said okay, he got the picture.

He continued. "Our organization, the Institute, is the clandestine intelligence task force of the Department of Defense." He paused to let that sink in. "In the chain of command, we report to the Joint Chiefs of Staff. I'm an army colonel, and I'm the Institute's operations officer."

"Oh, so you're from the Pentagon?"

"We don't work at the Pentagon. We're outside-the-Beltway. In fact, you can count on the fingers of one hand the number of people in the Pentagon who even know we exist. The secretary of defense, of course, and very few others.

"Our overseas bureaus are commanded by military officers. We don't permit those officers to engage as spies. A matter of plausible denial. Are you with me?"

I nodded, speechless and comprehending little of what he was describing.

"You are being considered for a job as a case officer. We plan to insert you into a location somewhere in East Asia. We think you'll blend in. That part of the story they've fed you is true." He stared at me with raised eyebrows, as though asking me to comment. I pondered for a moment.

At last I asked him what a case officer did. Was it dangerous? I sort of hoped it might be.

"No. It's not particularly dangerous. You'll handle foreign agents. They'll do the dangerous work. You will manage an important part of your agent's life."

I nodded as if I understood. At this point it sounded like a movie I'd seen starring Richard Burton.

"I will recommend to the commanding officer of the Institute that we invite you back for a final interview. Management knows about you because of your last two interviews and from the background trace. They do want to meet you. When can you leave for Washington?"

A surge of adrenalin. "I'm free to leave soon," I replied. My voice was strained all of a sudden. "Say within a week."

"Fine. Here's a check." He withdrew an unsealed envelope from his attaché case and handed it to me. "Purchase a one-way ticket to Dulles. We'll issue your return ticket on arrival. Meet the Institute's managers. Sign a few agreements. There will be an officer to guide you through all of it. This won't take you more than three days. Afterwards you'll fly back to San Francisco, say your goodbyes, cancel your lease agreement, so on and so forth. Then you return to the Washington area and begin your training."

I looked at the $500 check in my hand, issued to me by Monarch Executive Staffing. This was all coming fast. Pack up and leave San Francisco within a week. Move to Washington D.C. New places and new faces.

"You know, Roy, you would be the youngest case officer we've ever hired. Just twenty-six, right? But in your case, we'll make an exception. You have the background. And leave it at that." He looked at me, cocking his head to one side. Again, he waited for me to comment.

"I do have one question, Colonel Wright."

"Shoot."

"Why did you claim you were the largest ship owner in the world?"

"Well, that describes the United States navy. And the navy is one of our most important customers." He chuckled at this double entendre. "We expect you'll be involved in clandestine maritime operations. Your experience on that freighter, as a radioman, is one factor." They knew, of course, about my two years of active duty on a navy cargo ship, the *USNS Wake Forest*. I wondered if they had learned of my more recent visits to the seamen's union hall. They had.

"Oh, and by the way, Roy, one requirement for this particular position is that you remain single. We anticipate you'll travel a lot. No time, really, for any kind of family life. Any plans to get married in the near future?"

"No, not any time soon." And there it was. We had a deal.

We made arrangements that I would phone him as soon as

I had my flight details. We parted on that note and agreed to meet again in a few days. As we stood up, he told me to call him Pete. He explained that we never refer to anyone in the Institute by military rank.

# 3

JULY 1973

I CALLED PETE WRIGHT COLLECT FROM A PAY PHONE, AS instructed. He confirmed that Brian Bradford would meet me at the airport and get me checked in to a hotel. I would meet the managers the following morning. I should pack light because I would fly right back to San Francisco.

Brian met me and greeted me with a wide smile and hearty "welcome aboard." As we drove to the hotel in Alexandria, he revealed his true name and position to me. He was Gus Pomeroy, the Institute's East Asia desk officer.

Those were the most exhilarating two or three days I had ever spent in my life. I met the Institute's senior leadership, the management team, around a large oval conference table at the Monarch office. This company, Monarch Executive Staffing, was established solely for the purpose of recruiting civilians to work undercover as case officers. It was one of ten or so front companies used by the Institute throughout the world. I was not invited to the Springfield headquarters during this trip.

That would come months later, after I had completed my training.

The commanding officer, Frank DuPont, was a major general in the air force. He, like everyone else in the room, wore a civilian suit and was introduced *sans* military rank. DuPont was a stocky, bald, unthreatening figure. He smiled easily. There was an air of low-intensity good cheer about him. He smoked a cigar throughout the meeting.

The CO led off by welcoming me with a handshake and a pat on the shoulder. He introduced me to the others who were standing around the table. There was no way for me to determine who was civilian and who was military. When we took our seats, Pete Wright sat, impassively, to Frank DuPont's left. I sat at the opposite end of the table.

Tom Hiatt, the senior civilian and deputy director of the Institute, sat to the CO's right. Hiatt was, because of his background, almost a coequal of General DuPont, number two in the Institute's pecking order. Hiatt had been a high-ranking CIA field officer who organized an assortment of covert plots in the 1950s and 60s. I learned later that he specialized in orchestrating military coups and popular revolutions across the Middle East during those twenty years, in cahoots with the British SIS. Rumor had it that he'd plotted an assassination or two back in the day, before that sort of thing was prohibited by law. The legend around the office was that after retiring from the Agency, Hiatt had been offered a sinecure with a major American oil company in one of the Arab states. He'd turned the job down to help set up the Institute and to become the task force's permanent number two man. Once a spook always a spook, someone said.

Like many of the Agency honchos of that era, Tom Hiatt

was Ivy League. Yale or Dartmouth. He didn't look the part. He was no suave 007 playboy. He stood well under six feet. He was tubby, rather crabbed, and wore black horn-rimmed glasses that partially disguised the discolored bags under his eyes. He had a full walrus mustache which, like his thinning hair, had turned to gray. During the entire meeting Hiatt maintained an ill-humored frown. He didn't ask me a single question; he simply puttered with his unlit black briar pipe and stared at me. His expression shouted out that this rookie, meaning me, had yet to prove himself. Which, of course, was true.

The first question that the general asked me was what news magazines I read. I replied that I read *The Economist*. He nodded, indicating that he was satisfied with that answer. I recall that I couldn't hold a cup of coffee without my hand shaking. So after one tentative sip, I left it untouched. My case of stage fright wasn't soothed by the demeanor of Tom Hiatt.

Someone at the table asked me what I thought of the Vietnam War, which at that time in July 1973 was supposed to have wound down. I replied that it was a civil war involving Vietnamese nationalists, and that we had made a large mistake getting mixed up in it. The CO commented that he agreed with me. The five or six others at the table nodded.

"We don't do tactical intelligence," the CO said, referring I guessed to Vietnam. "The Institute concentrates on the big picture: Red China. The Soviets. Warsaw Pact. North Korea. In a word, we collect *strategic* intelligence." He paused to take a puff on his cigar and blow a smoke ring skyward. I watched it rise to the ceiling, intact. "We are hiring you, Roy, to help set up a maritime humint operation in Southeast Asia. As a case officer, you will recruit clandestine agents to collect actionable strategic intelligence for our armed forces, mainly the navy. With me so far?"

"Yes, sir."

"You will live and travel undercover in foreign countries. We understand you speak the languages in some of those places." He paused again to take a large draw on his cigar and to blow a cloud of smoke overhead.

The room was now thick with aromatic smoke. I saw Tom Hiatt stuff a pipe cleaner into the stem of his unlit pipe and go through the motions of cleaning it, jamming it in and out, and appearing bored to distraction.

The other men around the table, with the exception of Hiatt, then took turns asking me the odd softball question or two.

"I understand you'll return to San Francisco in a couple of days," DuPont said. "Nice city. And let me admonish you that everything discussed here is classified at a high level. Before you leave this office today we'll have you sign off on that." The general then stood up and snuffed out his pungent cigar in the ashtray in front of him. We all stood, and I shook hands with everyone.

I was left in the office with a pretty, smartly dressed young woman, about my age, who I learned was a marine corps captain working undercover as Monarch's office manager. Her name was Margie. She also serviced the post office box in Baltimore where I had mailed my resume and those two questionnaires. By now Margie would have known every intimate detail of my personal life.

There were half a dozen documents and agreements to sign, including a declaration that I would never reveal the Institute's secrets. The small print described the punishment I could receive, *in camera*, if I ever violated the Espionage Act and disclosed my activities to anyone outside the Institute. And there was a contract.

Margie pointed to the pages and said, "I'm not sure if they explained this to you in your meeting now with the brass, but you are *not* being hired as an employee of the United States Government, Roy. We are engaging you as a contractor. You're off the books."

I pondered that for a moment. "Oh? What does that mean?"

"Plausible denial for the Institute. You will be paid a salary that is equivalent to GS-13 to start. We call it CS-13. The contract is for seven years."

"Seven years?" I said.

"Yes. That's the legal limit for any contract written up in the United States. A contract that binds a person to someone else for over seven years is considered slavery. Seven years is the best we can do."

"Kind of like a seven-year itch?"

"Well, you can always renew your vows." She smiled at me.

I studied the contract for a few minutes. It was the final document on the pile in front of me. It did spell out that I was not a U.S. Government employee in any way, shape, or form, with all the ramifications (and lack of benefits) that entailed. I shrugged and signed on the dotted line. The CS-13 pay was, I soon learned, more than adequate for an unmarried, entry-level spook.

"Tonight you have a date with a psychiatrist, Roy," she said after I had finished signing everything.

"A shrink?"

"It's the final requisite. Dr. Rosen is a retired military doctor. He's cleared with the Institute. So you need to be up-front with him. He knows why you're here. His office is in his home in Georgetown. I'll drive you there. And we'll have dinner afterwards."

Well, if the questions asked by my earlier interviewers were intimate, this meeting with Dr. Rosen in his comfortable Georgetown home was over the top. Topics included sexual preference, drugs, masturbation, whoring around overseas, my propensity for stealing secrets (or not), and my strained relationship with my father. I wondered if Margie received a copy of the transcript. For around one hour of the three-hour session, he had me hooked up to a polygraph machine. At last, to my relief, he told me we were finished.

Margie waited outside and met me when it was over. She took me to dinner nearby at one of D.C.'s hot spots on M Street. I started the evening off with a chilled double Polish vodka, no ice. Margie liked her red wine.

"I'm not sure I passed," I remarked. I was relieved to be dining alone with Margie, and at the same time unnerved by the earlier session with Rosen.

"Everybody feels that way after their meeting with the shrink," she replied with a shrug. "Most of our case officer candidates pass the test."

"And some don't?"

"Yes, but it's rare." She looked at me coyly over her wine glass. "By the time you get this far in the process, Roy, it's almost certain you've been hired."

The next morning Margie handed me a roundtrip ticket for Dulles/SFO/Dulles, with the return date in one week. I had apparently passed the test of the night before. I was on the team. And I was going to work as an Institute case officer.

I rode a taxi alone to the airport, then I had a couple of beers and dinner at a bar and considered my situation.

I had reached that proverbial fork in the road and made a fateful choice. I would leave my comfortable San Francisco life behind.

# 4

---

JANUARY 1974

I WAS DEEP IN A DREAM WHEN THE INCESSANT RINGING
started. There followed a pounding on the door. I glanced
at the clock on the bedside table. It was a few minutes past
two o'clock in the morning.

"Who is it?" I called, as I rolled out of bed.

"Hotel security. Open the door, Mr. Kentfield." I had used
the assumed name when I'd checked in to the hotel.

I squinted through the peephole and saw a hand holding
up a badge of some kind. As I unchained and unlocked the
door and began to turn the knob, the door thrust open
violently.

Two men dressed in black from head to toe shoved me
back into the room. One of them, the taller one, grabbed me
by the arms and handcuffed me with plastic strips behind my
back. The other one placed duct tape over my mouth and
pulled a hood over my head. I could barely breathe through
my nose. They'd found my overcoat and wrapped it around

me, buttoning it up like a straitjacket. I was then frog marched down the long hall. We descended to the ground floor in a freight elevator and exited the hotel into a back alley. There they pushed me into the rear seat of a car and we drove off at high speed. We must have driven for fifteen minutes before we stopped and they led me into a dimly lit warehouse. It was eerily quiet, no sound of traffic. Neither man had said a word.

They removed my hood, the gag, the straitjacket, and handcuffs after we entered a room. They left their black ski masks on. The room was around ten feet square. A dim yellow lightbulb in the center of the ceiling provided illumination. The one scarred wooden table with three folding chairs was placed in the center of the room. Otherwise, the room was bare and windowless. And unheated. I sat on one side of the table and the two hooded thugs sat opposite facing me. I could just make out their eyes through the slits.

I had not uttered a word. Rather I'd done some sober planning during the ride from the hotel, conjuring up a cover story for the impending interrogation. They allowed me to slip my overcoat back on.

After we were seated at the cigarette-stained table, the tall one began in accented English. "You listen to me. We can do this the easy way. Or . . ." I remained silent, staring straight ahead. "You tell us who you are and what you've been doing here the past two days. Trust me, we're going to find out one way or the other. Clear enough?"

I muttered that it was clear.

"I can't hear you," he shouted behind his black hood.

"Yes, that's clear. I can explain," I replied, raising my voice.

"We're listening, asshole," the shorter one chimed in, hands folded in front of him on the table.

"Okay, then. Listen. I arrived here two days ago to meet a woman. I wrote love letters to her for months. My pen pal." They looked at each other. I had composed this line during the fifteen minutes it had taken to drive from the hotel to the warehouse. "I've spent the last two days waiting to meet her. She never showed up."

Silence. They stared at me. "And where were you supposed to meet this 'pen pal'?" one of them asked, using his fingers as quotation marks.

I explained that she and I had agreed to meet each other at a well-known restaurant five blocks from my hotel. I had mailed her a photograph in one of my letters. She would have recognized me.

"I waited, off and on, for two days inside that restaurant. She never arrived. And never tried to contact me at the hotel either. I think maybe she's married. She got cold feet." The two stifled guffaws behind their hoods. They seemed amused by my "cold feet" idiom.

"What's her name? Address?" the shorter one demanded. He slapped one hand on the table top. The other one held a pen, preparing to write my answer on his notepad.

"Her name is Anastasia Molotov. I can't remember her address. I didn't think I'd need it. And, you know, if she really is married, then it probably isn't her true address anyway. Right?"

"No. I think that is bullshit story. You're an American spy," the tall one shouted. "Why do we know this? We saw you meet your agent in that bar next to the public market yesterday afternoon." He folded his arms over his chest. "Don't deny it, *Mister Kentfield*, we've been following you from the day you arrived. Explain."

So they'd had me under surveillance and they had

watched me make the meeting the day before with the tall man. He passed me information in a brown envelope as we sat at the bar and drank a beer together. The meeting lasted no more than ten minutes. We'd left the bar separately.

"Look, I was depressed. I'd flown all this way to meet Anastasia. She'd stood me up. A no-show. I mean, what more can I say. I planned to marry this woman. Arrange her visa. We've been writing to each other for, let's see, about three months."

I was winging it, improvising a solo in an unfamiliar key. "I found a saloon near the market. I needed to have a few drinks, drown my sorrows. And I met this guy, a stranger, sitting at the bar. I never did get his name. I wanted to talk to someone, practice my Russian." I hesitated here before I said in a quiet voice, "Speaking Russian won't do me much good now. I've lost Anastasia." I made a gesture of throwing my arms up in frustration.

The interrogation continued for half an hour. The two thugs tried their best to trip me up. I stuck to my story, a cover-within-a-cover. At last the tall one looked at his partner and gave an almost imperceptible nod. And at that point they both tore off their hoods. Right away I recognized these two Green Berets from the school. I'd seen both of them playing liar's dice and telling war stories at the bar in the Officers' Club.

"Hey, I know you guys." I grinned with relief. They snickered.

"Well done, Mr. Mancini. You win this round." The taller one reached across the table and shook my hand. The two-day tradecraft exercise in Boston was over with. We conducted a brief postmortem and they drove me back to the hotel. I graduated from the spook school one month later with highest honors.

# 5

---

M Y OP PLAN RECOMMENDED THAT I OPERATE overseas under commercial cover. That is, I would not work out of an embassy or a military base as most of our case officers did under official cover. The advantage in my non-official cover was that I would not be working under the thumb of the military officer I reported to. Being the independent character I am, that appealed to me on the face of it. The downside was that if ever I was apprehended in a foreign country, I could not claim diplomatic immunity and seek refuge in a U.S. embassy or at an American military base. Worst case, the Institute would deny knowing who I was and what I was up to. I'd be up the creek without a friend if ever I was caught in the act. The very definition of plausible denial.

We met to discuss my cover in August three days after I'd put the finishing touches on the operation plan. There were five of us at the long, polished mahogany conference table:

Tom Hiatt, Frank DuPont, Pete Wright, Gus Pomeroy, and me.

Hiatt removed a briar pipe from his jacket pocket and started to poke at it with a fresh pipe cleaner. We all looked at him, waiting for him to begin.

"All right, Mancini," he said at last. "We've studied this happy horseshit you call an op plan. Explain it to us. Your mission, we all know, is to collect intelligence on the naval order of battle in Red China, the Russian Far East, and North Korea. A large area. I don't see here how you can accomplish that. Proceed."

"My plan is to live and work in Southeast Asia as a businessman." I glanced at my notes. "I'll reside and do business in a country under my true name. I've selected the country, and a town, where I can take up residence and operate a trading company. Buying and selling coffee beans. My choice of the country is geographic." I paused for effect. "I've selected Malaysia. Its location is central to the ports on the South China Sea and the Indian Ocean littoral where I'll spot, recruit, and run my agents. Now, when I meet my agents and run them into the denied areas, I'll operate under a separate cover. I'll switch to a different identity from the one I use in the coffee business in Malaysia."

"Stop right there. Let's clarify this," Tom Hiatt shot back at me, waving his pipe in front of him. "You'll travel from your country of residence, let's say Malaysia, to the countries where you'll conduct clandestine meetings using two identities. How and when will you make the switch—from one cover to the other?"

"I'll exit Malaysia using my true name. And I'll use my true name clearing immigration controls at my destination. I'll also conduct my legal activity, the coffee trading business, using my true name. I'll likely run that business out of a hotel room. In any given day, I could be changing identities two or three times—from coffee trader to clandestine operator, and back again."

General DuPont rolled an unlit cigar between his fingers, deep in thought.

"Explain this in more detail, Roy," he said, breaking his silence.

"Sir, I'll register a coffee trading company in Malacca and arrange the trade finance there through a Malaysian bank."

Tom Hiatt put up his hand and looked over at a skeptical Pete Wright and then back at me. "Hold it. Let's go back. Explain some of these concepts to everyone. Don't be vague. First off: Why coffee? What kind of trade finance are we talking about?"

"The reason I chose to be a coffee trader is because all the countries in my area are either producers of coffee beans or consumers of coffee. I can travel to any producer country in Asia and Africa and pose as a buyer of coffee beans. And I can sell those beans to the roasters in the consumer countries. Coffee is one commodity that can serve as a commercial cover anywhere in the world." I looked across the table at Pete Wright. He gave a nod of approval in my direction. I avoided Hiatt's menacing gaze.

"Roy," Frank DuPont cut in. "Explain to me how you plan to finance this, uh, coffee business. You mentioned something about Malaysian banking."

"Right. We'll name our company Coffee Traders International, CTI for short. A customer, that is a roaster, places his order for beans with CTI. I will have him open a letter of credit to us through our bank in Malacca. Say the value of his bean order is $50,000. And the beans cost us $42,000." I paused to let that sink in.

"That's a sixteen percent profit," Hiatt said after poking on his calculator.

"Yes. It will all be transacted through our bank with letters of credit. We collect $50,000 from our customer after the beans have been shipped. Soon after that, we pay the supplier, say in Jakarta, $42,000. We have a profit, in this example, of $8,000."

Everyone at the table nodded. Tom Hiatt stared at the job he was performing on his pipe.

"Sounds good." Frank DuPont looked at me and asked, "So how much do you know about the coffee business?"

"There are Arabica beans and there are Robusta beans. Arabica is grown in the mountains of Indonesia and is higher priced. It tastes great without being blended. Robusta is shipped in bulk to the multinationals, and it's used for blending the cheaper brands of coffee. The rot-gut they serve you in diners. It has a bitter taste. I won't waste my time trading Robusta. I'll specialize in Arabica."

"What now, *gourmet coffee*?" Pete Wright quipped. Everyone, except me, chuckled thinking Pete had made a joke.

"That's right, Pete," I replied, making eye contact with each of them in turn.

"Sounds like you've done your homework on the coffee trade," remarked Tom Hiatt after everybody had stopped the chuckling.

"Yes, I have enough knowledge to get this business started, enough to convince a bean seller, a customer, and a banker."

"Another question about your commercial cover, Roy," Frank said. "Name the locations in your area where you'll travel for this Arabica coffee business."

"I'll buy the beans in the Indonesian islands of Java, Bali, Sumatra, and Sulawesi. I speak the language." I smiled to myself, imagining a career visiting those exotic places. "I can contact the buyers in any other country in Asia where I need to conduct my undercover clandestine work."

"And the profits that accumulate in that bank account in Malaysia?" asked Pete Wright.

"I'll use those profits to fund my activity in the region. Our legitimate coffee business will help finance the clandestine intelligence effort."

Tom Hiatt said, "Let's move on. Tell us about the cover you'll use for the clandestine meetings and for running your agents."

"I'll set up a maritime research company and register it in Hong Kong. The company will conduct port studies. I'll approach a lead, a *potential* clandestine agent, with an offer to work for me as a freelance representative. I plan to offer him a financial incentive of a couple hundred dollars or so if he reports on what he observes in various ports. At first I'll ask him to report innocent, unclassified information: cargoes handled, civilian shipyard activity, equipment improvements, and so forth. Eventually, after I have him hooked, I'll recruit him to work for us in the denied areas. I'll teach him tradecraft and train him on how to use a camera without being caught. My clandestine agents will for the most part be foreign merchant marine officers whose ships load or discharge cargoes in the USSR, in Communist China, North Korea, and the Warsaw Pact countries." I paused to let the concept sink in, staring at Tom Hiatt. "I'll get them used to the joy of being paid well for their efforts. We can expect in most cases an agent's motivation will be financial gain."

Tom Hiatt looked at me with, for the first time, an approving grin. Frank DuPont and Pete Wright sorted through the notes they had been scribbling on the margins of my thirty-page op plan; Gus Pomeroy leaned back in his chair and stared at the ceiling. I sipped some water out of a bottle.

Frank DuPont placed the tips of his ten fingers together as he sat back in his chair and looked straight at me. He was silent for a moment. And then he struck a match, rolled the flame around the end of a fresh cigar, and lit up.

"Why have you selected Malacca," he finally asked behind a cloud of smoke, "of all places in Asia, to live and work?"

"I would be inconspicuous in Malacca. I could operate my coffee bean business out of my home and under the radar of the Malaysian Special Branch. It's a small city. Some call it a 'sleepy hollow.' I'd be comfortable operating in that milieu."

I neglected to mention that I had sailed from Singapore to that coastal town with my father during a school holiday when I was a child. Old-world and multicultural Malacca had left a lasting impression on me over the years.

There was no need to discuss this personal reminiscence, or my fascination with Malacca's beguiling 600-year history. Rather I needed to describe how the city was strategically located for the Institute's purposes.

"The city's location is at the center of Southeast Asia. It's a perfect place to set up shop."

Tom Hiatt was the first to respond. "Malacca *is* a rather surprising choice, Roy. It's a sleepy little town. I've passed through it once or twice. Good local food as I recall. Any rate, I think you've made your case. I can go along with it." He stuffed his briar pipe into the side pocket of his jacket, as a final point, and looked to his left at Frank DuPont.

"Yes, a slow-paced town like Malacca would be a fitting place to organize your commercial cover activity. You don't need to operate your trading business in a port city like Singapore where you'll be simultaneously running agents under a separate cover. I can see the benefit of keeping the two apart," Frank said. And with a stern demeanor he continued. "But listen, Roy." He pointed a wooden matchstick at me. "You have got to stay in close contact with your boss, Lieutenant Commander Steve McCoy. Do I make myself clear? You don't go running around Asia roughshod without keeping McCoy informed."

"My plan, Frank, is to pass through Singapore every time I take off and return from a mission. And during the stopover I'll meet with Mr. McCoy. He can give me instructions and I can brief him on my activities at those frequent meetings."

Gus Pomeroy lightened things up. "You'll work well with your boss, Mancini. He plays clarinet."

"All right," the CO continued, leaning forward in his chair. "Malacca it is. Thank you, Roy, for your well-researched op plan." He looked at each of us in turn. "We need to make a decision today. The new director of Naval Intelligence is on my back to provide a humint capability in that area. I have a meeting scheduled with him this Friday. So if you'll leave the room now, Roy, I need to discuss all this with Tom, Pete, and Gus. And we'll come to a decision. Stand by at your desk in case we need to clarify anything with you."

After an hour Frank's assistant, an air force master sergeant in mufti, came to my office and asked me to follow him back to the conference room. I entered and Frank asked me to take a seat.

"We've decided to sign off on your op plan," the general

started out. Each of the others nodded. Gus gave a thumbs up. "In theory it's well written. But the execution is going to be challenging. You will be spending a whole lot of time in airplanes, hotels, and safe houses, juggling your identities. It's vital that you keep all your cover stories and aliases straight and not let them tie you up in knots. Any rate, I will brief Admiral Zinger on the plan when I meet with him on Friday. Meanwhile, we want you to go to the Panama Canal. You need to get comfortable boarding foreign cargo ships. And there's no better place to do that than in the Canal Zone. We have an army officer down there, Major Sommers. You'll check in with him and spend a month undercover as a U.S. Customs officer trainee. That cover will allow you to board any ship that transits the Canal. Any questions about that?"

"Yes, sir. When do I leave?"

"Book a commercial flight to Panama" Pete Wright replied. "Take the train from Panama City to Cristobal. That's over on the Atlantic side of the Canal. We'll have Sommers meet you at the train station and get you settled in."

The meeting was adjourned. Gus and I walked back to his office.

"A warning, Roy. Sommers won't win any prizes as 'Mister Geniality,'" Gus said as we sat at our desks in his office. "Pete Wright ordered him up here for a verbal reprimand sometime last year. I don't know why he's still with the Institute, but you'll need to go along and *get* along with him. He'll be your boss for a month."

"Thanks for the heads up, Gus. What's his problem?"

"Seems Colonel Wright and Major Sommers have a personality conflict. And given their respective ranks, the colonel has the personality and the major has the conflict."

# 6

SEPTEMBER 1974

I TRAVELED TO PANAMA USING A PSEUDONYM, LOUIS Francisco, and a freshly minted passport in that name.

At the airport I grabbed a taxi that took me to the squalid Panama City train station, just in time to hop aboard an eastbound train. The two-hour trip along the length of the Canal was uneventful.

The train chugged in to the Cristobal station in the late afternoon. The American zone. At that time, in the mid-1970s, the Panama Canal was a United States territory administered by the Panama Canal Company. That company employed scores of Americans to run the Canal and various and sundry activities inside the Zone.

Major Jonathan Sommers was undercover as the military liaison officer to the Panama Canal Company. Which meant he had little or nothing to do except gaze out his window at the ships lining up in the anchorage waiting to transit the Canal from the Atlantic to the Pacific. The Institute provided him and his wife, Julie, with a comfortable villa in Coco Solo, a country club membership, household staff, and a secretary. Typical for the pampered expatriates who lived and worked in the Zone.

I don't know what task he otherwise performed for the Institute. I suspect he'd been passed over and this was his last hurrah prior to being sent out to pasture. Nevertheless, as a civilian case officer, I required military supervision and Sommers was the man. I was told I would recognize him at the train station because he'd be wearing his army uniform with a major's insignia. And there he was.

"Do you always dress like a bum, Mancini?" he asked me as I walked up to him, preparing to shake his hand. He was not speaking in jest. And he should have known better than to refer to me by my true name.

I glanced down at my aged cowboy boots, faded Levi's, and casual Hawaiian shirt. I was about to make a smart rejoinder when I remembered Pomeroy's advice, to "go along and get along."

"You must be Major Sommers. Nice to meet you, sir," I exclaimed, ignoring his initial greeting. There was no handshake.

Gus Pomeroy had accurately described Jonathan Sommers as a prissy s.o.b.

Fortunately I did not have to deal with him often because I was kept busy boarding foreign ships as they entered the Canal, under my cover as Louis Francisco, U.S. Customs officer trainee.

I boarded six or seven vessels every single day, including Sundays, for one month. There were the well maintained, immaculate and freshly painted Scandinavian freighters— Swedish, Danish, and Norwegian. There were the seedier cargo ships flying the flags of convenience: Cyprus, Panama, Liberia, and Somalia. And every nationality in between—the Russian, Japanese, South Korean, German, British, Dutch, and Brazilian freighters and oil tankers. I didn't waste my time boarding any American ships. We rode in a speedboat out to each ship as it arrived at the anchorage.

I boarded the ships with a posture of authority. I was, after all, a U.S. Customs officer and the Canal was American territory. The first thing I did after arriving on board was seek out the captain of the ship. I would introduce myself and pass the time of day with him. I'd ask him where his ship was coming from and where it was headed after it passed through the Canal. I'd peruse the crew list and make a mental note of the crew's nationalities. Sometimes, the captain would offer me a gift, which I gratefully accepted—a bottle of Chilean wine or a box of forbidden Cuban cigars. More often than not, I established a friendly rapport with the ships' officers.

The higher-ups at the Institute had sent me to the Canal Zone in their belief that I needed to gain experience dealing with foreign ships and officers. In truth, the trip to Panama turned out to be a pleasant one-month tropical holiday. By day I would board ships and shoot the breeze with the officers about their experiences at sea, and by night I would carouse in the bars and restaurants in Colón.

Colón was the somewhat raunchy, multiracial city in the Republic of Panama and not part of the American Zone. Throughout that month I struck up a few friendships and practiced speaking Spanish with Panamanians on that side of the tracks. And that did not sit well with Major Sommers. He reported to Pete Wright that I was "fraternizing" with locals, and he thought that was a risky thing for me to do.

What the managers at Springfield may not have realized was that I could also use my cover in the Canal for spotting potential clandestine agents.

I realized soon, after less than a week of boarding, that Filipinos dominated the crewing industry. Seventy percent of the ships I boarded in the Canal had Filipinos in the crew—as officers and as seamen. I asked a captain on a Liberian-flagged freighter why this was so. "Three reasons," he explained. "We Filipinos all speak English, sort of. We work hard and are considered competent. And we are cheap to the ship owners." I expected that I'd spend some time in Manila in the not too distant future.

Soon after breakfast, and three weeks after I had arrived in Cristobal, our U.S. Customs team boarded the speedboat and headed out to the anchorage. Two of us climbed the ladder of the MV *Pacific Star* as she was slowing and preparing to drop anchor.

The vessel was a ten-year-old tramp general cargo ship sailing under the flag of Cyprus. She was about 20,000 dead-weight tons. The Cypriot flag did not denote the nationality of the vessel's owner.

Flags of convenience are used to disguise the identity of the ship's owner so that he can avoid paying taxes. This owner also gets away with paying low wages to a polyglot multi-national crew. And he limits his liability by registering each of his ships under a separate shell company. These ships masquerade around the world as being home ported in countries like Cyprus, Liberia, and Panama. The *Pacific Star* was owned by a rich Swiss businessman who owned four other cargo ships, each of them registered under a separate company at a lawyer's office in Limassol, Cyprus.

The captain of the *Pacific Star* was a stout, saturnine Greek. He was unshaven and had bloodshot eyes at half-mast that morning. He wore a soiled, untucked, short-sleeved shirt and greasy black trousers. His lopsided captain's cap had a company insignia. He seemed unwell and not in a mood to chew the fat. I suspect he wanted to get the customs and immigration formalities over with so he could go back to bed.

He handed me a copy of his crew list, and I scanned through the nationalities of the crewmen. The three other ship's officers were from Egypt, Syria, and Turkey. I noticed that the radio operator was an Indonesian.

I handed the crew list back to the captain. "By the way, where did you load your last cargo?" I asked.

"We load it in Cuba," he replied with his thick accent. I figured his final night out in Havana might explain his bloodshot eyes.

"And your next port of call?"

"We discharge the sugar in North Korea," he said without looking me in the eye.

We learned later that the freighter's Swiss owner had fixed a two-year charter with the North Korean government through the Baltic Exchange in London.

I saluted the captain and left him on the bridge.

I now had one destination aboard that ship, the radio room, which was tucked behind the wheel house. I realized that having an Indonesian agent on a ship that sailed to North Korea could be my golden opportunity. As luck would have it, the young man was alone in the radio room, smoking an aromatic clove cigarette and listening to a local music station on a portable radio. I intended to do whatever it took to strike up a friendly rapport with the man.

"*Selamat pagi.*" I greeted him good morning in Indonesian, then asked him how he was. "*Apa kabar?*"

He was astonished by my speaking his language. The first step in gaining one's confidence.

"*Baik, baik,*" he replied, meaning he was fine. He stood up and broke into a big smile as we shook hands. He invited me to sit down. I introduced myself as Louis Francisco and told him my friends call me Cisco. I pulled up a chair.

He laughed. "Like Cisco Kid!"

And this gave me a good laugh too. I asked him how he knew about the Cisco Kid. He explained that his school teacher in Bali used to have her students read old American comic books as a way to learn a little English. Our conversation continued in Indonesian.

He turned down the music on the radio and asked me why it was that I spoke Indonesian. I explained that my mother was from Indonesia. He was evidently delighted to be able to speak his language with someone. I glanced at the clock in the radio room. It showed that I had twenty minutes before I would have to leave the ship with the other customs officer.

He told me his name was Komang. He was twenty-three years old and he had been to sea for over a year on the *Pacific Star*. He had studied to be a radio operator in Surabaya, and he had joined this ship in that busy East Java port when the previous radio operator had gone AWOL.

He had a wife back in Bali, living in the small fishing village of Amed on the east coast of the island. Komang had been born in Amed. But rather than fish for a living, like all of his friends and relatives did, he had decided to further his education in Surabaya and go to sea. I remarked that I was interested in astrology as a hobby and asked him when he was born. It so happened we were both born in the same month, December. So I now had his name and occupation, and I had elicited his date and place of birth. Enough information for the Institute to start a background trace.

I had to make a decision. And it was an obvious choice. I would ride this ship through the Canal to Panama City and assess the possibility of recruiting Komang as my first clandestine agent. I had to inform Sommers of my plan, knowing he'd be livid when he found out I had stayed on the *Pacific Star* through the Canal without clearing it with him first. He'd made it pretty clear all month that he disliked me in principle. This latest stunt, I knew, would drive the major nuts.

I excused myself from Komang so that I could step outside and write a note to Sommers. I passed the sealed note to the real customs officer, and asked him to hand deliver the envelope to Major Sommers. By now the American customs officers were familiar with my strange training regimen.

My note to Sommers explained that there had been a development that caused me to ride the *Pacific Star* through the Canal, and that I would return to Cristobal within two days. At the bottom of my note I wrote:

*Urgently require background trace for Komang Surya, D.O.B. 12/02/1950 P.O.B. Amed, Bali, Indonesia. Radio operator MV Pacific Star.*

My next move was to tell the captain that I planned to stay on the *Pacific Star* until the ship reached Panama City, on the Pacific Ocean side of the canal. He shrugged and told me to follow him below, leading me to the owner's stateroom. This was the relatively posh cabin reserved for the owner of the vessel in the unlikely event he ever visited the tramp ship. Meanwhile, it could be made available to selected guests. And since I was a U.S. Customs officer, as far as this captain knew, he made the room available to me for the period it would take to transit the Canal.

I returned to the radio room.

Komang was still there—puffing on an Indonesian clove cigarette and listening to music on his radio. I had noticed a framed photograph on a shelf beside the radio equipment. It portrayed a beautiful young Balinese woman dressed in full ceremonial regalia. I mentioned the photograph to Komang.

"That's my wife, Putu," he said with a certain sadness. "This photo was taken at our wedding ceremony in Amed. I miss her so much."

Komang stared out the porthole for several moments. He seemed to be in another world.

He looked again at the photograph of Putu. "I want to return to Bali. I want to make babies with Putu. And I miss my family. I'm not sure I can continue this life at sea much longer. It's a lonely job. Sometimes I think my life is passing me by, in the wake of this ship."

He paused, then continued. "There are Indonesians who have no problem leaving our country. They see it as an opportunity. But for a Balinese, it is difficult to stay away from Bali for long. We have our unique culture. It is profoundly a part of us. And it's hard for me to be separated from that."

I needed to change the subject. His desire to leave the ship and return to Bali did not conform to my plan of recruiting him as an agent with access to seaports in the denied area. I would have to make it worth his while to remain on board the freighter for the long term. And I began to think for the first time of the risks I would ask him to take for me.

I told Komang that I had some work to do in Panama City, and that I would ride *Pacific Star* through the Canal. He was pleased to hear that. It was clear that he enjoyed the opportunity to speak Indonesian again. He hadn't spoken that language —not to mention his distinct Balinese dialect – in over a year.

The *Pacific Star* would wait at anchor until the late afternoon before she could begin the westbound transit because the eastbound ships heading to the Atlantic Ocean and the Caribbean Sea had priority in the morning. I knew that the fifty-mile trip to Panama City would take about ten hours, so there was no need for me to rush the recruitment of Komang. What's more, I would have to wait a couple of weeks while the Institute conducted the background trace. This was the time to become Komang's friend. As luck would have it, I discovered that he liked to play chess. We adjourned to the crew's mess hall where there was a chess set.

It was apparent from the beginning of our first game that I was a more experienced player than he was. So I made a point of playing subtle blunders to keep our games even. Other crew members gathered around the table to watch us play and keep a running commentary on our moves. Two of them chuckled at my blunders. The crew were a motley assortment of nationalities—Filipinos, Arabs, Indians, and Burmese. Each spoke his own uniquely accented brand of English. The mess hall smelled like an unsavory blend of Indian curry, fried fish, fuel oil, cigarette smoke, and body odor.

At five o'clock in the afternoon, the ship got underway. I suggested to Komang that we climb to the bridge for some fresh air and to view the sights along the Canal. The American pilot had arrived. He took command of the ship as it passed through the Canal.

I have never been a cigarette smoker. But during that month in the Canal, I had smoked one or two of those Cuban cigars that had been given to me as gifts. And now standing outside on the bridge of the underway freighter with the breeze blowing around us and the sun about to set over Gatun Lake, it seemed the perfect time to light up one of those pungent cigars. I offered one to Komang, but he preferred his own spicy clove cigarettes.

The passage across the massive Gatun Lake at sunset was an adventure. We passed ships in the lake that were heading in the opposite direction, toward the Atlantic Ocean. Veritable ships passing in the night, never to meet again. Another cargo ship followed us through the Canal, 300 yards astern. As the sun set, all the ships switched on their navigation lights together.

Throughout much of the ten-hour journey, I befriended Komang. He took me into his confidence—his courting of Putu from their early teens, his original desire to escape the confines of the small fishing village in east Bali, and now his intense yearning to return home. The money he made sailing on *Pacific Star* could not compensate for the loneliness he endured when he thought of his wife, his family, and his friends in the village. I listened with rapt attention to his dilemma and spoke only to cue him.

Toward midnight, and before he retired to his stateroom for the night, I upped the ante. I explained to Komang that there was a chance we would meet again. I told him I had accepted a job offer that would take me to Asia. I said I had not revealed this to the U.S. Customs Service and that he was the first person I had confided in. I requested that he keep it a secret. He pledged that he would. It is never too early to get a potential agent conditioned for the secret world.

I told him I would like to stay in touch by ship's radio. I listed down his ship's call sign and we selected a radio frequency that we would use together. I gave him the hour of day, Greenwich Mean Time, when I would attempt to make contact. We now had in place the germ of a clandestine communications scheme.

"And by the way, Komang, my new job involves maritime research and the collection of port and shipping information. I pay the people who help me collect the information. I can arrange to send money to Putu, five hundred dollars a month, if you'll be my representative. But we have to keep this secret."

Komang was elated, not only for the confidential sideline job and welcome financial bonus, but also for our friendship that would continue into the future. He wrote down the name of the bank in Denpasar where he kept his account. I told him to expect my call on his radio in a few weeks, after I arrived in Asia.

I spent the remaining hours, from midnight until three in the morning, on the bridge and in the wheelhouse with the American pilot and the ship's Turkish chief mate, drinking coffee, smoking a Cuban Cohiba, and experiencing a feeling of accomplishment as the *Pacific Star* plowed slowly through the dark Canal.

The pilot had arranged for a motor boat to pick us up as the vessel sailed beyond the Miraflores locks. The pilot and I climbed down the ladder of the moving ship and hopped aboard the launch as it glided alongside. The boat made a sharp turn away from the freighter and raced through the black water back to nearby Panama City. The *Pacific Star* sailed into the Pacific Ocean and on to North Korea.

I checked in to a hotel in downtown Panama City in the small hours of the morning, slept until noon, and then took the familiar train back to Cristobal in the afternoon. I had phoned Sommers earlier. He ordered me to meet him at his home so that he could debrief me as soon as I arrived.

I'd anticipated his anger. I listened to him rant about my lack of discipline, my impertinence, and the unlikelihood that I would succeed as an intelligence officer. I was embarrassed for his wife, Julie, who was in the next room and within earshot of his diatribe. After listening in silence for ten minutes, I asked him if he had forwarded the information about Komang Surya to Springfield. With a sigh, he acknowledged that he had.

There is a lasting memory of Panama that I do carry with me through life. Sommers and Julie had invited me to dinner at their tony country club to celebrate Julie's thirty-second birthday on my last night in the Canal Zone.

Julie was a very pretty woman, a petite, dark-eyed brunette. She had a fit, well-proportioned figure, and she dressed with cool, tropical good taste. Julie had impressed me as being pleasant enough and cordial in a rather formal sense during the few times we had met at their home. She was a regular tennis player at the club, and we had discussed the sport together on occasion.

We sat at a table for three in the clubhouse dining room. After the main course, before the birthday cake was delivered to the table and as Jonathan Sommers pontificated about one thing and another, Julie began rubbing her bare foot up and down my leg beneath the tablecloth. I stretched my leg to make it easier for her toes to meander high up the inside of my thigh. It took an effort for me to contain my breathing when the tips of her toes struck home. Indeed we struggled to keep our eyes off each other as the sensual foreplay continued over the champagne toast and singing of Happy Birthday. It was timely, I suppose, that I departed the Panama Canal Zone the next day.

# 7

---

## THE GULF OF ADEN

THE SKY AT ONE O'CLOCK IN THE MORNING, 136 miles west of the Yemeni island of Socotra, was pitch dark. There may have been a sliver of a moon. If so, the acrid haze that blew north from the Horn of Africa disguised it. There were no other lights as far as the eye could see.

The Suez Canal remained closed as it had for the past six years, as payback for the Egyptians' defeat in the 1967 war with Israel. This had once been a busy shipping lane with scores of merchant ships sailing to and from the Canal. No longer. A small vessel at this time could wallow in the middle of the Gulf of Aden unobserved, day or night. And that was why the fishing trawler without a national flag or a name was here, gliding over the swells at a speed of four knots.

As a precaution, the trawler displayed no running lights. The single navigation light shining on the craft rode atop the fifty-foot mast. The commander of the vessel, his foreign guest, and the five Palestinian crew members were silent as they scanned the horizon. The wizened commander stood erect and held a flashlight and a compass at his side.

"Wadi, over there, to the left. I think I see it," the mate beside him whispered in Arabic.

The forty-five-year-old commander's eyes were not good. He was loath to wear spectacles around his men, and especially in front of his guest. He gazed into the distance off the port side of the trawler. The men waited. At last others saw the sinister profile of a submarine a few miles off the port bow.

"I see it, Ahmad," the commander said.

Wadi Haddad switched on the flashlight and blinked the recognition signal in the direction of the submarine. The sub flashed back a reply from the top of its tall black superstructure. One could barely perceive the dark shape of the Foxtrot-class submarine as it approached on the surface. When it was near, the crew noticed that B-427 was painted in white onto the sub's black superstructure.

The commander held the Soviet submarine in view through his binoculars.

"Open the hatches," he ordered. "Prepare to take on cargo. Ahmad, get the lines ready." The sub was now less than one mile distant, approaching port side.

Wadi Haddad's Russian code name was *Natsionalist.* The KGB didn't know he knew.

He uttered to himself, "All profess to be nationalists."

Wadi pondered on the most fickle creed of all: Muslim nationalism. It stretched from distant Indonesia to Pakistan, into Afghanistan and through the Arab and Persian worlds. The clashing Sunnis and Shiites hate each other. And onward, west to North Africa and the south of Russia. So many unconnected races and cultures in disarray, cultures with little in common except for the pillars of Islam, if that.

And he reflected on Arab nationalism. Nasser had tried and failed. There were too many rivalries and jealousies in the mix. And leaders who loathed one another. And who paid lip service to Palestine's cause, Palestine's liberation.

"There is but one true nationalism, the only meaningful one: Palestine," Wadi Haddad sneered, grinding his decaying teeth.

The commander had been born in what today is northern Israel. The term *Israel* made his blood boil. His family's home had been destroyed in the 1948 Arab-Israeli war when he was twenty-one years old. They fled to Lebanon, and Wadi had battled against Israel as a guerilla in the underground for the past nine years. The KGB recruited him in 1970.

"Prepare to toss the lines," the mate shouted in Arabic.

Two Russian sailors appeared on the rocking deck of the submarine. Thick mooring lines were thrown to the sailors on the sub.

"Set the fenders. Hurry up."

Rubber truck tires were dropped between the trawler and the submarine to prevent the vessels from coming into direct contact.

Commander Wadi looked on. He thought of the times he had performed this maneuver in the past three years. Five, six times? Always with a submarine. Always the same KGB officer, the infidel who called himself Vladimir. The Russian would signal him to come over to the sub, not an easy trick on a pitching sea. Vladimir never dared to crawl over to the trawler. Another reason Wadi crossed to the submarine was because of the alcohol that his case officer swilled during their meetings. His crew would not have been comfortable with that.

Vladimir stood at the top of the superstructure with a flashlight. He turned it on and pointed it at Wadi's feet, motioning for him to come over. A narrow metal ladder was stretched from the sub to the trawler, and, as always, Wadi crossed to the submarine like a dog on all fours. He spat into the sea and recalled the expression, "Beggars can't be choosers," then banished that thought. Vladimir was waiting for him, alone, at a table in the officers' mess.

The first thing Wadi noticed was that, as usual, the vain Russian had his shirt unbuttoned, showing off his muscular white physique, feigning it was because of the heat. Wadi knew his own build was sickly by contrast. He could just make out the strange tattoo on Vladimir's powerful chest. The drawing of a dagger, a Muslim Kris.

Wadi greeted the Russian officer in Arabic. Vladimir replied in the same language, and asked, *pro forma*, if the commander was well as he poured himself a glassful of vodka from the half-empty bottle in the middle of the table.

"Join me, Wadi?" the Russian asked in Arabic. He pushed a shot glass across to the Palestinian and stared at him with watery blue eyes.

Wadi Haddad stared back with a caustic glare. The Russian knew well that he did not drink alcohol. This was the same ritual they went through at every one of their meetings— Vladimir would push a small glass of vodka at him, and he would decline it.

"I'll pass," he muttered.

"All right then," the Russian continued unabashed, "here is the packing list for the weapons we are supplying you tonight." He slid the list across the table. Wadi snatched it up and read it.

*150 AK-47 rifles*
*10 shoulder-fired surface-to-air missiles*
*20 Beretta 9mm handguns with silencers*
*50 anti-tank grenades and RPG-7 launchers*
*100 radio-controlled mines*
*50 sets of night-vision goggles*
*60 gallons of fuel for the trawler*

The Palestinian nodded after reading the list. "This is what we were expecting. No more, no less." He tucked the packing list into his pants pocket.

"Good. Now let's review our operations—past and future. I understand you have a guest aboard your fishing boat, one who is known as Carlos the Jackal. Why did you not bring him with you to the submarine tonight?" The Russian held a grin in place.

Wadi shrugged. "He wishes to keep a low profile. If you want, *you* can crawl over to the trawler on your hands and knees and make his acquaintance."

"Not necessary, my friend. I understand that you are training him in your methods. Am I correct?"

"Yes. In Baalbek."

"You know, Wadi, my people relish plane hijackings, like the ones you pulled off three years ago. Those airliners you snatched in one week and landed in Jordan. What were they? TWA, BOAC, Pan Am, Swissair? And then you blew up the planes on the ground. Brilliant." The Russian chortled and drained his glass of vodka. He believed his Arabic became more fluent, less inhibited, the more he drank.

The Palestinian replied with a baleful look on his face. "Yes, that is what we did. It was a great success."

"Okay." The Russian drummed his fingers on the table. "We supply the weapons. And the cash. Can we expect more activity in the future from the Democratic Front for the Liberation of Palestine? My people want to know your plans. Deploying this submarine to arm your group is expensive, and risky. Understand, we want to see results. We want the world to see the events in newspapers and on television. We need to terrify them—the Americans, Europeans, and the Israelis. Don't get complacent, my dear Wadi. In today's world, when nuclear arms have made military force obsolete, terrorism should become our main weapon." The Russian was no longer grinning.

"Trust me, Vladimir. With Carlos the Jackal we are going international. The massacre in Munich last year and the one in Ma'alot this year should have pleased you, did it not? Have patience. We must plan carefully."

"We know a thing or two about careful planning," Vladimir mumbled in Russian. He poured himself another glassful of vodka, his fourth. He stared at the Palestinian and shrugged his shoulders. "That is all I have to say, Wadi." They stared at each other, neither trusting, nor particularly liking the other.

"Then I shall return to my boat. I can show myself out." Wadi stood, reached for the packing list in his rear pocket, and left the room.

Vladimir remained seated at the table and sipped his drink, satisfied that he had pulled off yet another successful arms transfer and meeting with his agent, the most dangerous terrorist in the world. The irony was that no one in the West knew this Palestinian's name. The Russian, intoxicated now, laughed to himself. He absent-mindedly buttoned his shirt, covering his chest and the tattoo.

Wadi crawled back to the trawler on the ladder and was helped aboard by the mate and the Jackal. He glanced forward and noted that the hatches had been closed, the cargo loaded.

"Cast off," he ordered, "Set your course to the Red Sea at full speed."

The fishing trawler would sail north through the Red Sea until it reached the Gulf of Aqaba. At the port of Aqaba the cargo would be loaded onto waiting trucks, under cover of darkness. They would drive north through Jordan, parallel to the Israeli border, until they reached Syria and then Lebanon. Vladimir had issued Wadi sufficient cash to make payoffs at the borders. Final destination: Baalbek, Lebanon.

# 8

---

GOOD AFTERNOON, GENTLEMEN. HAVE A SEAT." THE director of Naval Intelligence, Admiral Johnny Zinger, greeted the two men from the Institute. "Nice to see you again, Frank."

"Afternoon, Admiral. I believe you know Tom Hiatt, the Institute's deputy director," Frank DuPont said.

"Yes. We've met. Glad you could be here, Tom."

Tom Hiatt stared without expression at the fourth man in the room, who was seated beside Admiral Zinger.

"Tom, the admiral said, "I suspect you might know George Sikelman, being that you're ex-CIA. George is now chief of staff of the President's Foreign Intelligence Advisory Board. The chairman of that board has requested he attend meetings of this sort. The president doesn't want to see any more "loose cannons," as he puts it. George's job is to randomly monitor the military's humint collection activities on behalf of the Board. Do I have that right, George?"

"Correct, Admiral. The new president is adamant. He wants to put the scandals of the past years behind us. He has given the Board authority to monitor the clandestine activities of both the CIA and the military branches. A lot of what has come out of congressional hearings has been particularly embarrassing to the executive branch. There are to be no more Howard Hunts. The president's words."

Hiatt continued to stare at George Sikelman. He knew him. He had never trusted him. Senior officers at the Agency had called him "Clark" behind his back. With his perfectly trimmed moustache, freshly barbered dark hair, and expensive three-piece suits, his dead ringer resemblance to the actor Clark Gable was uncanny—except that he spoke English with a foreign accent.

Hiatt and Sikelman had both joined the Agency during the first year of the CIA's existence. Sikelman had been an interrogator with army intelligence in Europe during World War II. He was born in Hungary of Hungarian parents and spoke fluent Hungarian and German. At the end of the war, the army sent him to Hungary with the mission of recruiting former Nazis, Germans and their Hungarian collaborators, to spy against the Soviet Union.

What Tom Hiatt didn't know, and what was not known among senior army and CIA staff, was that George Sikelman was Jewish. And that the task of recruiting and running these Nazis, who had done their utmost to kill every Jew in Europe, made him sick to his stomach. Literally. Sikelman became a double-agent in 1949. That year he was recruited by the Soviet NKVD, the predecessor to the KGB, under a false flag ploy.

The NKVD case officer who recruited Sikelman was, like Sikelman, Jewish—one of the very few in the Soviet intelligence services. The Russian lied to George Sikelman and told him he was a Zionist and that he was engaging George on behalf of the new state of Israel. Sikelman agreed to do whatever was necessary to neutralize, and in many cases terminate with extreme prejudice, the ex-Nazis he was recruiting to operate against the Soviets. It was only a matter of time until Sikelman learned that his true paymaster was the NKVD, eventually the KGB, and not Israel. By that time the Russians had a firm handle on the Hungarian-American spy. He was now, in 1974, the most highly placed KGB "mole" operating inside the U.S. intelligence community.

"Hello, Sikelman. Long time, no see," Tom Hiatt uttered at last to the man sitting across the table from him.

"Tom. Congratulations on the new job. I'd heard you left the Agency the same time as Helms. Seems you've landed on your feet," Sikelman replied with a bland smile.

Hiatt ignored the comment. He was not at all comfortable having George Sikelman involved in this meeting.

Admiral Zinger glanced at his watch and continued. "Let's discuss your pending operation in Southeast Asia, Frank. You have the floor."

General DuPont briefed the admiral and Sikelman on aspects of Roy Mancini's operation plan. They would recall later that the PFIAB chief of staff took copious notes during the briefing.

The target, DuPont explained, was the naval orders of battle of the Soviet Union, the Peoples Republic of China, and North Korea. Mancini would operate under two separate covers—from Malacca, Malaysia—and he would undertake maritime missions in the seas and ports of China and the USSR, as well as the Indian Ocean littoral.

Admiral Zinger interrupted DuPont at mention of the Indian Ocean.

"Frank, this reminds me. We need to add a target. Lately our submarines on patrol in the Indian Ocean have identified suspicious activity in the Gulf of Aden. We've picked up Russian submarines. And in that confined area, these subs don't appear to have any mission we can determine. We know they're Soviet subs because our skippers have observed the markings on the superstructures during the few times the Russian boats have surfaced. Foxtrot and November-class submarines. Their objectives remain an enigma. We need the Institute to do what it can to unravel the mystery."

"Well, Admiral, Mancini's trading cover can take him to East Africa. Kenya and Ethiopia are coffee producers." General DuPont made a note.

"This may be sheer coincidence," the admiral said, "but these Soviet submarines appear a month or so before there's some major terrorist event where the Democratic Front for the Liberation of Palestine is identified as the culprit. You recall the hideous Ma'alot massacre last May. There was a Foxtrot submarine observed at night on the surface near the Red Sea a month prior, in April."

Tom Hiatt said, "We never assume a coincidence."

"All right." Admiral Zinger looked at the man sitting beside him. "Unless you have something else to add, George, I believe we can adjourn this meeting. The navy needs the Institute's human intelligence to augment what we're getting by other means."

Sikelman shrugged. "Mancini's mission sounds okay to me. I'll inform the Board. Good luck with it."

When George Sikelman left the Pentagon fifteen minutes

later he did not return directly to his office at the Old Executive Office Building beside the White House. Instead he drove to a pay phone in downtown Arlington. He phoned the picture framing shop that was owned by his Russian cutout.

"Orlov Gallery," the man answered the phone with his heavy Slavic accent.

Sikelman responded. "This is Rene. Is my stunning Monet completed yet?"

Igor Orlov hesitated before answering. "I will check. And call you later."

George Sikelman waited precisely one hour before again phoning the gallery.

"This is Rene. Is my stunning Monet completed yet?"

"It will be completed in the morning on the seventh of next month."

The message informed Sikelman that his Russian case officer, Boris, would meet him on Sunday (the seventh day of the week) at 4:00 in the afternoon. The meeting would take place along a trail in Rock Creek Park.

That Sunday George Sikelman parked his car just off 16th Street at 3:30 in the afternoon and walked into the park. He conducted active counter surveillance along the park's paths for twenty-five minutes before entering the trail that Boris had selected two years earlier for their infrequent meetings. At precisely 3:58 he stood beneath a tree, looking up and feigning an interest in bird-watching. He tucked a copy of the *Baltimore Sun* under his left arm. This was the safety signal that would indicate to Boris that his agent was not being followed. They had synchronized their wristwatches that morning with a BBC broadcast. At 4:01 Sikelman saw Boris walking up the path toward him. They greeted each other and continued walking together.

Boris insisted they conduct their meetings in German, a language in which they were both fluent.

"So George, you must have something very interesting for you to request a personal meeting. Am I right?" the Russian asked.

"Yes. And it should be worthy of a generous bonus." Sikelman smirked as he said this. He had been handled by six different Soviet case officers over the past twenty-five years. By now he had a sense of the tail wagging the dog in terms of his relationship with the Russians.

Boris chuckled. "You are already paid very well . . . we shall see. What do you have for me?"

"There is a new intelligence agency under the auspices of the Department of Defense. Like your GRU. It's called the Institute."

"We know. I hope you did not disturb my Sunday afternoon, George, just to report that to me."

The American scoffed. "Of course not. I attended a meeting at the Pentagon on Friday where the Institute's commanding officer and deputy director briefed Johnny Zinger about a new mission, targeting the Soviet navy."

"Go on."

"They are sending a case officer to Asia next month. He will run agents into Russia to observe and photograph naval shipyards and warships with emphasis on your Pacific Fleet submarines."

Boris stopped walking and held Sikelman by the arm. "You have the details? The case officer's name and where he will be based?"

"Of course I do. I took notes. Here." He removed sheets of paper from inside the folded *Baltimore Sun* and handed them to Boris. The Russian quickly placed them inside his jacket.

The two men walked in silence for a few minutes. The American waited for the Russian to speak.

At last Boris said, "You must order the new counter-intelligence chief at the CIA to keep the Institute's case officer under close surveillance in Asia. Understand? And have the CIA report back to you, and only to you. You come up with a reason for that, George. Maybe CIA and the Institute are less-than-friendly competitors, like KGB and GRU. You are good at planning that sort of thing."

Sikelman thought for a moment before replying. "It is fortunate, Boris, that James Angleton will soon leave the Agency or I wouldn't attempt this. Angleton may be paranoid, but he's smart. Perhaps the new chief, Angleton's deputy, will wish to ingratiate himself with my Board. He might go along with my request. I'll update you through the dead drop.

"And before I forget, there's another thing you should know. Your submarines in the Gulf of Aden are easy for the U.S. navy to identify because of the markings on their super-structures. Foxtrots and Novembers. That's from the admiral. He wonders what those subs are doing up there since the Suez Canal is still closed and they're not performing any obvious mission. Zinger suspects a link to Palestinian terrorists."

"That information could be bonus worthy, George. I'll pass it along to the naval attaché at the embassy."

The Russian case officer handed his agent an envelope containing fifty untraceable $100 bills. He knew better than to ask his agent for a receipt. The two men parted in separate directions.

The next day George Sikelman paid a visit to Langley and on behalf of the PFIAB ordered the future head of counterintelligence to place Roy Mancini under close surveillance, beginning with his departure from the U.S. and continuing with his activities throughout Southeast Asia. The CI deputy chief had no choice but to comply and curry favor with the President's Foreign Intelligence Advisory Board.

# 9

---

OCTOBER 1974

M Y PLANE TOUCHED DOWN AT SINGAPORE'S
airport at midnight. It had been a long day with a
flight departing from Dulles, connecting through
Los Angeles and Tokyo, and on to Singapore. I had persuaded
the Institute to upgrade me to business class for these flights so
that I could better live my cover as a successful coffee merchant. Gus Pomeroy shook his head in disbelief when the CO
agreed to that unusual request and ordered the travel department to rebook my flight. A case officer had never been known
to fly business class anywhere in the world as far as Pomeroy
knew. It might have had something to do with the box of
Cuban Cohiba cigars and bottle of absinthe I had smuggled in
from Panama for the general.

I took a taxi from the airport to the Raffles Hotel on
Beach Road. It had been nearly twenty years since I'd walked
hand-in-hand with my father through the grand portico of this
1887 French Renaissance building. The colonial façade was as

I remembered it. The bearlike turbaned Punjabi doormen, outfitted in their faux British military attire, were the same imposing gentlemen I had playfully saluted as a child. They held the taxi door open for me, and I entered the high-ceilinged lobby beneath the slowly revolving ceiling fans overhead.

The tuxedoed Chinese night manager, bowing his head and smiling, beckoned the uniformed bellmen who ran up to grab my suitcase from the trunk of the cab. The alert and friendly young ladies at the reception desk, I'd known them all before at the Raffles Hotel, so many years ago. As I approached reception my mind wandered to the famous British authors and adventurers who had stayed at the Raffles during their Singapore sojourns. Among them: Somerset Maugham, Graham Greene, and Rudyard Kipling.

"Good evening, Mr. Mancini. Did you have a pleasant flight?" The attractive Chinese receptionist greeted me with a welcoming smile and the whiff of an English accent as I handed her my American Express card.

I smiled in return, happy to be here at last.

"I did, yes, thank you," I replied.

"May I take your passport please? You can sign the register here." She handed me a card to fill in.

"My passport? Is that necessary?"

"Oh, yes. We need to make copies of the front page and of your arrival visa."

"That's interesting."

"Hotels in Singapore must forward these pages to the police, straightaway. It's the rule." I reached into my briefcase, removed my passport, and laid it on the desk. She took it to a back room where she copied at least the two pages she had described. I knew now why I would need a safe house in Singapore to run my agents.

After a minute she returned and handed my passport to me along with my room key.

"Your suitcase has been delivered to your room, Mr. Mancini. You're on the second floor. Mr. Chin will show you the way. Good night and pleasant dreams."

I turned and found the gentleman in the tuxedo standing a few feet behind me. He nodded and asked me to follow him.

"We'll take the lift at the end of the hall, Mr. Mancini." He pointed, allowing me to lead the way.

We walked down a hallway, past the Long Bar, which was empty, and past the spacious gardens of the Palm Court, now dark. We took the elevator to the second floor where I entered my room. My suitcase had been delivered and was placed on a luggage rack. I wanted to tip Chin on behalf of everyone who had helped me on arrival. I reached into my pocket and pulled out the bills from my taxi change, offering it all to him.

"Oh no, sir. We're not allowed to accept cash gratuities at the Raffles. But thank you for your kind gesture." He spoke with a flawless private school English accent. I wondered if he might have studied at my old primary school, the Stamford Raffles Academy. I smiled inwardly at the thought.

"Well then, good night and thank you," I said. He turned and walked back down the deserted hall. I closed the door.

I stripped off my clothes, brushed my teeth in a jet-lagged daze, and dove between the fresh, cool white sheets of the large canopied bed. It had been a long, thirty-hour day across several time zones, exactly halfway around the world, from Virginia to Singapore. I fell asleep within seconds.

The next morning I ordered room service and took my

breakfast in the shade on my balcony, with a view of the great harbor before me. Cargo ships and oil tankers lay at anchor as far as the eye could see. Beyond those ships in the distance were several small islands. What I sensed was opportunity. I couldn't guess how many of these ships might sail to seaports in the denied area: Communist China, the USSR, and North Korea.

As I finished breakfast and poured myself a second cup of coffee from the pewter pot, I tried to envisage how I might begin to accomplish my mission: the recruitment of spies who sailed on ships that lay at anchor in this very harbor. Boarding those ships, as I had done in Panama, was not an option. I had no reason I could think of that would permit that. I'd need to come up with a plan.

I recollected my meeting with Komang. He was ripe for recruitment. When I found him again I would raise the stakes by revealing what I needed him to do for me: report on the naval activity in the "denied areas": North Korea and its Communist trading partners.

And that brought to mind the company that I was about to purchase in Hong Kong, the company engaged in maritime research, where I would operate using my alias, Louis Francisco. That passport was hidden in a secret false bottom of my briefcase.

My first official task that morning was to introduce myself to my new boss, Lieutenant Commander Steven McCoy. His office was at the U.S. Embassy. I wondered how he would compare to the ill-tempered army officer in Panama I had reported to in September. At any rate, he was a fellow musician. A positive sign.

I decided to walk from the Raffles to the embassy. I was

dressed for the climate in a new pair of tennis shoes, loose-fitting khaki slacks and a fresh polo shirt. I desired now to wander by some of the spots I'd known in Singapore and see if I remembered them, or more accurately, find if they were still there.

I walked across the bridge near the mouth of the Sing-apore River and spotted the statues of the two lions at the river's entrance that symbolized Singapore—the Lion City. Boat Quay lay at the other end of the bridge. Here were the Chinese shop houses and below them, at the river's edge, the row of hawker stalls that sold food representing every ethnic group in the city. Chinese noodles, fried rice, sweet and sour fish. Malay rojak and chicken satay. Indian biryani, a flat hot bread called naan, and spicy curries. And an array of fresh tropical fruit and hot and cold beverages. A hawker who was native to the cuisine operated each stall. The aroma along Boat Quay was a savory blend of all these dishes and spices. I found myself inhaling deeply, exhilarated, as I walked along the riverside, breathing the atmosphere.

I took a stool at a beverage stall and ordered a *kopi-o*. Here I could look out on the busy river traffic, at the sampans and barges filled with inbound and outbound cargoes. There were the deeply tanned and sinewy crewmen on those passing boats shouting at each other in their various unintelligible Chinese dialects.

The grizzled Cantonese hawker poured the hot, sweet coffee that I'd ordered into a water glass and sloshed it in front of me. A portion of the brew splattered and landed on the saucer. I paid him his twenty-five cents. Now, the trick was to hold the impossibly hot glass and drink from it, without burning your fingers. I don't know how the locals do it. I waited a minute or two for the coffee to cool down before lifting the hot glass to my lips. There is a local custom, I recalled, that says the coffee is not up to par if the hawker doesn't splatter it over the brim of the glass, making a mess before he hands it to you.

I continued walking up Boat Quay past more fragrant hawker stalls until I reached another bridge. I crossed back again to the north side of the river. I'd forgotten how hot and humid it gets by nine o'clock in the morning. After a further twenty-minute walk, I arrived, sweating, at the U.S. Embassy and entered the cool lobby.

After a ten-minute wait, a uniformed Marine sergeant with the name tag "Dubrowski" arrived in the lobby.

"Mr. Mancini?" he asked.

"That's me."

"May I see some identification, sir?" He stood in front of me at attention.

I handed him my passport, which he studied, looking first at the photo and then at my face, and back again at the photo.

"Thank you, sir. Please follow me," the Marine said as we passed one by one through a security scanner. I followed Dubrowski to the elevator and we rode to the third floor.

"Mr. McCoy is waiting for you in his office." He led me to an open door and knocked.

"Come in, come in, Roy. It's good to meet you." Steve McCoy stood up from his desk and walked over to me to shake hands. He was a tall, slim man, well over six feet. With a fair complexion and a toothy grin, he had a fun-loving expression on his face. I figured him in his mid-thirties. I'd been told he was single and a Naval Academy graduate. He had served on a guided missile destroyer as an intelligence officer prior to his current job as the Institute's point man in Singapore. His embassy cover was, ironically, Southeast Asia Coordinator for the Military Sealift Command, the operator of the navy's cargo ships I had sailed on years earlier.

"I've received good reports about you from Pete Wright." He glanced at the Marine. "Sergeant, would you please bring us a couple of coffees." The Marine sergeant left the room and closed the door.

"Likewise, Mr. McCoy," I replied, standing inadvertently at attention. "I look forward to working with you."

"Call me Steve. And relax. I hear you're a jazz musician. Terrific. Have a seat and cool off. Did you walk over?" He was observant.

"I did. I wanted to see what I could remember of the city from twenty years ago, when I lived here. The stroll over made for a pretty hot workout."

"Mad dogs and Englishmen."

"Noel Coward, right?"

"I thought it was Kipling. Whatever. It was one of those characters that used to hang out at the Raffles Hotel." He made a hand motion to brush aside the issue. "So let's get to know one another."

"Fire away."

"I hear our man in Malacca is going to live the life of an international coffee merchant."

"Well, I'm banking that it will serve its purpose. I should be able to plausibly visit any country in the world buying and selling coffee beans. At the same time I'll create a second cover as a maritime research consultant."

"So I hear." He stood up again and started to pace the floor in front of his desk. He was holding a copy of my operation plan in his hand.

"I have read your op plan. I'm impressed. You've shown imagination. Let's discuss the implementation phase now." He sat down in an armchair beside me and laid the document on the glass coffee table in front of us. "What's your first step?"

I described to McCoy how I needed to find a place to live in Malacca, move in, and unpack. Coffee Traders International, CTI, had already been formed by the lawyers in that town, and they only needed to copy my passport and get my signature on some documents. The "red tape" was minimal. I would open a company bank account in Malacca. After the account was open with a couple hundred dollars, one of the Institute's cover companies in Europe would wire transfer fifty thousand dollars to it. I would draw on those funds to finance my operations.

My next move would be to follow up with the company formation in Hong Kong. I was in the process of purchasing an off-the-shelf company from an accounting firm there. The firm I was in touch with created companies that it "put on a shelf" and sold to persons who wished to hide their identity. I was buying one of those companies and only needed to change its name. I would also establish a banking relationship in Hong Kong. And in the future I would pay our clandestine agents their wages from that account.

I reminded Steve that I would need to lease a safe house in Singapore under my cover name, Louis Francisco. It would be too risky to meet my agents in hotel rooms. He said he had the funds for that. They had been wired to his office's account a week earlier.

"You'll have to decide on a code name for yourself, Roy."

"*Arabica*." I had already thought of that.

"Has a nice ring to it." He wrote it down. "All right, from

now on you sign off on all your reports as *Arabica*. I'll inform Springfield."

I nodded.

"Now, regarding Komang Surya, your Balinese lead. We need to assign him a cryptonym. We never want to communicate his true name in a report or in a cable. Any ideas?"

McCoy was right. Intelligence agencies worldwide and throughout history had been compromised by "moles" and double agents who had been able to scoop up and expose to the enemy the identities of agents working undercover. The purpose of code names for case officers and cryptonyms for their agents was to prevent the exposure of their true identities in the event the agency had been penetrated by such a "mole." Or if the spy agency's communications system had been compromised.

I recalled the cigarettes that Komang smoked. "Let's call him *Clover*."

"All right." Steve wrote down Komang's cryptonym.

"There is a matter of protocol you need to follow," Steve said. "The CIA is the authority for all American clandestine activity worldwide, outside the U.S. We need to coordinate with them so we don't stumble over each other's feet."

"Meaning?"

"Meaning that when you visit a country to brief or debrief an agent you need to pay a courtesy call to the local CIA station."

"So I stroll into a U.S. embassy and ask the receptionist if I can have a word with the CIA?" I smiled at the absurd idea.

"No, no. There will be a CIA officer under diplomatic cover. The attaché for cultural affairs or something like that. You'll know his or her identity beforehand. I'll arrange it so they know you're in town. The meeting takes fifteen minutes. They want to be kept informed when we operate on their turf. You don't need to reveal anything about your cover, or any specifics about your agents. To be honest, we don't entirely trust the Agency. They only need to know that you're the Institute's case officer and that you're in town to do some business."

"Fair enough, if that's what we need to do."

"Oh, and one other thing. We don't recruit British subjects. They're off limits. And the Brits don't recruit Americans. It's an understanding we have. It goes back to the 1940s, agreed to at the highest levels. So don't waste your time pursuing any English ship captains."

"I understand."

"Do you have a name for the cover company in Hong Kong?" he asked.

"Not yet. I need to give that some thought."

"Here's what I suggest. Why don't we meet each other at your hotel for drinks this evening? We can find a private spot somewhere and come up with a name. Meanwhile, for the rest of the day you can renew your acquaintance with Singapore or catch up on some rest."

I had the sense then that Steve McCoy was keen on leading, vicariously, the kind of life I was about to live: cover stories, secret agents, safe houses, business class travel to exotic places, and plenty of money in Malaysian and Hong Kong bank accounts.

"Sure, that sounds good. Two heads are better than one. Let's come up with a name," I said.

"Fine. Meet at the Long Bar at five-thirty and have a sling or two. Dinner somewhere afterwards."

# 10

―――――

I LEFT THE EMBASSY BEFORE NOON, AND RECALLING THE adage about Englishmen and mad dogs walking in the noonday sun, I hailed a taxi.

We drove past the Cricket Club where I had learned to play tennis on the pristine grass courts as a kid. Nearby was the old Parliament building that looked as though it could have been transplanted from London. On our right we passed the large *Padang*, the massive well-tended grassy field that these former British colonial cities maintain in the center of town. The traffic that hummed along on Saint Andrews Road was orderly, one might even say polite, every vehicle traveling within the speed limit. My overall impression of Singapore so far, above all else, was that it was a city-state defined by its orderliness.

A few minutes before the scheduled meeting at five-thirty, I took the stairs down to the lobby. As I walked down two floors, I could hear the hushed voices and the occasional men's laughter from the Long Bar, which was off to the side.

I conducted a brief, imaginary dialogue with myself as I descended.

"An entrepreneur. That's what you are now, Roy, a globe-trotting Arabica bean merchant. Live your life well as a young American trader, out to make his fortune in Asia. You can forget the rest of the spook business for a minute, but never lose track of your coffee trading legend. Never lose that focus. If you can live your Arabica coffee bean cover, the rest of it, the undercover intelligence work, will fall into place."

"A soldier of fortune, is that what you think you are now?" The sarcastic voice of my father exclaimed in my head as I continued down the stairs.

"No, Dad. But close. I am out to make a success buying and selling coffee beans. At the same time I'm engaged in something I'm good at but not allowed to tell you much about. I think you'd be proud of me."

"Well then, son. A warning. Don't fuck up. Don't get sent home with a blown cover."

I broke off this whimsical conversation as I reached the bottom stair. A quick glance at the reception desk and I saw the same pretty Chinese lady was on duty who had checked me in the night before. We smiled at each other and I gave her a brief wave. The two uniformed bellmen, standing at ease, greeted me with slight bows of their heads as I made a right turn into the Long Bar.

McCoy was standing at the far end of the bar. The room had been appropriately named; it might well have had the longest solid African mahogany bar in existence. There were no stools but a brass rail ran along the floor, the length of the bar. A customer was expected to stand with a foot on the rail. There were rattan table settings beneath rotating ceiling fans for those who chose to sit and drink. A long mirror extended across the entire wall behind the bartenders. The mirror was convenient for a patron who was standing at the bar and wanted to see who was walking up, or seated, behind him.

There were six men at the other end of the bar, talking with posh London accents. The Englishmen wore suits and ties despite the heat and humidity. Steve and I nodded to each other, and I walked over to him.

"Greetings. And welcome to Singapore's oldest and finest drinking establishment." Steve turned to me. He had changed into civilian clothes. He wore a batik short-sleeved shirt and loose-fitting white tropical pants.

"I see you're drinking a Tiger Beer. What, no Singapore Sling?" I commented.

"Too sweet. All that cherry brandy. It's for tourists. What can I get you?"

"The same. Make it a Tiger." Steve motioned to the bartender standing in front of us to bring another bottle.

A party of four matronly western women entered the bar together, talking audibly and fanning themselves. I could see them in the mirror in front of me. They took their seats on the rattan dining chairs at a table beneath a ceiling fan. A white-jacketed Chinese waiter rushed to their table to take drink orders.

"Did you hear the story about the live tiger that entered this bar?" Steve asked me as he too stared at the chattering women in the mirror.

I laughed. "You've got to be kidding."

"True story. One day these British rubber planters were having lunch here. Or it may have been in the Tiffin Room next door." He pointed to the hotel's cool white restaurant beside the bar. "And in strolled a real live, honest to goodness, tiger. Escaped from a zoo or the jungle. I think one of the planters got up and nailed it with his shotgun."

"Those were the days." I took a long delicious swallow of the cold Tiger beer.

"So let's discuss Hong Kong," he said in a lowered voice, glancing at the six men further down the bar.

I looked at the mirror in front of me to make sure we were not within earshot of anyone.

He continued in a quiet voice, "We need to come up with a name don't we?" His use of the plural did not escape me.

"Yes, we do."

"Well, as I was standing here, before you arrived, I came up with an idea. You see all those bottles beneath the mirror. Must be a hundred of them."

There were indeed. Every brand of spirit—scotch, gin, brandy, vodka, liqueurs ... even the odd bourbon.

"This is going to be fun. But first, let me order you another beer. It will take some creativity on our part." He signaled for another beer and pointed to me. The bartender removed my empty bottle and placed a fresh cold one in front of me. He walked away from us speaking Hainanese to his colleague at the other end of the bar. I recognized the dialect. Our family's chauffeur and cook had spoken it with each other.

"Let's pick a name from those bottles. And we'll come up with a name for the new company. Do you follow me?"

It occurred to me that McCoy and Sommers, both officers of comparable rank, could not have been more different in their approaches to clandestine intelligence collection. Steve was starting to impress me. We had been cut from the same cloth. I appreciated a fellow wit who liked to improvise, who could be spontaneous and not take himself too seriously. "All right. Let's name the company."

"You go first," he said.

I scanned the bottles that were lined up in front of us.

"I like the scotch bottles. The names have a certain eminence," I commented. "They convey tradition." I looked Steve in the eye. "Although this can't appear to be a name that we created in some barroom. No need to inform Springfield how we came up with this, is there?"

"Nope. And, yes, one of those scotch brands might appear like some old-school firm that goes back generations. So I second the motion. Scotch it is."

I focused then on the several brands of scotch whiskey along the bar below the mirror.

"I like Haig and Haig, sounds like a proper family business," I said. "On the other hand, that might sound too obviously like a brand of whiskey. We'd better compress it to Haig & Company. That's it, Haig & Company Limited. International maritime consultants."

And thus the name of the Hong Kong firm was born at the Long Bar of the Raffles Hotel.

"Well, lo and behold. The CIA station chief just entered the room." Steve was looking at the large mirror in front of us. I followed his gaze and saw three men walk in and sit down at a corner table. "That's Hunter Lenihan. He's the one wearing the tropical white suit, bow tie, and Panama hat. Looks like he's auditioning for a part in *Casablanca*. A good man. Tells me he worked with Tom Hiatt in Beirut ten years ago."

"Does he know about me? That I'm here?"

"No. there's no reason he should ... yet. When you come back here to recruit or debrief an agent I'll have to clue him in. But right now, he doesn't have a need to know." I saw Lenihan and McCoy make eye contact in the mirror.

"Who's the guy sitting beside Lenihan? The tough-looking hood in the brown shirt?"

Steve glanced at the mirror before answering. "His back is to us. I can't tell."

"I saw him walk in just before they sat down. He was on my flight yesterday. I'm sure of it."

"Interesting coincidence. He's Agency from the looks of it. I recognize the older guy with Hunter. Oscar, one of his case officers. I don't know the one in the brown shirt."

I stared for another moment at the mirror. The man kept his back to us.

"During the flight from L.A. to Tokyo I'd needed to go to the head. The lavatory door was locked, so I waited. Finally the door opened and this guy, the heavy-set, dark-haired one sitting there with Lenihan, walked out, zipping up his fly. I remember he stared at me. I didn't think anything of it until now. I forget names. I don't forget a face."

"Like I said, a coincidence."

"Perhaps."

"You know, Roy, this is a peculiar relationship we have with the Agency. The Chairman of the Joint Chiefs, who we report to in the chain of command, is higher up the White House totem pole than the director of the CIA. I think if push came to shove over a clandestine collection issue that affects the military, the Chairman might prevail. But at our micro level, the CIA sets the rules. We need to keep them informed and receive their blessing for a lot of what we do. What I'm saying is, it behooves me to keep on the good side of Hunter Lenihan."

McCoy motioned for the bartender to bring him the check.

"Let's have dinner. I'll introduce you to the American Club up on Scotts Road." We finished our beers. McCoy paid with cash. No tip was left on the bar. I took one last look at the pock-marked face of the man on the plane.

# 11

———

I N THE MORNING I SELECTED A MALAYSIA-BOUND taxicab at the Arab Street taxi stand, a half a mile from the Raffles. The drivers wait here to get return fares to Malaysia. The Mercedes Benz taxi I chose was from Malacca, so the driver was happy to get a fare back home. He'd arrived in Singapore with a passenger earlier that morning. I placed my suitcase in the trunk and put my trumpet case and locked briefcase on the back seat. I sat in the front.

The driver introduced himself as Sammy. He was a dark-skinned Tamil Indian, about forty years old, who spoke pitch-perfect English. At that time all the schools in Malaysia used British English as the medium of instruction. And beyond that, the Indians of Malaysia—Tamils, Malayali and Sikhs—prided themselves with their mastery of the language. They often spoke English at home.

As we began the journey north, I told him I was planning to live in Malacca.

"Splendid idea," Sammy exclaimed. "You'll find Malacca

so much more hospitable than Singapore. Less rigid. It is low-key and the people get along well together. And we thankfully don't have a sultan."

"That's what I've heard. I'm looking forward to settling down there for a while."

We passed through Malaysian Immigration and Customs control on the north side of the causeway without incident.

"May I ask you, sir, are you married?"

"No. I'm single," I said as we left the city of Johor Baru behind us and headed for the coast.

He nodded and drove on through the state of Johor for a while. "I can offer you some advice," he said at last.

"Sure. I'm all ears." It was going to be a three-hour drive. Why not learn a thing or two along the way?

"You know Malaysia has three main cultures, religions, and races. A fourth, if you include the Portuguese of Malacca. That is our nation's strength, and also our weakness." I could tell that I was about to get an education. And one that you won't receive in a textbook or at the local library.

He continued. "The reason there is so little intermarriage among the races—Malays, Chinese, and Indians—is not because of our race. It is religion. All because of religion," he stated, tapping the fingers of one hand on the steering wheel. He paused for a long while.

"Go on," I urged as I reflected on the adage that if you want to know what's going on in an unfamiliar locale, ask your taxi driver.

"Let me start with the premise that if intermarriage were easy in Malaysia, we would not have the hostility that exists now between the three races. You know about the anti-Chinese race riot in May 1969?" he asked.

I answered that I remembered reading about it at the time I was studying at UH.

"It was bloody, brutal. One good thing we can say is that peaceful Malacca was spared. But in Kuala Lumpur you had Malays attacking Chinese with every weapon imaginable. It was a bloodbath. Sure, the Chinese shopkeepers can be arrogant. Those in the towns' public markets manage to be quite rude to a non-Chinese."

"How did the riot start?" I asked. "Who was at fault?" I recalled the stories of the Singapore riots that took place when my family lived there in the 1950s. That violence had been the reason behind our permanent move to the United States.

"We don't know for sure how the riot started in Kuala Lumpur. It depends on who you ask. The Malays say they were insulted. They are a sensitive people. The Chinese claim, on the other hand, that the riot was planned in advance by the Malays. Premeditated murder. We Indians have always played third fiddle to both the Malays and the Chinese in this country. You know, a pox on both their houses." He gave a short malevolent laugh.

I thought then how similar this Chinese-Malay chasm was to the Jews and the Arabs who continued to fight each other in what was once Palestine, both of them blaming the other for the terror and war in 1948.

"You see. Look around. This is a beautiful country. So rich with natural resources." He swept his hand toward the sides of the road.

And that was true. We were driving up the coastal road now. On either side of us there were vast rubber tree plantations. Forests really. All the trees showing the traces on their trunks of resin taps. And before we reached Batu Pahat I looked to my left and there was the calm, deep blue-green sea, the Malacca Straits. I observed a solitary cargo ship sailing north. To the right as we sped up the coastal road was another plantation, this one thick with palm trees.

"When we left Johore I told you I would give you some advice," he said now. "You seem like a jolly good fellow. I don't want you to have any trouble because you are not familiar with the culture here."

"Right. The last thing I need."

"Okay then," Sammy continued. "You say you will live in Malaysia. Let's say that you are attracted to a pretty, young Malay woman, close to your own age. Perhaps you meet her in a coffee shop. Or on a town bus. Or at the post office. It is sure to happen. She will be dressed in a colorful batik sarong. She will smell fresh. You will start a conversation, and one thing will lead to another. You develop a mutual attraction. Opposites attract, and so on. Do you follow me?" He turned and looked to see if I was listening.

"Sounds good so far."

"Just wait. You ask for her phone number so that you can stay in touch. The next day you give her a call. She is alone at home, so the two of you can speak English together without anyone in her family being suspicious. You tell her how beautiful you think she is. She's flattered. And before you know it, you have made a date to meet each other at a restaurant in town. And let me remind you that every Malay in Malaysia *must* be a Muslim. That's the law here. If she is a Malay, she is a Muslim. No exceptions."

How different Malaysia was from Indonesia, I thought, where my Indonesian mother was a devout Christian.

"As you may have guessed, I am telling you this story from first-hand experience."

"Something like this happened to you?"

"Did it ever. You become infatuated with her. And she with you. What you don't realize is that the two of you have drawn the attention of the religious police. They wear plain clothes, always prowling around, so you would not have any idea that they have you and this pretty, young Malay woman under surveillance. But they are watching you. And they follow you after you finish your meal."

"It's starting to sound a lot like Saudi Arabia."

"Yes, it's bloody similar. So you invite her up to your flat to listen to some pop music on your stereo. She knows what she is getting into, but she agrees to join you anyway. She is crossing the line into *Khalwat* territory, and not only that, but *Khalwat* with a non-Muslim. It's taboo."

"Look, I understand Indonesian, Sammy. But that is a word I don't know. *Khalwat?*"

"It's a Malay word. Or perhaps an Arabic word that doesn't apply to Indonesia. It means an unmarried man and woman, either one or both are Muslim, and they are alone together and in *close proximity* to each other. They may not even be having sex. They could indeed have all of their clothes on. They are relaxing in the man's flat listening to pop music on his stereo. Doesn't matter. The religious police have decided that they are in close proximity, *Khalwat*, and it is time to make an arrest."

"You've got to be kidding me."

"No, alas, I'm not, because that is what happened to me fifteen years ago. The religious police followed us, the Malay woman and me, to a hotel room. We had been seeing each other for a few weeks on the sly. This time we had not been in the room for five minutes when they pounded on our door. We were frightened. I opened the door. Three men walked in, arrested us, and took us to a police station." Sammy stopped talking for a moment as he relived the episode.

"Go on," I urged.

"You see, here in Malaysia, a Malay is subject to Sharia law when it comes to this sort of thing. The Muslim woman I was with did not stand a chance. We had been caught red-handed. To make a longer story short, we were fined a staggering amount of money. I had to borrow from my family. And that wasn't all. The Sharia judge ordered me to convert to Islam and marry the woman. No if, ands, or buts. I was a Hindu." There was silence as we drove on over a river through the city of Muar.

"I was forced to go through the whole thing. Convert to Islam. Get myself circumcised. It was painful for me at that age. I was twenty-five. And then I married the woman. We got divorced five years later. I'm still a Muslim because it is illegal in Malaysia for a Muslim to convert to another religion. I cannot return to being a Hindu. They call someone who converts an apostate. An apostate would face serious consequences in Malaysia."

The drive continued on in silence for a long period. Up ahead and off to the right were lush green plantations and the jungle. I saw rugged mountains further to the east.

"We'll enter Malacca soon," he said at last.

"I'm curious, Sammy. How long have you been driving a taxi cab?"

"Five years. It was difficult for me to obtain a license to own a taxi. The government departments are Malay. They reserve most of the licenses for fellow Malays. I waited for two years before I finally got the license and bought this taxi." He made the motion with his thumb and forefinger of having to pay someone under the table.

"My family has a successful business in Malacca, by the way. A travel agency in the center of town. It's called Royal Travel and Tours. I should be running that business by now. But I was ostracized by the family when I converted." Sammy shook his head reflecting on his bad fate. "My family is Hindu. I have a younger brother, who of course continues to go to the temple with my parents. As a Muslim I could not be seen praying there with them. My parents lost hope. They turned the business over to my younger brother. He runs it now. Go meet him some day. Anyway, I tried working at various jobs over the years. Eventually I bought this taxi. At least I'm earning more now than I did in the past going from job to job." He drove on in silence for several minutes.

"Mr. Roy, where do you want me to drop you off?"

"I'll be staying at the Majestic Hotel. Do you know it?"

"Of course. It's the grand old hotel of Malacca. I think it has been around for something like fifty years or more. It's about a mile up the river on *Jalan Bunga Raya*." I knew that translated to Street of Great Flowers. The Malay and Indonesian languages are related, though not identical, as, say, Spanish is to Portuguese.

"I hope you keep in touch. Any time you need a taxi, be sure to give me a call." He handed me one of his calling cards. I told him I would be sure to do that.

"You can also use my family's travel agency, Royal Travel, when you need to. My brother and I are still close. I don't have any bad feelings. What happened was my fate. It's *Karma*. That's Hindu, by the way." He said this with an ironic smile.

We entered the town of Malacca. There were no high-rise buildings. It appeared to be a city of antiquated one-story shop houses. It also seemed to be a city populated primarily by Chinese judging by the written characters on most of the shops and by the people sauntering along the narrow sidewalks.

"Here, look, we are now arriving in Little India. Don't blink or you'll miss it," he said a moment later, pointing to the shops along the road. "It takes up only about one block. You see there, all the people are Indians. If you were walking here, you'd smell the sweet incense. It's different from the Chinese incense at the shops we just passed."

The clothing stores in Little India all displayed colorful saris and sarongs. I saw an array of red and green chili peppers laid out in baskets at a food shop. Most of the people along the road were swarthy Tamils. Many of the men wore sarongs wrapped around their waists. The women wore colorful saris, and many of them seemed to have jewelry pierced through their noses and either a black or a red dot plastered onto the forehead.

Sammy read my mind. "You are looking at the Indian women, I see. Pay attention to the color of the dot on the woman's forehead. If it is red, that means she is married. If it is black, she is still single, and fair game." He laughed. He was delighted to be back home. We made a right turn onto *Jalan Bunga Raya.*

Indeed there is no place in Malaysia that has more charm than Malacca. The town lies on the sea at the mouth of a narrow, winding river which runs slowly beneath a four-century-old bridge before it flows into the Straits. The north side of the river has the ancient Chinatown and the ornate seaside homes of the Straits-born Chinese merchants. On the other side of the bridge, south of the river, one finds the large red houses in the middle of town that the Dutch built when they ran Malacca during the seventeenth and eighteenth centuries. And on a hill above those red buildings stands the ruins of the fort built by the Portuguese, who controlled the Asian spice trade from here in the 1500s until their defeat by the Dutch.

The first Chinese arrived even earlier, in the 1400s.

No other locale in all of Southeast Asia has a more beguiling history than Malacca. The tolerant and peaceful town has always drawn breath, through boom and bust, from its enlivening mix of Portuguese, Malay, Chinese, Eurasian, and Indian citizens. This was the intoxicating setting where I planned to make my home base as an undercover spook.

"Well, here we are. The Majestic Hotel."

We turned into the hotel's driveway. The façade of the building was a blend of down-at-the-heels British colonial and Malacca Chinese, with the name of the hotel written in English and in Chinese characters above the portal. Across the narrow street was the slow-flowing Malacca River.

Sammy opened the trunk of his ten-year-old Mercedes Benz taxicab and hauled out my suitcase. A bellman rushed up to assist. I removed my trumpet case and the briefcase, which contained my valuables and my second passport, from the back seat of the car.

I handed Sammy the forty dollars for the three-hour journey and added a five-dollar tip.

"Thanks for the ride, Sammy. I'll be in touch with you when I need to return to Singapore."

"Be sure to do that, Mr. Roy. I am at your service. Goodbye for now."

# 12

---

AS THE TAXI DROVE OFF, I FOLLOWED THE BELLMAN into the hotel lobby. As I approached the front desk, a thought occurred to me. I had planned on spending a week or so looking for an apartment or a house in Malacca. Now I realized that with all the tasks I had on my plate, I did not have time to waste home-hunting in the town. I needed to get the businesses set up here and in Hong Kong. And I needed to locate Komang and the *Pacific Star*. The sooner, the better.

The Chinese man at the reception desk greeted me with a cordial smile.

"Good afternoon," I said. "Say, I have a reservation for a couple of nights. Name is Roy Mancini." I took my passport and American Express card and placed them on the desk. "I'm wondering, would you have a suite available for a long-term stay? Something I could pay for by the month?"

The receptionist glanced at a ledger and ran his finger along a list before replying.

"We do have one suite available. And, yes, we could

arrange a monthly billing. I would have to calculate that for you. Would you care to see it now, Mr. Mancini?"

"Sure. Let's take a look. You can have them bring the suitcase up to the room." I anticipated that I would take the suite regardless.

We took the elevator to the top floor and walked down the passageway to a room at the end of the hall. As we entered, I saw a large window with a view to the other side of the river. I walked over to the window and looked down. There were fishing boats with dragons' eyes painted on their bows, plowing up and down the river. I'd never seen those eyes on boats anywhere else in my travels. I commented on it.

"It's uniquely Malacca. The Chinese owners paint them on their boats to ward off evil spirits when they venture out into the Malacca Straits. It can get stormy out there, and they believe those dragons will keep them safe. See the iguana down there?"

"Iguana?"

"Yes. The river below has iguanas. If you look down, you may see some of them sunbathing or swimming about. They're harmless."

I looked around the interior of the suite. We were standing inside a large living room with a sofa, coffee table, and matching armchairs. And on one side of the room there was a large writing desk and a couple of antique hardwood cabinets, one containing a television set. The carpet was well worn but appeared to be clean, and there were paintings of local scenes on the walls. An open door led to the bedroom, which had a king-size bed, more furniture, and ample closet space. No kitchen, but I hadn't planned on doing much cooking for myself in Malacca.

"This is fine," I said. "If you'll figure out a rate for me, you can charge it to my credit card. I expect to stay for a while in Malacca."

"If I may ask, sir, what do you do?"

"I'm in the coffee business. Buying and selling. I expect to travel a fair amount, so my staying here in the hotel is a good choice. And I like the river view. Do you need me to go back to the lobby to sign anything?"

"No, Mr. Mancini. You can sign in the next time you go downstairs. And welcome to the Majestic."

I made two phone calls that night. One was to Sammy, asking him to pick me up the next afternoon and drive me back to Singapore. That would give me time in the morning to complete the registration of Coffee Traders International with the lawyer.

The other call was to Steve McCoy at his home in Singapore. I asked him to book a flight for me from Singapore to Hong Kong and to have the Institute's Hong Kong office reserve a room for me for three nights at the Peninsula Hotel. McCoy had been informed of my agreement with Frank DuPont that any flight with a duration of over three hours could be booked business class.

The urgent business in Singapore was to make radio contact with Komang. We had agreed when we met in the Panama Canal that I would attempt to contact his radio on the *Pacific Star* at 1:00 in the afternoon, Greenwich Mean Time. That would be 9:00 p.m. Singapore time.

McCoy had arranged to have a shortwave radio installed in his embassy office. It was now a matter of contacting Komang by voice transmission at the selected time of day. I would ask him what his next port of call was and get his estimated date of arrival.

We had been able to monitor the itinerary of the *Pacific Star* using the Lloyds of London Shipping Index. That guide kept an up-to-date record of the voyages of every cargo ship and oil tanker in the world. In a true emergency, we could request the U.S. navy's satellites to do that job. But on a routine basis, it was better not to burden the navy. They had more important missions for their satellites. So we used Lloyd's commercial shipping service.

"Welcome back, Roy," Steve greeted me when I arrived in his office the next day. "That didn't take long. Everything okay in Malaysia?"

"Couldn't be better. I chose to remain at the Majestic Hotel a little longer. I've got more important things to do right now than to go house-hunting. First off, we need to find the position of the *Pacific Star* and its next port of call. Can we check Lloyds?" I was eager now to locate Komang and to start making plans to meet and recruit him.

"I've got it here." He reached for the gray paperback booklet on his desk. "Give me a second. This just arrived." He thumbed through the booklet until he found the ship. He glanced at it and handed it to me.

I read in Lloyd's that *Pacific Star* had departed from Belawan, Indonesia, in North Sumatra. Destination unknown.

Steve said, "You know we learned that the *Pacific Star*'s owner … what's his name?"

"Rolf Beckmann."

"Right. It looks like we may have hit pay dirt with your guy. Beckmann fixed a two-year time charter in London with the North Korean government for this ship."

"Fan-fucking-tastic!" I exclaimed. "Two years in and out of North Korea! I've got to get *Clover* to stay on the ship for the duration. Let's try to contact him at nine o'clock tonight. That's 1300 hours GMT. We need him to tell us his ship's next port and ETA. I'll plan to meet him."

"You've got his call sign and the frequencies you agreed on?"

"Yeah, got it. In my head. Call sign is P3C4G. We'll use 12 megahertz tonight," I said. The excitement of the hunt. "Make a note. Whenever we call him during daytime we use the 20-meter band." Steve wrote the frequencies down on a pad.

"I've booked you on the Cathay Pacific flight to Hong Kong tomorrow morning. Departure 0900 hours. You arrive early afternoon. The Peninsula is confirmed." Steve shook his head in mock amazement. "I'll trade jobs with you, Roy. The 'Pen' is the finest hotel in Hong Kong."

"Nothing too good for a coffee bean hawker." I laughed.

I continued in a serious vein. "That'll give me enough time to get over to the island and meet with the accounting firm that's setting up Haig. I'm going to arrange for that firm to act as the nominee directors and shareholders so my name won't appear anywhere on the company's records. Ditto for the company in Malacca."

"Where are you staying tonight?"

"The Raffles. Meet me later at the Long Bar for a drink? I'll buy you dinner at the Palm Court. Afterwards we return here and try to connect with *Clover*." We would begin referring now to Komang by his cryptonym.

"You're beginning to sound like a local, Roy. Okay, I'll meet you at the Raffles at five-thirty. Go out and enjoy yourself for the rest of the afternoon."

I reserved a table for dinner in the Palm Court restaurant for 7:15. A waiter led us outside past the hotel's several bird cages to a table set beneath palm trees along the rim of the hotel's vast lawn. The sky was clear and filled with stars and a full moon. McCoy and I ordered drinks and dinner.

Without appearing conspicuous, I glanced around at each of the tables and the dinner guests. As I did, I saw the man from the plane walk onto the lawn. He appeared to ask the maitre'd for a table. The host looked over the settings and led the man to a table close to the swimming pool. He sat with his back to us. Dinner for one.

"My mysterious companion from the plane, the one we saw at the Long Bar, just sat down." I motioned with my head in the direction of the man's table. McCoy looked and saw his back.

"Interesting. The Agency must be putting him up here at the Raffles."

"Right. A coincidence." I said.

We took our time over dinner and had a liqueur afterwards. As I signed the bill and we got up to leave, the man remained in his seat, his back turned to us.

I deliberately left my notebook under a napkin on the table as we stood up to leave. After taking four steps toward the hotel, I turned around abruptly, giving the appearance of remembering something I'd left on our table. As I did, I looked at the man from the plane. He was staring at me with something like a glare on his dark visage, then quickly turned his head. There was no doubt in my mind now that I was being followed and that the surveillance had begun stateside. The CIA had me in their sights for some reason.

McCoy and I returned to his office at 8:30. The short-wave radio set was hidden in a closet. There was a state-of-the-art transceiver, two sets of headphones, a recording device,

and a microphone. The antenna led up to the top of the embassy building and was disguised among the vast array of
antennae.

At 8:50 we turned the set on and dialed in to the
frequency 12 MHz. I began repeating the *Pacific Star*'s call sign
at 8:55. At 9:05 Komang replied that he was P3C4G and
asked who was calling. I replied in Indonesian that I was
Cisco. I did not wish to waste time with insecure chitchat. I
asked him for the ship's position and next port of call. He
replied that the ship was currently sailing in the Java Sea north
of Jakarta. The next port of call would be Surabaya, and they
would reach that port in less than twenty-four hours.

"Where will the ship go after Surabaya?" I asked.

"We will load rice in Bitung, in North Sulawesi. I don't
have an ETA for Bitung. It depends on how long it takes to
load timber in Surabaya."

"Copy," I replied. I quickly improvised a plan. There
would not be time to meet Komang in Surabaya. I would get
Haig set up in Hong Kong first, while *Pacific Star* was loading
in Surabaya, and then I'd fly to North Sulawesi. "See you in
Bitung. I'll send a note to the ship. Over and out."

"Copy that," he said. We signed off. The entire conversation had taken no more than one minute.

Steve removed his headset, turned off the recorder, and
gave a puzzled smile before asking me what we had talked
about. He of course had not understood our conversation in
Indonesian. I told him I would continue with my plan to fly to
Hong Kong the next day, requesting that he monitor *Pacific
Star*'s port call in Surabaya—arrival and departure dates. He
could arrange that through our military attaché in Jakarta.

After I set up Haig & Company, I would fly from Hong

Kong to Manado in North Sulawesi. And from Manado I would travel by road to Bitung. I needed to know the ship's departure date from Surabaya. I could then estimate her day of arrival in Bitung.

# 13

---

ONE CAN NEVER FORGET HIS FIRST APPROACH AND landing at Hong Kong's old Kai Tak Airport. About five minutes prior to touchdown, the plane made a radical right turn in order to avoid the barren mountains to the left. At the same time, the plane threaded its way beside Kowloon's tall multi-story apartment buildings on the right. This is one approach that would not have been attempted on autopilot. It took a highly focused pilot to navigate the twists and turns, land on the runway, then brake hard and come to a full stop before plunging into the bay at the end.

I arrived in the afternoon at the Peninsula Hotel on Nathan Road in Kowloon. The first thing one notices on arrival are the pristine late-model Bentley automobiles lined up in the hotel's driveway, limousines that are available to take discriminating hotel guests wherever they need to go.

As I entered the magnificent lobby, trailed by the bellman who carried my suitcase, it was apparent to me that this was a place where Hong Kong's upper crust gathered to meet and greet. The tables were occupied by prosperous-looking hotel guests and local aristocracy enjoying what they refer to as "high tea." I had to remind myself as I walked through the lobby this first time that I did indeed belong in this lofty milieu.

As soon as I unpacked, I left the hotel and walked to the Star Ferry terminal, four blocks from the hotel.

The ferry boat cruises across the harbor carrying passengers, first-class seats above and second-class below. The cruise is picturesque and can be thrilling as the ferry navigates among the large cargo ships and local craft that plow ahead of it through Victoria Harbor. One can sit on a bench and see, in addition to the cargo ship and Chinese junk traffic in the harbor, the majestic Hong Kong Island skyline ahead. On land and at sea, there is a sense of motion, of intrigue, of the world's business being transacted.

I walked from the Star Ferry pier on Hong Kong Island to the Prince's Building where the auditing firm had its office. I had phoned from Singapore and asked them to expedite the formation of Haig & Company. They were expecting me. The company was British, as were many of the professional services in those days.

An efficient Cantonese receptionist, Miss Wong, escorted me to the office of the managing director, Percy Beresford-Churchill. He was attired in a gray, pinstriped three-piece suit and wore a wide red and blue striped necktie. He had a florid complexion, indicative of many a long lunch, a full head of barbered gray hair, gray eyebrows that curled upwards, and a matching regimental mustache. He was in his late fifties or early sixties and appeared the embodiment of English class and financial success. His urbane demeanor would give a client a sense of confidence—whatever was discussed in his office would not be repeated beyond these walls.

"Good afternoon, Mr. Francisco," he said in upper-class, London-accented English as he stood up and crossed the room to shake my hand. "I trust you had a pleasant flight."

I caught myself in time from replying in the same theatrically accented English.

"Yes, I did. Cathay Pacific is super," I said.

We sat down in cushioned, expensive-looking armchairs at a polished mahogany coffee table in the center of the room. After ten minutes of small talk on the subject of Hong Kong and its attractions, we got down to business.

He opened a folder on the table in front of him. "We have organized your company documents here. You have indicated that you wish to have our firm act as nominees—as shareholders and as directors. We are of course prepared to do that." He spread each of the documents out in front of me.

"It's a simple process for us. We form companies like this every day of the week. Our address will be your office in Hong Kong. We'll hang a plank with your company name on it out front. Our receptionist, Miss Wong, whom you met, will perform as your secretary, answering phone calls, and receiving cables, mail, and messages on your behalf. You need only provide us with your forwarding address and contact numbers." He sat back and gave me a broad smile. "You are, of course, the beneficial owner of the company, and we have documents for you to sign that establish that fact. No one outside of this office need know a thing about it."

"That sounds like the setup I have in mind."

"And as you may know, whenever your business transactions are offshore, outside of Hong Kong, there will be no tax on your profits."

I asked him to explain that.

"I understand you are in the consulting business."

"Yes. Shipping."

"Indeed. Let's say your client is domiciled in a country outside of Hong Kong. They remit your fee to a bank here in Hong Kong. You pay no tax on the money that gets deposited here. However, if your client is based in Hong Kong, then it would not be considered an offshore transaction and you would have to pay a fifteen percent tax on that profit."

I nodded, aware that none of that was relevant since there would be no actual clients. "That's fine. I need an offshore company. And you're holding the company's name for us: Haig & Company Limited?"

"Done," he replied. "All the paperwork is in order. You only need to sign a couple of documents, we take a copy of your passport, and you are ready to do business. You indicated that you might wish to set up a bank account in Hong Kong. We will expedite the registration process so you can do that."

"Yes, I'd like that. It would make it easy for me to pay your fees from the funds here in a local account."

"Splendid. Have you given any consideration to a banking relationship?"

"I have. I'd like to open the account with the Hong Kong and Shanghai Bank."

"Good choice, indeed. The senior managers of the bank are friends of mine. Fellow members of the Hong Kong Club. I would be only too happy to arrange an introduction."

Within three days we had formed Haig & Company as a legal offshore company, ready to engage in maritime research anywhere in the world. The receptionist, Miss Alice Wong, would be my point of contact at the Prince's Building office.

On the third day I opened Haig's U.S. Dollar account with the main branch of the Hong Kong and Shanghai Banking Corporation. I deposited four hundred dollars in cash from my wallet, and one of the Institute's cover companies would top it up with more money. I planned to draw funds from that account to pay my clandestine assets their fees and expenses.

I phoned McCoy at home at ten o'clock at night. He informed me by way of our prearranged code that the ship had docked in Surabaya. Estimated time of departure was four days later, on November 2nd. I estimated that the ship would arrive in Bitung on November 5th or 6th.

Two days after my meeting with Percy Beresford-Churchill I sat at a table in the grand lobby of the Peninsula Hotel. I was alone, having a cool drink, and observing the women who sashayed through the lobby. They were of all ages and assorted nationalities: European or American, Chinese, Malay or Filipino, Indian and South American. Most were dressed expensively. I glanced at the tables around me where Chinese, Arab and Western businessmen huddled together over coffee or tea, speaking in soft tones, perusing documents. There was a table where an exhausted middle-aged American couple, tourists from a cruise ship, drank iced tea as they studied a map. I had ordered business cards for myself the previous day from two separate printers in Kowloon, and I was killing time before I would walk up Nathan Road and pick up the new cards. All of a sudden, the plan came to mind.

I had to formulate a communications system with Komang when I met him in Bitung. I could not depend solely on the incomplete Lloyds Shipping Index; I needed to have much better real-time information of the *Pacific Star*'s port calls. I therefore had to create a link where I could communicate with Komang, using a cutout by shortwave radio, one where he initiated the calls. And this system would include the use of a clandestine ham radio network. The pattern of that network appeared to me now.

I would recruit Komang a.k.a. *Clover* as a clandestine agent in Bitung. And I would provide his wife, Putu, in Bali, with a ham radio. He would make a voice call to Putu in Amed from his ship when he had information for me about his itinerary. They would speak with each other in the complicated Balinese language that would be unintelligible to anyone on his ship who might be eavesdropping. Putu would relay Komang's information to me, not in Balinese, but in the language that I spoke and understood—Indonesian. She would make the call from her clandestine shortwave radio to McCoy's radio in Singapore.

The message from Komang through Putu to me would be quick and simple, one that should not take more than thirty seconds for Putu to relay to Singapore. It would give me his ship's last port of call in the "denied area." This would be followed by the next port of call where I could plan to meet him, the estimated date of arrival at that next port, and finally a code indicating a level of urgency.

The dicey part of the plan would be secreting an illegal radio in Bali. Indonesia was an authoritarian military dictatorship run by former General Suharto, his family, and their army cronies. I knew the security-conscious Indonesian military would not allow amateur radios in the country. I would have to smuggle the radio components and antenna into Bali, delivering them to Putu at her home in the east coast fishing village of Amed. Putu could be at considerable risk. I'd have to train her thoroughly.

This plan occupied my mind for several minutes. I lost track of the sashaying women, the earnest businessmen discussing their business deals, and the occasional tourist entering the lobby from the street. I was on to something. I had filled in one of the holes that had concerned me in regard to running Komang in and out of North Korea. I was confident that I could recruit him as an agent, but the recruitment was only the start of a successful, long-term operation. Our communications with each other would be key to the mission.

I stood up searching for my waiter. When I caught his eye, I made the signal with my thumbs and forefingers that I needed my bill. I sat down and scribbled in my notebook, "K/P/S/M," shorthand for the one-way direction of our clandestine radio traffic: Komang/Putu/Singapore/Mancini. The waiter arrived; I signed my bill and left the hotel in search of a pay phone. I found one beside the Star Ferry Terminal.

The Institute had an office in Hong Kong that was commanded by an air force officer, Major Geoffrey Davis. Under normal circumstances there would be no reason for me to check in with him when I was operating in Hong Kong. He commanded three case officers in the colony whose missions were to collect intelligence on the Chinese People's Liberation army missile forces, the air force and the army. I knew from my stint at Springfield that these case officers were busy running agents inside China. The only need I might have for contacting Major Davis was if I had to cable McCoy in Singapore with some sensitive information. I now had that need.

I phoned Davis's direct number at the consulate.

"Hello?" the woman's voice on the other end answered.

"Hello. I'd like to speak to Geoffrey Davis please."

"May I know who's calling?" she replied. This phone number, I knew, was unlisted.

"My name is Roy Mancini. I work with Steve McCoy. You made a hotel reservation for me in Hong Kong this week."

She told me to wait. I fed another Hong Kong dollar into the pay phone and waited. People pushed and bustled behind me, heading for the nearby toll booths, rushing to board the next ferry boat to the island. At last, Davis answered the phone.

"May I help you?" he asked in a brisk, neutral tone of voice.

"Yes, sir. My boss told me you could help me out. I need to send him an urgent message." He would have known my name from the exchanges we had had between his office and Springfield when I was assisting Gus Pomeroy on the East Asia desk. We had never met each other.

He hesitated for a few seconds. "All right. Come over to the consulate this afternoon. We'll see what we can do. When you get here, tell the receptionist downstairs that you have an appointment with Cynthia Roman in the military attaché's office. Miss Roman will be expecting you." He hung up the phone.

I boarded the Star Ferry and rode it across the harbor and took a taxi to the United States Consulate building, a five-minute drive from the ferry terminal. I arrived at three o'clock, relieved that there would be enough time for me to draft my cable and get it sent to the Singapore office, with a copy to Springfield.

Cynthia Roman met me in the lobby. She was a slim and quite pretty Asian woman, about my age, who I later learned was Filipino-American. She was a navy petty officer, working undercover as the secretary to the Deputy Assistant Military Attaché, which was Geoffrey Davis's cover job at the consulate. She led me through the security procedures on the ground floor, then the key-padded and fingerprint-recognition doorways on the third floor that lead to the Institute's sterile office suite.

Miss Roman informed me that Major Davis was in a meeting and could not be disturbed, and that she could assist me in preparing my memo to the Institute's Singapore office. She led me to an empty desk and handed me writing material.

"This will be short," I told her. "I hope you can send it this afternoon."

"Major Davis will need to review it first and sign off on it," she answered. I was reminded that this was an office that was unused to receiving visitors and that hospitality was not a priority. I could have used a cold drink.

My message to McCoy stated that I needed him to order a low-power, easy-to-use shortwave radio set with an antenna. I gave him the brand and model of radio that I wanted. It needed to be delivered to his Singapore office as soon as possible. I wrote that I would leave for North Sulawesi in two days, signing off with my code name: *Arabica*.

Cynthia Roman escorted me back to the lobby. She never asked me about what I was up to in Hong Kong. She didn't have a need to know. Truth be told, I wanted to spend more time with her.

Before saying goodbye to each other, she smiled and offered me her hand. I took it and thanked her for her assistance. That's when the man in the plane walked up to an elevator beside us, unaccompanied. He pushed the button and looked straight ahead, waiting for the door to open. I unconsciously held on to Cynthia's hand and stared at the side of the man's head. Cynthia made no effort to pull away from me. Finally, just as his elevator door opened, I asked the man if we had met somewhere. He looked at me strangely, shrugged his shoulders, and without saying a word entered the elevator and punched a code into the keypad. Just before the door closed, he raised his right hand in front of his face and gave me the finger, mouthing "fuck you."

Cynthia was puzzled. She continued to hold on to my hand. "Is everything all right, Roy?"

"I wish I knew. Thanks again, Cynthia, for your help."

We parted, leaving a lot unsaid.

My next chore was to find a photo store and purchase a top-of-the-line Nikon SLR camera and zoom lens. Komang would need that. I also had to pick up my name cards that I had ordered at two separate printers: one that identified me by true name as the managing director of Coffee Traders International with an office in Malacca, Malaysia, and the other that introduced me as Louis Francisco of Haig & Company Limited, with offices at the Prince's Building in Hong Kong.

All errands accomplished, I booked my flight from Hong Kong to Manado via Jakarta at a small travel agency tucked away on the mezzanine floor of the Peninsula Hotel.

# 14

---

NOVEMBER 1974

I DIDN'T WANT THE CHAMPAGNE-FUELED FLIGHT IN
business class to end until the party was over. The comely
Indonesian flight attendant and I spent much of the time
playfully seducing each other. Back in the day, the flight
attendants were uniformly young, pretty, charming, and single.
She slipped me her Jakarta phone number soon after the plane
began its descent.

A day, indeed an entire nation, of stark contrasts. The
decrepit Jakarta airport was a hellhole in November 1974. I
waited for several hours in a drab, hot transit area for my connecting flight to Manado. The sullen immigration control officer who chopped an entry visa into my passport gave the
impression he would just as soon place me on the next plane
out of Indonesia and send me back to wherever I came from.

At last, Manado. One can stroll in front of the hotel here,
savor a fresh offshore breeze, and look out at the deep blue
Celebes Sea and volcanic islands to the north. A river winds its
way through the middle of the city to the sea.

I experience a satisfying feeling when I'm in a town on a river. The river adds an aura, a unique personality, to the locale if you have the time to pause and watch its life and the flow. I am also happiest along a seaside. I can't imagine living anywhere else. My psyche needs that panorama of a calm blue-green sea or a wild ocean. And so much the better if there are islands and boats offshore to tease the imagination. Add to the mix a brilliant sunset, which in the tropics drops below the horizon in the blink of an eye.

I BOOKED A TAXI AT MY WATERFRONT HOTEL THE NEXT morning. I anticipated that the *Pacific Star* would arrive in Bitung that day, and that I would make contact with Komang while the ship was in port loading rice.

I placed writing material and envelopes, along with the Nikon camera and the zoom lens, in a backpack. I wore jeans, a white tennis shirt, a baseball cap without a logo, and dark glasses. I planned to first case Bitung for a suitable meeting place. That done, I would write a brief note to Komang and somehow get it delivered to him on his ship.

The road from Manado to Bitung winds its way through green forested hills and fragrant clove plantations. North Sulawesi is the clove capital of the world. The spice is exported world-wide, as it has been for hundreds of years, first by the Portuguese and later by the Dutch colonizers. The trade is now controlled by Chinese middlemen. Those cloves are used also to flavor the tobacco in the aromatic Indonesian cigarettes, the kind that Komang had been smoking when I met him in Panama. The trip from Manado to Bitung took two hours including a brief stop at a roadside stand where I purchased a sack of cloves for good luck.

Bitung is a small, dusty, and nondescript port town. The main activity is deep-sea fishing and the processing of canned tuna. The large fish are caught in abundance in the nearby Celebes and Molucca Seas. A shipping channel runs between the town and a large island to the east.

The taxi dropped me off four blocks from the Port Area where I began my search for a meeting place among few choices. It was ten o'clock in the morning, hot and humid. I trusted because of my tan complexion and black hair I would not be conspicuous as a *boolay*, a white foreigner. I entered a restaurant called *Warung Gossip* and spoke to the waitress in Indonesian. I thought I could be mistaken for a local, albeit of a mixed European bloodline. I ordered coffee and surveyed the restaurant. There were few customers and the place seemed to be as good a spot as any in this small town to meet Komang. I wrote the note for Komang, signed it "Cisco," and sealed it in an envelope.

I needed to find the shipping agent for the *Pacific Star*, so I walked along a sidewalk in the direction of the port. Soon enough I located the office on a street that was two blocks from the gated entrance to the docks. I entered and removed my dark glasses. A bulletin board hung on a wall at the back of the office, and I could make out that the *Pacific Star* was listed near the bottom. The ship had arrived in port that morning, and she was due to remain there for two more days. I walked to the counter and nodded to a clerk who was busy typing documents.

"*Selamat pagi,*" I greeted him good morning. He looked up and asked if he could help me.

I replied in Indonesian. "I would like to send a letter to the *Pacific Star*. Can you arrange that for me?"

"Yes, I can do that. Do you have it with you?"

I reached into my backpack and removed the envelope that was addressed to Komang Surya, Radio Operator, MV *Pacific Star*. I handed it to the clerk.

"Oh, he is Indonesian," he exclaimed in surprise upon seeing the Balinese name on the envelope.

"Yes. He's a friend of mine. How soon do you think you can get this note to him?"

"I can take it to the ship after I finish with these." He motioned toward the papers that he had been typing. I thanked him and discretely handed him an ample gratuity in a separate envelope.

The note asked Komang to meet me at two o'clock that afternoon at *Warung Gossip*. I listed the street address, adding that if he was unable to meet me that day, he should try to meet me at two o'clock at the restaurant the following day, and every day that his ship was in port.

A case officer learns in this game how to wait for long periods of time in strange, foreign places without becoming conspicuous or raising suspicion among the locals. This is even more challenging if one is waiting to meet his agent in a small town like Bitung. I now had more than three hours before my two o'clock meeting with Komang.

The gaudily decorated pony-drawn buggies called *bendis* were everywhere. This horse-and-buggy contraption appeared to be the only means of public transportation in Bitung. I flagged one down when I stepped outside the shipping office. There is just enough room on a *bendi* for two passengers. I hopped in and told the driver I wished to sightsee and that I could pay him by the hour. We negotiated a price and he seemed happy to have the steady fare. He whistled and made a clucking sound with his tongue, gave the pony a swat on its rump with a switch, and we took off at a trot down the main road, heading to nowhere in particular.

At last I asked the driver to go north up the coast road and out of town. The view to my right was of the main shipping channel and Lembeh Island a few miles off in the distance. Inter-island ferry boats, a small cargo ship and fishing vessels with their catch of tuna were sailing in the channel from points north. We passed thick groves of trees on our left. And there beside a red-flowered cluster of clove trees I spotted a small restaurant, a *warung*. I asked the driver to pull over. It was past noon, so I invited him to join me for lunch. Meanwhile he fed his pony with a handful of carrots he had stored in the back of the buggy.

The restaurant had three tables, and we were the only customers. The owner, an emaciated, gray-haired elderly woman, cooked and served us lunch. I realized at once that this was an ideal setting for the imminent recruitment meeting I was planning that afternoon, preferable to *Warung Gossip* in the middle of town.

The driver and I shared a tuna curry with fried rice and washed it down with a large bottle of the local *Bintang* beer. The meals cost me a total of three dollars equivalent in the local Rupiah. Satisfied with the meal, and with the bill for lunch, I commented aloud in English, "This is the life." The driver and the old woman gave me a puzzled look.

At a quarter after one, I asked the driver to take me back to Bitung. We arrived in the center of town at fifteen minutes to two. I paid the driver and walked the three blocks to *Warung Gossip*.

Komang was not yet an agent, so there was no need to go through a lot of tradecraft drills, safety signals, two-minute rules, and so forth. I was prepared now to wait for him at the restaurant for as long as it took in the event he could not get off his ship early. I was pleased when I saw him walking up the sidewalk from the direction of the Port Area at a quarter past two.

As I watched him approach, I heard the ubiquitous soundtrack of ponies' hooves on the road outside. Komang was a heavyset man of average height for an Indonesian, about 5'8". He may have put on weight because of his sedentary life on the vessel. He had a swarthy complexion and smooth untroubled facial features. His black hair was cut short. He now wore khaki cargo pants, heavy leather shoes, and a green short-sleeved shirt. His dark glasses were pushed rakishly up onto his head. He held a placid expression as he walked into the restaurant and looked around the room for me. I was sitting at a table in a far corner in the back, verifying that he was not being followed as I watched him enter. He spotted me and his face broke into a wide smile. I stood up happy to see him and motioned for him to join me.

We greeted each other warmly and shook hands. "Hello, Komang. Great to see you again."

"Hey, Cisco Kid. Welcome to Bitung. How do you like this place?"

"Seems like a nice place to be from. Do you know the town?"

"No. My first time here," he replied.

"Let's get ourselves a *bendi* and take a ride. How much time do you have ashore today?"

"I'm off for the rest of the day. There's not a lot for a radio operator to do in port."

"Well then, let's go sightseeing. It's nice here, outside of town."

We waited on the side of the road until a *bendi* pulled over for us. We boarded the buggy and I told the driver to take us north, up the coast road. He whistled and snapped his pinto pony into a fast trot. Komang lit up a clove cigarette and sat back and smoked, relaxed and happy. I did not want to discuss anything about our plans now because of the proximity of the driver. I knew the ride to the *warung* would take no more than thirty minutes. After five minutes we reached the coastal road beyond the lackluster environs of Bitung.

I turned to Komang. "I know of a small *warung* up the road. We can have refreshments there and discuss business." He nodded, but said nothing. I gathered he was happy just to be off the ship and back on Indonesian *terra firma*.

# 15

---

A S WE CLIP-CLOPPED UP THE ROAD, WITH THE occasional car or truck passing us to the right, I thought about my impending pitch. A successful recruitment of Komang would be predicated on his motivation, as it is with every clandestine agent. I pondered now about what could possibly motivate him to agree to work for me in secret, putting himself at great risk in the denied area ports and aboard his ship. It was unlikely that he would be motivated by the few hours of friendship we had established in the Canal Zone. A feeling of friendship, or even a sense of adventure, was not going to be enough to induce him to put his life on the line, taking surreptitious photographs and keeping incriminating reports about submarines, warships, and shipyards in Communist China, North Korea, and the Soviet Union. An arrest for spying in the denied area would result in a sentence of life in prison, if not execution by hanging.

Ideology? There are agents who spy because of a desire

for freedom or Western democracy. And so they agree to betray the totalitarian regime in their homeland. That would not be the case with Komang, who was devoted to his island of Bali. I knew enough about the island's culture to know that the Balinese believed that the Hindu gods, plural, had placed them at the center of the earth, that their own unique religious beliefs and customs were superior to all surrounding cultures. A person with that kind of singular pride was not going to risk everything in life over an alien ideology.

I considered the motivation of financial gain. An Institute cover company in Europe had remitted $500 to Komang and Putu's bank account in October. Komang may not have been aware of that. In fact, he had done nothing for me yet to earn it. I knew that $500 per month was what he was paid as the radio operator on the *Pacific Star*. So the additional $500 a month would double his income. That might be sufficient pay for providing the kind of innocent maritime information we had discussed in Panama. But would this additional $500 be enough for him to risk his life in the "denied areas" for me? I doubted it.

I turned to Komang and asked, "Have you received any news from Putu?"

His relaxed visage turned to a dark frown. "*Adu*," he said, expressing his frustration. "The mail in Korea is terrible. I received only two letters from her this year. And she had written those three months before they were delivered to me. Imagine that."

"Could you phone her from Surabaya?"

"Ha. If only Amed had telephones. But, you know, we are a simple fishing village. There are no telephone lines. The government tells us they are working on it. So we wait, and then we wait some more. The Suharto children are probably holding the money that is supposed to be spent on our phone lines."

"I think we can work something out," I said. He gave me a baffled look.

Ten minutes later I spotted the small *warung* beside the grove of clove trees on our left. I asked the driver to stop in front of it, negotiating with him to pick us up three hours later. He said he would return then, and I agreed to pay him double the usual rate *after* he returned and drove us back to Bitung. It was 2:45 in the afternoon.

Inside the restaurant we ordered iced *cendol,* the, sweet, cold coconut milk drink of Indonesia.

"Komang, I'm looking forward to working with you as a partner in this business I'm now engaged in. You remember, I left the customs job in Panama?"

"Yes, I remember. We talked about it in the Canal. About a new job in Asia."

"My new company has deposited $500 to your account in Denpasar. It was credited last month." Komang was surprised. He hadn't received any news about the deposit.

"Komang, we want to increase the monthly amount we send to you and Putu. I don't believe $500 a month is enough for what we want you to do." He looked confused. He knew he had not yet performed any tasks for me.

"We need to define the information you provide to us. I wasn't specific in Panama." I paused to sip my drink. Komang lit a cigarette. He exhaled over his shoulder, knowing by now that I didn't smoke.

"Okay, let's talk about it," he said.

"We want you to collect information on the navies, the

warships, of Communist China, the Soviet Union, and North Korea."

There was a long, awkward silence. I continued to hold intermittent eye contact with him. He lifted his glass of *cendol* nervously and took a long drink.

At last he exclaimed sotto voce, "You want me to spy?" He glanced at the old woman behind the food counter who was out of range.

"In a word, yes, Komang. We would like you to help us keep track of those countries' naval capabilities. Keep an eye out for their warships and submarines and report new construction in their shipyards."

He abruptly changed the subject.

"You know, Cisco, you speak Indonesian almost like an Indonesian. You have a slight accent if I listen to you closely, but you are fluent enough. When I met you in the Panama Canal I was surprised by that. You were a customs officer. And I figured, since it was the Panama Canal, you must be an American." He paused and took a long drag of his cigarette, blowing smoke over his shoulder again. "Is that correct? You are an American?"

I nodded, wondering where this was going. There was a further silence. My pitch had startled him and I was troubled by that. After a long pause he said, "We have loaded cargoes in China and Russia this year. After we discharged that Cuban sugar in North Korea, we sailed to Shanghai."

I was relieved now to be back on track. I said, "We know your ship is on a long-term charter to the North Korean government. So you should be visiting their trading partners often: Communist China and Russia. I would like you to work for me when you're in those ports. I brought you a new camera." I nodded toward the chair where I had laid the backpack. "I'll train you on how to use it while we're here. If you agree to that, Komang, then we can discuss a monthly salary for you and Putu."

"How much will you pay me, Cisco?"

"I can raise your salary from $500 to $2,000 a month." He made a quick mental calculation, converting U.S. dollars to Indonesian rupiah.

I now added the surprise feature while he was still reacting with some ambivalence to my pitch.

"I will give Putu a shortwave radio so that the two of you can talk with each other often." A happy smile appeared on his face. The ice had been broken.

"Fantastic, Cisco," he exclaimed. The old woman looked in our direction. He lowered his voice. "Yes, I will work with you. Let me know what you need."

"Great. Let me explain to you how this will work. I want you to write a letter to Putu today. I will deliver it to her in Amed this week, after I leave Bitung. You introduce me and explain to her that I'm going to train her on how to operate a shortwave radio. You need only tell her you're doing some freelance work for me. Like a consultant."

"Yes, I understand. Keep the part about spying secret." He grinned.

"Exactly. Putu will have to get a passport so she can travel to Singapore for her training."

"She can apply for one."

"Right. We'll pay for it. And my company will provide her with a letter of support from Singapore. The Indonesian government might need that before they agree to issue a pass-port. After I train Putu with the ham radio in Singapore, and she returns to Bali, you'll call her. She'll monitor her short-wave radio at certain times of day."

"Okay. That's clear."

"Now, here is the code we'll use. Please listen closely. At the beginning of your conversation in *Balinese*, you convey numbers. The first set of numbers will be the latitude and longitude coordinates of the Communist port you've recently visited. The second set of numbers will be the latitude and longitude of your *next* port of call, where we can meet each other. The third set of numbers will be the estimated date of arrival at that next port. The final number indicates the urgency. We'll talk about that later."

"Yes, I can remember that. But I think Putu might get confused by so many numbers."

"She won't have to understand the meaning of our code. She only needs to write down the numbers as you say them to her. She will then make a call to my radio in Singapore. All she will have to do is translate and repeat those same numbers in *Indonesian*, not in Balinese, so that I can understand them."

I continued, "Her radio in Amed won't be licensed. Putu will need to keep it secret. No one in Amed, or on your ship, can know that you and I are working together to gather this kind of information. I will teach Putu about security."

"You mentioned a camera." Komang glanced at my back-pack.

"Yes. I will train you today and you'll keep the camera. But first, you need to write the letter of introduction to Putu and seal it." I handed him blank paper, a pen, and an envelope. I waited fifteen minutes as he wrote the letter, sealed it in the envelope, and addressed it to his wife.

"Do you know your next port of call, after Bitung?" I asked.

"Yes. We're loading rice here, and we'll discharge it in Nampo, in North Korea." I was pleased to see that Komang's body language now indicated to me that he thought of us as co-conspirators. He was motivated. Not by ego, nor by ideology or money, but by the opportunity to stay in close contact with his wife using his ship's radio. They don't teach that one in the spy schools.

We walked away from the road, up a hill about a mile beyond the *warung* and inside a dense forest. The view to the east, beyond the trees, was of the main shipping channel and Lembeh Island, about five miles away. I trained Komang in surreptitious photography using the new Nikon and the zoom lens. He was fast on the uptake. It took him little more than an hour to demonstrate his knowledge of shutter speed, aperture openings, depth of field, focus, and use of the zoom lens. He practiced taking photos of cargo ships and fishing boats passing up and down the channel. He zoomed in on objects on the island. At last I was satisfied that he had mastered the camera sufficiently to accomplish that part of his mission.

I explained that if he saw or photographed capital warships or submarines in "denied area" ports or in the open sea, he was to assign the code number for *most urgent*, a three, to his clandestine radio message to Putu. Less urgent observations would rate a one or a two.

We continued to sit undisturbed inside the forest of clove trees, reviewing all we had discussed. The only other sounds were of birds and wild monkeys and the occasional traffic on the road far below.

I had a final instruction for Komang regarding our communications. "You must not use your ship's call sign. I want you to use the call sign *Perak* whenever you initiate contact with Putu. And in return, she will reply using the call sign *Mas*." He grinned at my selections, which translated to "silver" and "gold" respectively.

I handed him the backpack that contained the camera and lens and told him these were now his to keep.

"Don't show any of your shipmates the new camera, Komang. Keep it hidden. You don't want to draw any attention to yourself. By all means, don't trust anyone on your ship with our secrets."

"I'm not close to anyone on that ship. I'm the only Indonesian there, and I'm by myself most of the time. No one will know."

And with that, the recruitment and briefing of Komang Surya was complete. My first recruitment, a success, with an agent I admired for his intelligence and composed manner. I was confident the two of us would make a good team.

When we returned to Bitung, I reminded him to listen for my radio call after I set up Putu's radio. That brought another of his broad smiles. I tried to imagine what loving a woman as much as he loved Putu must feel like.

# 16

_____

NOVEMBER 1974

I DECIDED DURING THE RIDE BACK TO MANADO THAT I'D
put in some time wearing my coffee trading hat. There
was no better place in Asia to do that than Makassar, the
trading and shipping port city for premium Toraja coffee
beans. I had earlier made contact with an Arabica bean
exporter there. Now I needed to introduce myself to him
personally and establish my credibility as a coffee trader.

I took the short, nonstop flight from Manado to Makassar
early the next day. If I were to define a sketchy term like _exotic_,
I would envision Makassar, the enchanting capital city in
South Sulawesi.

After I checked into my hotel room, I stood on the
balcony and marveled at the fleet of large bat-winged
schooners that glided with the breeze just offshore—the last of
the sail-powered trading vessels in Asia. They appeared like
small pirate ships. I thought to myself that I may have selected
the world's most desirable occupation, Arabica bean trading in
a bewitching locale such as Makassar.

There are occasions when a place, or a song, grabs you deep and never releases you for as long as you live. You experience it, or you listen to it, and you think to yourself: *Eureka*. Makassar. I was to return often.

The flight to Bali the following morning connected through Surabaya, the great port city in East Java where Komang had joined the crew of the *Pacific Star*. It had been my good luck that the original radio operator abandoned ship and was replaced there at the last minute by the Balinese.

My parents and I had spent a week's holiday in Bali when I was eight years old, some nineteen years earlier. I remembered my mother's pleasure in returning to the land where she had lived and performed music as a girl. And where, at the age of eighteen, she had first met my father as she was singing with a band in one of the island's deluxe hotels.

My flight arrived at noon, and I found a modest hotel in Kuta. The beach was nearly deserted, with a few Caucasians, or *boolay*, tourists lounging beneath umbrellas on the white sand in front of the hotel. There was a small group of chattering, tan-skinned Balinese women, each one modeling her batik attire and peddling sarongs and swimming trunks to the foreign sunbathers. I could see the magnificent five-foot waves from my hotel room, and as I had neglected to pack a pair of trunks, I decided to go to the beach and purchase a pair from the Balinese garment hawkers. We bargained with each other in Indonesian, and I bought a pair made of USAID flour sack for a third of the asking price. These shorts had been stitched together from U.S. Government sacks that had at one time contained flour shipped to Indonesia as part of an American foreign aid program. I fastened them with a thin drawstring at the waist. They looked pretty hip, and I thought they were unique.

Well, one gets what he pays for. I dove into the sea and swam out through the large breaking waves until I was fifty yards offshore. I decided I would put on a show for the *boolay* tourists and the Balinese women on the beach by bodysurfing on those powerful, perfectly formed five-foot waves. I doubted they had ever seen bodysurfing; I had been doing it for years in California and Hawaii.

I saw the large wave start to form further outside and swam out to position myself so that I could start my strong swimming strokes at the optimum spot—where the wave would lift me as it curled and then carry me, with my arms tucked at my sides, to shore. As the big wave broke and began to launch me forward, my flour-sack shorts were stripped right off my body. I rode the wave to shore, conscious all the way of my predicament. When I stood up in the shallow water, I was buck naked.

As I sauntered up to the beach, my audience—foreign tourists and Balinese women—were laughing and cat-whistling. I walked toward them on the white sand and shouted a plea to the Balinese women to bring me one of their batik sarongs. The leader of the hawkers, a woman in her twenties with long, jet-black hair, ran to me laughing and wrapped a colorful sarong around my naked midsection. There was to be no bargaining. I paid the full price of five dollars and walked back to my hotel across the road. An hour later I returned to the beach and purchased a batik-designed backpack from the jolly Balinese ladies of Kuta Beach.

I left my hotel the next morning at six o'clock. The sky was turning from gray to a light blue with the sunrise. I carried only my new backpack.

I walked north for several blocks from my hotel, conducting counter surveillance along Legian Street. Satisfied that

I was not being followed, I stopped and hailed a taxi heading south. Rather than sit in the front seat beside the driver, I hopped into the back seat and told him in English to drive me to Amed. I had things to think about and did not wish to answer questions posed to me by a curious taxi driver. Also, Amed was a long three-hour drive from Kuta, so I figured I'd make myself comfortable in the back.

The Balinese taxi driver spoke little English. At the start of the journey he asked me why I was going all the way to Amed. I answered in English that I was going snorkeling. He didn't seem to understand "snorkeling." The trip proceeded in near silence.

Not knowing at first where Amed was located, I had looked it up on a map of Bali while I was in Springfield. It is on the far eastern shore of the island, in the shadow of Mount Agung, the largest active volcano in Bali. A peninsula that resembles a large pig's snout points out into the Bali Sea. On the bridge of that nose lies the village of Amed.

The taxi pulled into the town center at ten o'clock in the morning. I paid off the driver and he left. Komang had given me an address for Putu, but I had no idea where that was in relation to the village. The town itself was small and quiet. I didn't see any means of public transportation. According to Komang, his cottage was located at a beach and near a fleet of sail-powered fishing boats, which would all be pulled up onto the sand when they weren't out at sea.

I found a *warung* and ordered a breakfast of *nasi goreng*, fried rice Indonesian style, and a cup of Bali coffee. I conversed with the cheerful teenage waitress and complimented her grandmother, the chef, on her cooking. They seemed happy to entertain me, a foreigner who spoke Indonesian. In Bali any person who is not Balinese is, a priori, deemed a *foreigner*, even if they are an Indonesian compatriot from another island.

Breakfast finished and paid for, I asked the waitress if she knew of a particular beach I was looking for to go swimming, giving her Putu's address. She answered that she did indeed know the beach; it was about three kilometers farther down the main road. I asked if there was any way I could catch a ride to the beach, and her grandmother overheard us. She said something in a Balinese dialect to the girl.

The waitress turned back to me. "Yes," she said. "My brother can take you on his motorbike to the beach. I'll go find him." And before I could comment, she rushed out the front door and crossed the main road.

I thanked the chef. She smiled and nodded, placing her two hands together, prayer-like. I had the impression that older women like her did not speak Indonesian well, having only to speak the distinct Balinese language in faraway Amed.

The teenage girl returned riding on the back of a motorbike driven by her brother, also in his teens. They stopped in front of the *warung* where he gunned the motor. She motioned for me to join them. Instead of hopping off the bike, she indicated that I should get on behind her. We took off at a fast clip up the road, the three of us, my arms wrapped around the girl and holding on to the back of the driver's seat.

We reached the beach in less than five minutes. The brother and sister team offered to wait for me. I thanked them and I told them it wasn't necessary. I didn't want to offend their generosity outright by offering them money, so I asked if I could chip in for the gas. They laughed at that and said that they were happy to help out. They roared off back to town, her hair blowing behind her.

# 17

---

NOVEMBER 1974

THE CONTRAST BETWEEN THE BEACHES AND THE SEA at Amed on the remote east coast and Kuta on the Indian Ocean is evident. The ocean at Kuta has those large, rolling waves ideal for world-class surfing, while the sea off Amed is flat, calm, and pristine with barely a swell. Two different worlds. The lush coral beds offshore at Amed are a snorkeler's dream come true, alive with colorful tropical fish of every stripe.

I walked now along a narrow dirt path from the main road through a grove of coconut trees until I reached the sandy beach. The area appeared deserted with the exception of four dark-skinned children, two boys and two girls, who were cavorting in the sea a few feet offshore. Adjacent to the beach were several homes, some mere shacks, others a little more substantial. The beach itself was lined with thirty or forty outrigger sailboats, each one identical in design, about twenty feet in length with a tall mast and a boom with a furled sail. This was the fishing fleet that Komang had described to me. The fishermen were home, asleep after spending all night at sea.

I spotted a young man standing beside one of the boats. When I caught his eye, I waved and walked toward him. He looked at me in a friendly manner as I approached.

I greeted him. "Hello, mister. Can you help me? I'm looking for Putu, the wife of my friend, Komang Surya."

His mouth fell and his eyes opened wide. "Ah, Komang. You are a friend?"

"Yes. Can you show me where Putu lives?'

"Putu is my cousin." He was happy to hear that there might be news from the long absent Komang. "My name is Nyoman."

"Nice to meet you, Nyoman. My name is Cisco." We shook hands and he motioned for me to follow him up the beach toward a house nestled beside a cluster of coconut trees.

"That's Komang and Putu's house," he remarked as we got closer to the cottage. It was evident that he was curious about me, and that he would stay close by when I introduced myself to Putu.

As we approached the cottage, a pretty young woman stepped out the front door. She was tall, barefoot, the same height as Komang, about 5'8", and wore a red T-shirt with white shorts that stopped above her knees. She had a fair complexion framed by long black hair that was tied into a ponytail and fell to her waist. Her figure was perfectly proportioned, moderately athletic. Her dark, almond-shaped eyes were bright and expressive. In short, she had an unblemished natural beauty. I recognized her immediately from the photograph in Komang's radio room.

Putu smiled at us both as she said something to Nyoman in Balinese. My first thought was that Komang was a lucky man. No wonder he wished so much to return home.

Nyoman replied to her in Indonesian, which was the language that he and I had been speaking.

"This is Mr. Cisco. He is friend of Komang."

She stopped in her tracks. Nyoman's announcement had caught her by surprise.

"Welcome, welcome," Putu exclaimed at last, spreading both hands out to us. "Please come in."

"Thank you, Putu," I said, returning her smile. "I have a letter from Komang." I removed the envelope from my backpack and handed it to her. As she took it from me and read the handwriting on the envelope, her face, eyes, and sensuous lips broke into a beautiful smile. She led us into the house.

I had never met a people who smiled as naturally and were as good natured as the Balinese.

I somehow needed to suggest a way that Putu could read Komang's letter privately. She promptly went to the kitchen to prepare cold *cendol* and a plate of fresh fruit: rambutan, mangoes, bananas, and pineapples. When she returned I explained to her how I had met Komang in Sulawesi, and that he had recommended that I visit Amed to experience the spectacular snorkeling off the beach here, near his home. Putu, I could see, was eager to open the letter from her husband.

After finishing the drinks I made a suggestion. "Nyoman, let's go down to your boat and you can explain to me how you sail it and how you fish. I'm sure Putu would like to have some time to herself to read Komang's letter."

Putu laughed and said, "You're right about that, Mr. Cisco. Let me read his letter, and maybe have time to write a reply. You boys go look at the boats and come back later."

I would leave it to Putu to inform Nyoman that she and I needed to talk in confidence after she read the letter.

Nyoman was a proud boat owner. He had owned the craft for a couple of months and was delighted to be a new member of the village's fishing fleet. I told him I knew how to sail, and he invited me to join him and go fishing sometime. He explained that the fishermen all go out to sea in the late afternoon and don't return with their catch until sunrise the next day. As it happened, he was eager to get some sleep before going out to sea later that night. He left me at Putu's door and said goodbye to us both.

Putu and I now sat alone in her living room. Her calm expression was pensive as she held the open letter in her hand. I knew that Komang's letter had explained to her how we would set up a shortwave radio in Amed so that the two of them could talk to each other, and that she should follow my instructions as to how to acquire the radio set and get trained. He had mentioned in the letter that he was working part-time for my company, earning extra money. The stage was set for our three-way radio network.

"Putu," I began speaking in Indonesian again. "I want to thank you for giving us this chance to stay in contact with Komang and work together. He is excited. He misses you a lot and he's very happy that he will now be able to talk with you often."

"This is such a surprise. I am the one to thank you, Mr. Cisco." She poured us both some more of the cold coconut milk drink and sat down again.

"The radio, I'm afraid, will not be licensed because it's not likely the Indonesian military would allow it. We must keep this radio secret, Putu. Do you have a place to hide it here in your home?"

She leaned forward. I saw a wrinkle appear on her brow for the first time. At last she spoke. "Yes, there is a wardrobe in the closet in my bedroom. We put our valuables there. You may take a look to see if it is large enough for the radio."

I followed her into the bedroom. Up against the wall at the back of the clothes closet was a tall chest of drawers. Each drawer had a brass lock. Putu unlocked one of them.

"This is where I lock our valuables."

I doubted that the radio equipment would fit.

"I think it would be better to place the radio on top of this wardrobe. You can push the set back against the wall so that it's out of sight when you're not using it, and cover it with one of your sarongs."

She agreed, and we walked back out to the living room.

"We'll need to run an antenna from the radio up a coconut tree," I continued. "Let's take a look behind the house."

There were several tall trees behind the cottage. I recognized the possibility of running an invisible antenna from the radio transceiver in the bedroom over to one of the trees, and then lead the wire up one of them. I estimated the length of the antenna wire we would need for this, and I stood beneath a coconut tree trying to figure out how we could carry it up the tree without being seen. Would we have to string it up in the middle of the night?

"I know how to climb those trees," she said. "I've been doing that since I was a little girl. You see those small steps carved into the trunk?" I saw that there were small man-made notches in the tree. "I was kind of a tomboy when I was a kid." She laughed. "We often climbed those trees to gather the young coconuts before they ripen and fall. I could climb one of those trees and bring the antenna with me."

This was looking feasible.

We went back inside the house and sat again in the living room.

"Mr. Cisco, I don't know anything about radios."

"I'll train you in Singapore, Putu."

"*Singapore*! How will I ever get to Singapore?" The prospect of a trip to Singapore was exciting to this young woman from Amed.

"I'll give you an official letter that states we wish to hire you as a housekeeper for our guesthouse there. My letter will request that your government issue you a passport. I'll send it by courier later this week."

"You mean I will work as a housekeeper?" she frowned.

I laughed. "No, Putu. We'll only describe it that way in the letter we give you to make it easy for you to get a passport, to prove that you have a job guarantee. When you arrive in Singapore, you'll stay in an apartment and spend two weeks there learning how to use your radio. No housekeeping. When you finish, you'll return to Amed. And then you can begin talking to Komang. He'll call you from his ship."

"Will I have to spend our money, mine and Komang's, when I'm in Singapore?" she asked with a somber expression. This new venture was, for her, still somewhat complicated.

"No. You won't have to spend a single dollar of your own. My company will pay for your airfare, your lodging, and all of your meals." I paused. "And for some shopping. You may like to buy a few things while you're there."

Putu and I reviewed the plan. We would deposit enough money in her bank account so that she could pay for the passport, including a "tip" to the issuing authorities to expedite it. There would also be sufficient funds in her account for her to buy a 30-day return plane ticket: Denpasar/Singapore/Denpasar. She would have enough cash left over in her wallet in the event that a Singapore immigration control officer at the airport asked her to prove she had enough money to support herself during her visit. She could use that cash to spend on meals and shopping in Singapore as she pleased. When the training was complete, she would return to Amed. I would then deliver the radio equipment to her here, and she could begin using it right away to talk with her husband. She appeared overjoyed by this lucky twist of fate.

"After you have your new passport and purchase your plane ticket, phone me from a public telephone and give me your flight details so I can meet you at the airport. I'll leave the Singapore phone number with you now." I gave her McCoy's home phone number and told her she could leave a message on his answering machine with her flight number and date of arrival in Singapore. We repeated the full procedure to each other three times until I was sure she understood it and could recite the flight details in Indonesian and English.

"Mr. Cisco, this all seems too good to be true. What does your company do? What is Komang involved with?"

"We collect information about the shipping industry. If, for example, Komang is in a port and he sees a ship in a dry dock being repaired or under construction, he'll report that to us." I didn't expect Putu to understand why this malarkey would be important to anyone. I supposed the fact that it was confusing served its purpose.

It was now late in the afternoon. I told Putu I needed to return to Denpasar and wondered if she could arrange for a car to take me there. She asked me to wait while she went out and talked with some people. When she returned in twenty minutes, she was accompanied by an older man.

"This is my uncle Made." She pronounced it "Maday." "He will drive you back."

Made and I agreed on a price for the trip, and I left Putu a hundred dollars to cover her travel expense to and from Denpasar. She would find enough money in her bank account to pay for the passport and the airfare plus the pocket money we had discussed.

Putu's uncle Made was curious, if not suspicious, about my role in the Putu-Komang relationship. He knew I spoke Indonesian, and he questioned me continually during the first part of our drive back to Denpasar. I deflected his queries the best I could without appearing flippant and without revealing anything of my true relationship with the couple. He at last exhausted his curiosity, and we drove in silence along the coast for the final half of the trip.

I slipped a cassette into the car's player—Ravel's Piano Concerto in G. A fitting soundtrack for the idyllic scenes along the road. I was fascinated by the Balinese men and women, most of them dressed in splendid gold and white traditional attire and headgear as they walked to and from their Hindu temples. The women carried large, pyramid-shaped arrays of tropical fruit on their heads. Offerings to their gods.

I had always been enthralled by the gorgeous *adagio* movement of that Ravel concerto. And now, during this journey through the serene Bali countryside, it was the perfect accompaniment.

# 18

NOVEMBER–DECEMBER 1974

THE NEXT THREE WEEKS ADVANCED LIKE PRECISION clockwork. Putu picked up her passport, which she had expedited with a generous under-the-table gratuity to an official in Denpasar. The same day, she booked her round-trip flight from Bali to Singapore.

I leased our Singapore safe house as Louis Francisco, a two-room furnished flat on the eleventh floor of a building a short distance from Orchard Road. There was one bedroom, a bathroom, a spacious sitting room, and no kitchen. Putu would have her privacy in the bedroom, and I could train her with the radio equipment in the sitting room. She could have her meals at any of the several restaurants or hawker stalls along Orchard Road.

One could not miss Putu's dramatic arrival in Singapore. She wore a form-fitting, full-length, red and blue batik *kebaya*, and a white short-sleeved blouse, a fresh white flower placed behind her ear. She exited the baggage claim area pushing a cart with her one suitcase, a palpable confidence in her stride. One would not suspect this was the first time in this young woman's life she had ventured beyond the island of Bali. Her joy at arriving in Singapore was unmistakable.

I waved to her. She smiled happily and rushed in my direction.

I took the baggage cart and greeted her. *"Selamat datang di Singapura, Putu."* Welcome to Singapore. We agreed to drop her luggage off at the safe house and have lunch nearby. Keeping in mind that I was now operating as Cisco, we would not dine at one of my usual haunts.

We found a Malay Nonya restaurant on Emerald Hill Road, a ten-minute walk from the safe house. After lunch we strolled together along Orchard Road and I pointed out the areas she could visit to shop and relax during her free time. I made sure she knew how to return to the safe house on her own. And I made sure she had plenty of cash in her wallet. The Singapore immigration officer at the airport had, as I predicted, demanded to be convinced of that.

Late in the afternoon I walked her back to the safe house. I gave her the key to the flat, and we parted on the ground floor after agreeing to meet the next morning at nine o'clock.

She had discovered the hawker stalls for her breakfast that morning on a small lane off Orchard Road. When I arrived at the flat at nine o'clock, she answered the door barefoot, as is the custom, wearing a new blouse and a pair of jeans she had purchased the night before. I removed my shoes and entered the living room.

After unpacking the equipment, I placed my hand on the transceiver. "This radio is yours, Putu. It's the latest model, a Drake. It's small, lightweight, and portable. I can carry it to Amed in a suitcase, and that is what I plan to do."

The training session lasted for the rest of the morning. I explained how a transceiver served as both a transmitter and a receiver—all in one package. I showed her how to manipulate all the dials and told her that my plan was to transmit and receive on the twenty-meter band. Those frequencies would work well during daytime and would be effective for talking with Komang over a long distance.

During the days that followed, Putu became astonishingly proficient. She came to understand the concepts of frequencies, wavelengths, and positioning of the antenna. I explained the fundamentals of electricity to her because it was probable that Amed would have voltage fluctuations. Her motivation, the anticipation of soon being able to talk with her husband at sea, was evident.

One day toward the end of her training, I asked her to buy a commercial AM/FM radio for herself to take back to Bali. I gave her the brand and the model and some cash to make the purchase. She would use that AM/FM radio as a cover in Amed. The antenna, which she would run up a coconut tree, would be connected most of the time to that commercial radio. This would provide her with a pretext for owning an antenna: to obtain better reception when listening to popular music on radio stations in faraway Denpasar. The ham radio would remain hidden on top of the dresser. I reminded Putu often that all this surreptitious activity was because of a situation where her ham radio could not be officially licensed. It had to be kept a secret among the three of us. She would remain unaware of the actual work Komang was doing for me.

I explained that she must listen every day for Komang's call at 10:30 in the morning, and again at 1:30 and at 3:30 in the afternoon. Komang would identify himself as *Perak*. Likewise, she would identify herself as *Mas* when acknowledging his calls. She giggled at the use of the words "silver" and "gold." She knew to relay the numbered codes (latitudes, longitudes, ship's arrival date, and urgency) to *Bintang*, my call sign in Singapore.

"Mr. Cisco, may I talk with Komang after he and I do all those things with the codes?"

"Yes, of course, Putu. You may talk to each other about anything you want for thirty minutes." I had decided that thirty minutes was safe. It was unlikely that the Indonesian military would deploy radio monitoring equipment in Bali.

My plan was to send the radio inside a suitcase from the embassy in Singapore to the U.S. embassy in Jakarta. I'd ask McCoy to arrange it with the military attachés. I would pick the equipment up from the attaché in Jakarta, then drive in a rental car from Jakarta to Bali until I reached Amed. As a result, I would not have to clear customs with the incriminating gear in Indonesia, nor would I need to check the suitcase in at any airport for a domestic flight. As long as I wasn't stopped and searched by the police or military anywhere along the road to Amed, I should be home free. Just in case, I decided to disguise the shortwave set inside an operating radio/cassette player for the road trip to Bali.

After two weeks Putu returned to Bali. We were both confident in her ability now to operate the radio. She knew the codes backward and forward, in Balinese, Indonesian and, just in case, in English. Her command of English was indeed better than Komang's. She had spent those days operating the radio, often blindfolded, listening to the calls of ships at sea. Finally, I told her to expect my arrival in Amed within a week.

The day she left Singapore, I made radio contact with Komang. We knew from Lloyd's that his ship had recently sailed from Nampo and that it was destined for Shanghai.

When we connected, I told Komang that our plan was on schedule and that Putu had been well trained. I informed him that the radio would be set up in Amed in a few days. He needed to monitor his radio daily at our prescribed times for my next call.

McCoy sent the shortwave radio equipment hidden inside the radio/cassette player to the embassy in Jakarta by diplomatic pouch. I was ready for the next critical stage in the plan —delivering the radio to Bali.

I flew from Singapore to Jakarta. On arrival, the immigration control officer demanded to know what I was doing in Indonesia. I explained that I was there to purchase coffee beans in Java for export to the United States. He grudgingly stamped an entry cachet on a passport page and allowed me to enter the country.

I took a taxi from the airport to the embassy and phoned the military attaché from the lobby. He'd been expecting me.

The tortuous drive to Amed took well over forty-eight hours. There was a tense moment on the outskirts of Semarang in Central Java. A police checkpoint. I spotted it some 300 yards ahead of me. I slowed the car and inserted a cassette tape into the battery-powered player on the seat beside me and Beethoven's Fifth Symphony began to play within 100 yards of my arrival at the checkpoint. Cars in front of me moved forward without having to stop. It was my luck that the policemen motioned for me to pull over to the side of the road. I suspected my western appearance cued them to the possibility of enrichment.

Three policemen strolled over to my car after I stopped. I rolled down my window and greeted them in English. The leader ordered me to turn off the engine and to get out of the car. I complied and turned down the volume of the Beethoven symphony. Another one opened the rear door, removed my luggage, and began sorting through my clothing and toiletries on the side of the road. The leader asked in broken English to see some identification. The third one went to the passenger side of the car, opened the door, and reached in to fiddle with the volume of the radio/cassette player.

I knew better than to speak Indonesian with them as that would only serve to pique their curiosity. The leader asked me where I was going as he thumbed through my passport. I told him I was in Java in search of coffee bean suppliers, handing him my CTI business card. I added that I planned to holiday in Kuta, Bali. Meanwhile, the one on the other side of the car continued to stop and start the cassette player. He asked what kind of music I was listening to. I explained that it was western classical music. Then, without missing a beat, I asked him if he could recommend any good Indonesian music and if there was a store in Semarang where I could purchase cassettes. The leader translated my query for him. He thought for a moment before giving me his recommendation. He suggested a local pop group known as the Ekka Singers.

The underlying fact of the matter was that these three Indonesian gentlemen expected me to pay them a generous bribe before they would send me on my way. Their leader made it clear that I could avoid a trip downtown to police headquarters if I settled with them then and there. Anticipating this, I had stuffed $400 in twenty dollar bills into my wallet before leaving Jakarta.

I removed $300, figuring $100 a piece, and handed it to the leader. He counted it slowly. At last he motioned for me to hand over the remaining $100 he had seen me keep. Again, I opened my wallet and removed every last bill. He quickly stuffed the entire $400 into his pocket and nodded to his colleagues. The one behind me packed my personal items back into the suitcase. The third asked me if he could keep my Beethoven cassette. I bent down and removed it from the player, held it with both hands, and offered it to him politely with a bowed head.

The three of them walked away without another word. I got back into the car, started the engine, and gingerly drove away.

I stopped to sleep for three hours at a small, third-rate hotel on the outskirts of Surabaya, and again in Kuta after crossing the straits from Java to Bali on a ferry boat. On the third day after departing Jakarta, I covered the final leg from Kuta to Amed.

I drove slowly past the small town until I recognized the cluster of coconut trees that marked Putu's beach. I desired nothing more now than to dive into the calm crystal blue sea and soak. I was tired out and I felt grungy, having been on the road upward of fifty hours. I removed the player that contained the radio and walked through the grove of trees and toward Putu's cottage. I called out her name as I approached.

Putu was in a neighbor's home, next door. She heard my voice and stepped out the back door of the cottage. She was wearing the new Levis jeans outfit she had bought in Singapore.

She greeted me with a cheerful smile. "Welcome back, Mr. Cisco," she called out.

She said something to the effect of how haggard I looked.

"It's been a long drive from Jakarta, Putu. I'd like to take a swim," I said. "Let's see if Nyoman can lend me a pair of shorts."

"Better you wear a pair of Komang's." She went inside her home and I followed her there with the radio/cassette player.

"First, let's unpack," I said. I set the radio/cassette player on the living room floor and opened it up. She looked down at the array of equipment inside.

"Let's put the radio away now before anyone drops by for a visit," I suggested.

"Yes, follow me." She motioned for me to bring the player and radio into the bedroom. We placed all the shortwave equipment on top of the wardrobe and she covered it with one of her sarongs. After we returned to the living room, Putu went into the small kitchen and poured glasses of cool mango juice for both of us. I drained mine in a single gulp.

I then changed into a pair of Komang's shorts and dashed across the hot white sand, past the beached fishing boats, and dove into the clear glassy sea. Bliss! I swam with strong free-style strokes for fifty meters, out over the coral reef, and then dove straight down, eyes open, to a depth of four meters until I could touch the coral lightly with the tips of my fingers. Tropical fish of varied colors and designs darted away. After holding my breath for as long as I could, I surfaced and lay on my back, floating and revitalized—and for that moment, without a care in the world.

I heard children's laughter. I raised my head and saw the same four youngsters I'd seen during my first visit, frolicking in the shallow water. I swam to shore, ready now to get to work.

Putu had removed the antenna from her closet. She was

behind the cottage when I arrived. She told me I could find a dry towel in the bathroom, where I bathed with fresh water and changed into clean clothes. Meanwhile, Putu climbed to the top of a coconut tree, antenna in hand, and secured it to a branch. I stood below the tree and watched her as she climbed down with ease.

One idiosyncrasy a visitor notices on the island is that the Balinese women do the hard work, the heavy lifting. The women are the bricklayers here. The men of Bali, on the other hand, are inclined to take life easy.

"Okay," she said. "Now let's connect it to the radio. Let me set it up." She wanted to show me that she hadn't forgotten anything from her recent training.

I stood and watched as she laid out all the radio equipment and hooked up the antenna. She plugged the power cord to a wall socket, flipped the switch, and the radio came alive. She then switched to the 14 MHz band she would use in communicating with Komang. A proud smile creased her lips.

"Remember, Putu, I need to contact Komang and let him know you're now ready to receive his calls. He's expecting that. I'll drive back to Denpasar today and leave the car there. And I'll see if I can catch a flight to Singapore tonight. I'll call Komang on his ship first thing tomorrow. You must begin listening for *Perak* and the codes at the times we agreed on, starting tomorrow." She nodded. I sensed a slight nervousness.

I gathered our custom-made radio/cassette player in my arms. It had served its purpose well. We would store it in McCoy's office for use another day.

"So, I'll say goodbye to you for now," I said. "Better you not walk with me to the road." She understood. "See you again one of these days, Putu. And thank you for making this business possible." She stood still and watched me walk back along the path through the grove of coconut trees. I turned around and waved. She waved back, and then she put her hands together, prayer-like, and bowed her head.

I caught a flight that night to Singapore. The following day I made contact with Komang on his ship. I told him that Putu's radio was now set up, and that *Perak* should call *Mas*. The vital communications plan for the mission was now in their hands. And I was happy for them both.

# 19

---

I HAD SAILED TO SUBIC BAY A COUPLE OF TIMES, AND
partied off-base in the sin city known as Olongapo during
my two-year navy tour on the *USNS Wake Forest*. That had
been the extent of my interaction with the Philippines.

My objective now was to set up an agency that would send
Filipino merchant marine officers to ships that made port calls
in Communist China, the USSR, North Korea, and Warsaw Pact
countries—what the Institute referred to as the "denied areas."

The Manila airport was a sweltering madhouse, every bit
as chaotic as Jakarta's. At last I exited after more than an hour
and a half of wearisome immigration and customs processing.

I took a taxi from the airport to the stately Manila Hotel,
situated along the shore of Manila Bay. As I entered, a white-
suited pianist was playing a Chopin nocturne on a grand
piano in the center of the elegant lobby. I had indeed arrived
at a cool oasis in the midst of mayhem. I checked in as Roy
Mancini of Malacca.

After unpacking I returned to the lobby and walked

outside to the swimming pool where I swam a few laps. I then relaxed poolside, stretched out on a chaise lounge, and read the Manila newspapers until late afternoon. I wasn't reading the local news, rather I was studying the For Rent ads in each of the papers. I needed a safe house.

The sunset over Manila Bay is radiant. I'd never seen one like it before. Looking out at the blue hues, flaming reds, and changing shades of yellow as the sun disappeared over the horizon gave me a revived sense of calm, a fresh lease on life. In another instant it was twilight. I returned to my room overlooking the bay and took a long, hot shower. The grime of Manila of a few hours earlier had been lifted from body and soul.

I left the hotel on foot and wandered through the vast Luneta Park across the street. The park was alive with families and couples at play. Three promenading young women glanced coquettishly at me as I passed them. I was at ease.

I discovered a Spanish restaurant in the nearby Ermita district and ordered the specialty, a paella. As the guitar trio serenaded the tables with song, I ran through my mind the tasks I needed to accomplish before the end of that week.

The next morning I would lease a box at the Manila central post office. Then I would place an employment ad in a newspaper seeking a general manager for a new shipping agency. I needed to follow up on the real estate ads I had read earlier and rent a safe house.

I placed the ad in the *Manila Times* to run for one week:

```
We seek a general manager for an international
shipping agency in Manila. The successful candi-
date will be a merchant marine officer, holding
a captain's license. We pay a generous salary
commensurate with experience. Reply to P.O. Box
1742 Manila CPO.
```

I checked. The ad began running the following day.

I leased a safe house in a residential area south of Manila, the seaside town known as Paranaque. The four-bedroom furnished house with a swimming pool was located on the shore of Manila Bay. The Manila Hotel, in the far distance, was visible from the garden. I took the house for one year as Louis Francisco. An Institute cover company in Gibraltar wired one year's advance rent to the landlord that same week.

The net had been cast. There was nothing to do now but wait, a pastime I was learning to deal with.

During the day, poolside at the Manila Hotel, I read short stories by Somerset Maugham. At night I familiarized myself with the Ermita entertainment scene. Here there was an abundance of nightclubs, restaurants, small intimate bars and a jazz joint.

After three pleasurable days and nights, I went to the post office to see if the bait had been taken. I retrieved twenty envelopes from the post office box and carried them to the Paranaque safe house.

Over the next four days, the twenty resumes increased to a hundred. I studied each one carefully and created a short-list of five worthy candidates. Each one had the rank of merchant marine captain. The following week I interviewed the officers in five different hotel lobbies throughout greater Manila.

After a week I had reduced the number of candidates to one: Captain Ernesto Villarreal, the only captain I invited back for a second interview. We met in a busy five-star hotel lobby where he arrived at precisely our appointed time. I watched him walk in as I stood at a magazine kiosk where I could also keep an eye on the hotel entrance. I stepped away, waved to him, and motioned for him to join me at a table in a corner of the large room.

"Good afternoon, Captain," I greeted him. "Thanks so much for meeting me again."

"My pleasure, Mr. Francisco." I ordered a pot of coffee for the two of us and a plate of sandwiches. We spent a few minutes getting further acquainted until the coffee had been served.

Moving matters forward I said, "My firm realizes there's a demand for Filipino seamen and officers to man ships around the world. And please call me Cisco."

Captain Villarreal was in his mid-fifties. He had a light brown complexion and a full head of neatly barbered, prematurely gray hair. His height was six feet, tall for a Filipino. He was dressed now in pressed slacks and a long-sleeved business shirt. His shoes were expensive and well shined. Fingernails freshly manicured. He wore a gold wedding band.

"You're right, Cisco. Filipinos serve on ships throughout the world. It has become a big business, supplying crew from Manila."

"Well, Haig wants to take advantage of that. Our plan is to set up a crewing agency here in the Philippines, and we need a joint venture partner to run the agency."

"That sounds interesting. Are you suggesting that we partner in this?" He caught on that I was making a business proposal.

"Yes. And I'm thinking you would be the shareholder of record. You, Captain, would run the business. We'd be a silent partner, so to speak. What do you think?"

"I think it's possible. I have no doubt about the opportunities in running a crewing business, supplying seamen and officers to foreign ship owners."

"You won't have to put up the capital to start the company," I continued. His eyes brightened. "Haig will invest in the venture to get it off the ground. We expect that the agency will be profitable and will pay for itself within a year."

"I can assure you, Cisco, that we can make it successful."

I asked Captain Villarreal how much notice he needed to give to his current employer. He said he should give the company thirty days. I said in that case Haig would remit earnest money to his bank account right away. After he received those funds, he should give his thirty-day notice to his employer. At the same time, he would begin the process of registering the new company and securing office space. My company would send enough money to him so that he could sign a lease. We agreed that the Manila Port Area was the preferred location for the office. Next, I told him we would remit enough money for him to furnish the office and to hire a secretary and an assistant. We would pay him a salary of $2,000 per month, starting as soon as he left his current job.

"How can I contact you, Cisco? I want to let you know the status of each of those steps."

"I travel a lot, so it's better I call you. But I'll give you an emergency phone number where you can leave a message."

"I must say, you are making a dream come true. I've never had the money to go into business for myself. You will not regret this. And you can trust me."

To be credible I knew I needed to propose the percentage of the profits that Haig would expect to take from the venture.

"Here's what I suggest, Captain. We share the net profit fifty-fifty. I won't expect anything for the first year. After a year we do an accounting. If there is a profit, well and good. Now, what do you want to name our agency?"

He took a sip of coffee and replied, "Would you agree that we name it Villarreal Crewing Agency?"

"Sounds good to me." I raised my hand to get the attention of a waiter. "Go ahead and get the new company registered as soon as you receive the earnest money in your account. Here, let me write down this phone number you can call in an emergency. It's in Singapore." McCoy's second phone was only answered by a machine. "You can leave a message, and I'll phone you back. Only in an emergency."

Ten days later Steve informed me that the Institute had granted a clearance to recruit Ernesto Villarreal as an asset. An Institute cover company in Europe had sent the money to his bank account as I had requested. We hadn't asked Springfield to expedite his background trace. I learned later that Tom Hiatt had fast-tracked it.

I sat for a long while outside the house in one of the long wicker chairs beside the swimming pool as I contemplated the phone call and pitch I would make now to Villarreal. I looked out over the bay as the sun vanished below the horizon in a matter of a few minutes. There was a full moon that night. The stars were brilliant; the December breeze was cool. I thought to myself that this career of mine resembled a game of chess where I was playing the opening moves with the white pieces. And I intended to win with a strong attacking game.

It had been two weeks since we had last met. I phoned Captain Villarreal at his home at eight o'clock that evening. His wife answered the phone and asked who was calling.

"Please tell the captain this is Louis Francisco."

"Oh, yes." She put down the phone and I could hear her call out, "Erniiing ... it is your *priend*, Mr. *Prancisco*. Hurry,

Erning." She spoke heavily accented English, mixing up her Fs and Ps, as was customary in the Philippines.

The captain picked up the phone.

"Cisco. You are in Manila?" His English had only a slight accent.

"Yes, I am. When can we meet each other?"

"After work tomorrow? I leave the office around six o'clock."

"That would be fine. Let's meet in the same hotel lobby. Say, seven o'clock give or take, depending on traffic."

"I will be there at seven."

"See you then." We hung up.

I entered the luxury hotel at a quarter to seven. The captain hadn't arrived. I walked to the bank of elevators and rode one of them to the penthouse floor. The revolving restaurant was open. I walked in and sat at the bar, ordered an ice tea, and took in the early evening view of Manila as the room rotated 360 degrees. At five minutes to seven, I left and found a table in a corner of the lobby. Captain Villarreal walked into the hotel at five minutes past 7:00.

He spotted me soon after he entered and approached my table. Ernesto Villarreal wore a serene, self-assured expression. Seeing his features, his height and his visage, it occurred to me that he had more than a little Spanish blood in his ancestry. That evening he wore a long-sleeved light blue shirt and a necktie. As always, his graying hair was neatly combed. The consummate Manila businessman.

We ordered drinks from a waitress and settled back in our seats. The lobby was populated with Filipino and foreign businessmen and women, government big shots on expense accounts, and a hoi polloi of Makati socialites. I didn't plan to stay long.

"I've given notice to my boss. I'll leave in three weeks."

"Were there any problems?"

"No. He tried to persuade me to stay on, but I explained that I was going into business for myself, and that I had made up my mind."

"How long do they want you to stay?"

"I agreed to remain for one month. That was a week ago. They'll need to find my replacement and I may have to train that person before I leave."

We finished our drinks and I asked for the bill.

"Captain, I want to discuss this business of ours in a place where we have more privacy. I have rented a home in Paranaque. We can continue discussing the confidential details there." I paid the bill and motioned for him to follow me outside.

We boarded a taxi outside the hotel. The doorman asked me where we were going so that he could tell the driver. I told him I hadn't made up my mind and that I would direct the taxi driver myself after we decided where to go. Then I told the driver to head south on the highway that led to Paranaque. After ten minutes I gave him an address that was a couple of blocks away from the safe house. He dropped us off there, in front of a movie theater, and we walked the two blocks to my place.

These counter-surveillance procedures of mine might well have been an enigma to Villarreal. That was my point. Get him conditioned to security early in the game.

I unlocked the front door and turned on the lights. Through the large living room window we could see scores of lights from the fishing boats on Manila Bay. The rooms had been tastefully furnished. It looked like a home that had been lived in.

"This is nice, Cisco. I see you have a swimming pool," he commented.

"Yes. A lucky find. Make yourself comfortable and I'll get us drinks. Would you like a San Miguel?"

"No, thank you. A glass of water will be fine." He sat down on the sofa in the middle of the room. I went to the kitchen and returned with a pitcher of ice water and two glasses. I poured water for both of us and raised my glass to his.

"I suppose we can toast our venture with ice water," I said.

"Sorry, I'm not much of a drinker."

"Good to hear. Well then, have you found office space?"

"I have. I received the money in my bank account, and I've paid a deposit for an office in the Port Area. I can show you the space tomorrow." He removed the receipt for the office deposit from a thin folder he had been carrying.

"That's fine." I took the receipt, studied it, and handed it back to him. "I'll take a look at it before I leave Manila." I, of course, had no intention of ever setting foot in the crewing agency office.

He explained that he had accomplished what I had asked him to do—the company registration and the screening of a secretary and an assistant.

"Captain Villarreal, I need to discuss a matter we must keep confidential."

He looked at me, unfazed. "Yes. What is that?"

"I work for an organization that needs to have our ships' officers placed on vessels that sail to ports in Communist countries. I have to trust those officers enough that I can ask them to observe and photograph naval ships and activity and then report to me what they see." I made conversational eye contact, without too much intensity. He dropped his eyes and stared at his water glass for several seconds.

"Intelligence?"

"Yes. That's who we are. Our targets are the ports and seas around Communist China, the Soviet Union, the Warsaw Pact countries and North Korea."

I continued, "Your crewing business will operate legitimately just as we have discussed. We'll make it profitable for you. And the good news is that you won't have to share any of your earnings with us, or with anyone. All the profit will be yours to keep."

"I'm listening, Cisco. Tell me what you need."

I spent the next thirty minutes explaining how he would market his services and operate the business normally. The only added twist was that he would target companies whose ships sailed regularly to "denied area" ports. He needed to place vetted Filipino officers on those ships. I would guide him and identify those companies for him through my database. He might have to make trips abroad to meet with ship owners and sell his services.

"I'll give you an example, Captain," I said. "There's a shipping company in Hong Kong. Their vessels all fly the Panamanian flag. The true, beneficial owner of that company is the Peoples Republic of China, and those ships specialize in trading between Communist Chinese ports and the rest of the world—Asia, Africa, and the Middle East."

"What is the name of the company?"

"Chow Fatt Shipping & Trading Company Limited. Chow Fatt operates fifty bulk carriers and general cargo ships, and five or six oil tankers. You tie them up with a contract, supply those ships with officers and crew, and your agency would be off to a good start. And so would my group."

"You will be the one, Cisco, to recruit and train the ships' officers to spy for your organization?"

"Yes, that's right. You'll stay out of that. You just run your crewing business as you normally would and leave the intelligence work to me. Only provide me with the officer's name, his position on the ship, date and place of birth, and the name of the vessel you have assigned him to."

"It's a deal."

"And Captain, don't mention this to your wife or to anyone else. People have loose lips."

"Yes, I understand. Don't worry, Cisco. I won't endanger this business of ours. I have too much to lose."

"Yes, you do."

We raised our glasses of ice water and toasted to our future success.

"By the way, Cisco, do you know Mr. Sasha Popov? He's the manager here in Manila of FESCO, the Soviet shipping line."

I knew FESCO. It was a company that traded between Southeast Asia and the USA, offering the route's cheapest freight rates. I was aware they loaded and discharged cargo in Manila; I had boarded a couple of their ships in the Panama Canal. The officers on those vessels had all been mirthless Russians.

"No, Captain, I don't believe I've ever heard of him. Why do you ask?"

He grinned. "You might find him interesting. He's a rascal."

"Oh? How do you mean?"

"Well, he invited me out one night after a port association meeting, and I joined him." Villarreal continued to smile at the memory. "You know, I don't drink. But Sasha, he loves his alcohol. Like a fish. The vodka, you know. He took me to a place in Ermita where they play jazz music."

"Terry's Bar?" I had dropped in to Terry's a few nights earlier.

"Oh, you know the place? Well, Sasha is really into his wine, the women and songs, as you say. After he got tipsy that night, he sat down at the piano and played boogie-woogie jazz. He's pretty good. The customers, they all loved it. Everyone seems to know him at Terry's. And later a beautiful woman, a Filipina, joined him at the bar. She looked like a fashion model. They appeared to be intimate, caressing each other, holding hands and such. Her name is Flora. Anyway, I had to leave early and drive home. So I said goodnight to them and left."

"So this Mr. Sasha Popov, he goes there often? To Terry's Bar?" I maintained an indifferent expression and tone of voice.

"Well, everybody there seemed to know him: the bartender, musicians, and the women who work there at the bar."

"Thanks for that, Captain. I like good boogie-woogie piano."

Villarreal turned serious. He leaned forward and said to me in a conspiratorial tone of voice, "He's a Russian you know. Maybe useful to your company, Cisco? Know what I mean?"

"Sure do." My mind was made up. I would remain in Manila until I met the Russian boogie-woogie pianist, Sasha Popov.

# 20

---

MCCOY PHONED ME THAT WEEK. HE HAD SOME advice. Move out of the Manila Hotel. Listening between the lines, it was apparent that Springfield had no intention of funding both the safe house and an indefinite five-star hotel residence. I was directed to move into the house for the duration of my stay in the Philippines.

I left my trumpet in Malacca rather than hand carry it with me to Manila to avoid the hassle of clearing it through Philippines customs control. There were easier things to do than explain to a mercenary customs officer why I was bringing a trumpet with me into the country. I needed to find a music store that sold instruments and arrange to rent a trumpet for at least a month. As I checked out of the Manila Hotel for the last time, I asked the concierge where I could rent a musical instrument. He suggested I take a taxi to the other side of the Pasig River where I would find music stores on Escolta Street.

The Escolta section of Manila lies across a bridge on the more pedestrian north side of the Pasig River. The streets here were filled with *calezas*, the garish Filipino horse and buggy contraptions, Manila's facsimile of the *bendi* of Bitung. And there were hordes of passenger jeepneys that roared through the streets. These were the flamboyantly decorated World War II-style jeeps that had been converted to carry upward of fifteen passengers.

In this working and commercial section of the city, with few if any tourists about, I found a popular music store where I rented a fine trumpet for three months. I had a premonition that my jazz musician cover in Manila was going to last for a while.

After I arrived at the safe house, I left the following message on Steve's answering machine. "I'm about to load a shipment in Jakarta on a Soviet FESCO vessel sailing to the U.S. west coast. And I'm going to meet FESCO's Manila manager, a man named Sasha Popov, to negotiate a freight rate. Let me know anything you have about Mr. Popov before I meet him. Tell me if you think I can negotiate a good rate with the man. Reply soonest. I plan to meet with him this week." I spelled out the Russian's first and last names before I hung up the phone.

This message informed Steve that I needed a background check on the FESCO manager and I needed the results fast. He would forward this request to Springfield. Our analysts would do what they needed to do to identify and dig up the background of a Russian in Manila named Sasha Popov.

I knew one thing: the Soviets wouldn't waste a prime overseas position on a mere shipping manager. It was a good bet that Popov was either GRU or KGB. He would leave the nitty-gritty of the shipping business to his assistants while he worked undercover, running agents. The Philippines hosted two of the largest American military bases in the world at Clark Field and Subic Bay. Rich targets for Soviet intelligence.

Meanwhile, while waiting for Steve's response, I decided to make myself known at Terry's, the jazz joint in Ermita.

Late that afternoon and early evening, I puttered around the house wearing my comfortable Indonesian sarong, the one I'd bought from the Balinese vendor at Kuta Beach. I took a swim in the pool and finished a beer in the garden before sunset. Then I practiced playing my new trumpet for an hour. To get me in the right groove, I played a recording by Wynton Kelly, my favorite jazz pianist, as I showered and got dressed in casual attire. I took off to find a restaurant in Ermita. And to set the stage.

I would never call a taxi to pick me up at the safe house. It was more secure to walk a few blocks along the main road and hail a passing cab. Spycraft is about being conscious of what could go wrong, not allowing the black chess pieces to check one's forward movement.

The taxi dropped me off on Mabini, a one-way street. I walked along the sidewalk, against the traffic, until I found an Italian restaurant that was dark, candlelit, and half-full. There was a solo guitarist strolling among the tables, *de rigueur* for many of the Manila restaurants. I sat at a small table with a red and white checkered table cloth in the back of the room. I took my time over the pasta dinner and Chianti, listening to the music of the serenading guitarist, and observing the customers—mostly foreigners—come and go. At last, at nine o'clock, I decided to make my move. I paid my bill in cash and went out onto busy Mabini Street. I walked for a block before abruptly darting across the street, timing this move just in front of a speeding jeepney. Safely on the other side of the road, I cut into an alley and walked through darkness until I reached M.H. Del Pilar Street. This was the street in Ermita that was notorious for its hedonistic nightlife and bars of ill repute. I walked north and crossed United Nations Boulevard, to the somewhat less seedy end of M.H. Del Pilar. Terry's Bar was sandwiched between a curio shop and a bland, barely furnished Chinese restaurant. As I approached I saw a large brown rat scurry out of the restaurant.

I hadn't brought my trumpet with me because I didn't want to stand out yet. Rather, I would mind my own business at Terry's and nurse a couple of San Miguels before heading back to the house.

Terry's Bar was a dark, smoky hole in the wall, about twenty feet square. Anyone who entered the joint was noticed right away: by the bartender, the sole waitress, the customers, and by Terry himself.

Terry was a dark complexioned, weasel-looking man with a thin moustache, receding hair, and large ears. He was known around Ermita as a frustrated showman or a dilettante, take your pick. Give him a microphone and he would spend an hour singing his imitations of Frank Sinatra at full throttle. Depending on how much scotch he'd been drinking, he might move his pianist out of the way and take over the battered, drink-stained upright, and noodle his favorite tunes by ear. All of this to polite applause. When I entered the bar, he was strutting on the small stage beside the piano, waving his arms and belting, "I Did It My Way."

My eyes took a while to adjust to the darkness. I focused first on the five or six tables in the room. They were occupied by Filipino men and the dowdy, middle-aged women who worked the place for drinks. The seats at the bar were nearly all taken. At the end of the bar, beside the door leading to the toilet, I noticed an available barstool and headed for it. Passing behind each of the customers at the bar as I made my way, I noticed two foreign men accompanied by local women. I knew intuitively that neither of the men was Sasha Popov.

The bartender placed a napkin in front of me. He recognized me from several nights earlier and said, "Welcome back to Terry's."

"Thanks. Good to be back." I ordered a bottle of San Miguel beer.

"What's your name, by the way?" the bartender asked as he placed the ice cold bottle in front of me. He remembered that I didn't need a glass.

"Cisco. What's yours?"

"Jun. Nice to meet you." We shook hands, then he turned away to tend to a drink order from the waitress at the other end of the bar.

I was to learn that this sort of wide open hospitality, and unabashed curiosity, was customary in the Philippines. And Filipinos don't ever forget a face, or a name, or how one drinks his beer straight from the bottle.

Terry finished singing his Sinatra soundalike and took a bow. He then walked through the room and greeted people he knew at the tables. The mirror behind the bar, with the large Tanduay Rum logo stuck to it, allowed me to see him glide from table to table. The waitress delivered a glass of whisky on the rocks to him. He sat at one of the tables, lit up a cigarette, and drained half his drink in one swallow.

The pianist and bass player continued to play cocktail

jazz. Nice background music, familiar standard tunes, nothing too far out. The customers resumed their conversations.

I finished one more beer, paid my bill, and left the bar. I had accomplished my purpose, an appearance of enjoying the atmosphere at Terry's Bar. I was now acquainted with the bartender, which was propitious. It was a Saturday night in late December 1974.

I returned to Terry's the next night. The experience was similar. I talked at the bar with Jun the bartender; Terry sang Sinatra, a medley of ballads from *Only the Lonely*. I listened to the piano and bass duo for a while to feel how I might blend my own playing with them. At last I returned to the safe house soon after midnight.

# 21

---

DECEMBER 1974

O N NEW YEAR'S EVE I BROUGHT MY TRUMPET WITH
me to Terry's. I'd noticed earlier that amateurs
occasionally got up to play or sing, sometimes to
polite applause, as often as not to no applause. By now Terry,
the waitress, and the musicians knew me as Cisco. I was
beginning to feel like a regular. I walked in at ten o'clock and
determined right away that Sasha Popov was at the bar.

It wasn't because I recognized a man's voice with a
Russian accent. He was leaning forward and speaking audibly
with Jun, the bartender, in counterfeit American English.
There was a woman, a pretty, dusky Filipina, sitting on a
barstool beside him with her hand resting on his thigh.

"Hey, Cisco, Happy New Year," Jun called out as he saw
me enter. "What you got there?" He'd noticed my trumpet
case. Others at the bar turned to look at me.

"Oh, it's an item I picked up over in Escolta the other day.
I'll have to see how it plays here," I answered, keeping my eyes
off the husky blond man and the exotic-looking woman he was

sitting with. I glanced sideways at the pianist who grinned when he saw me with the trumpet case.

"Come over here. Have a seat. I want to introduce you to someone," Jun said with a wave of his hand toward an empty barstool. He'd already opened a bottle of beer and was placing it on the bar for me.

I stood behind the thickset blond. He turned around and stared, first at the trumpet case in my hand, then at me, then again at the case. A complete once-over, and a louche attitude.

"You a musician?" Sasha Popov asked coolly.

"Yeah, when the time is right," I replied. I moved to the empty barstool.

Jun introduced us. "Sasha, this is Cisco. The joint's going to jump tonight."

Terry sauntered over to me. "I didn't know you played, Cisco."

"We'll see, Terry, if I can keep up with your rhythm section." I looked over at Teo, the pianist, and Boy, the bass player. "Let me finish this beer to build my courage."

I sat two seats away from Sasha. I saw that he had a double shot of straight vodka in a glass with no ice in front of him. The woman was drinking something in a tall glass mixed with ice and tonic water.

"Give him the beer, on me," Popov mumbled to Jun. "Unless he can handle something stronger." Sasha looked into the mirror behind the bar, right at me. He smirked as he raised his glass in my direction.

"Thanks. Sorry, what was your name again?" I asked.

"My name is Sasha."

I raised my bottle in a salute to Sasha's reflection in the mirror. "To you, Sasha. Thanks for the beer. Next time the drinks are on me." I took a long swallow from the bottle.

Sasha turned to the beautiful woman and whispered something to her. I watched her bright smile in the mirror. Her catlike eyes caught mine for an instant. After Terry finished singing "Strangers in the Night," the musicians took a break.

Teo, the pianist, walked up to me. "Hey there, Cisco. You want to play the next set?"

I had a flashback to those nights eight years earlier in Tokyo and Saigon, when I was invited up to bandstands to jam with local jazz musicians. The same kind of dark smoky bars as Terry's, where local musicians had hung out and waited to play. I smiled at the memory. *Déjà vu.*

"Sure, Teo. Let me know when you want me to come up."

I turned to the Russian. "Sasha, let me buy you and your friend a drink."

He finished his vodka in one swallow. "Thank you." He pushed his empty glass toward Jun and made a twirling signal with his finger to refresh their two drinks.

"I am also building up my courage," he said, pointing at his refilled glass of vodka. "Maybe we play together."

"Let's do that. What do you play?"

"Piano." We conversed with each other through the mirror. "Cheers." He drained his two shots of Stolichnaya.

When Teo and Boy returned to their instruments after a break, the pianist announced that later in the set they would have a guest join them onstage.

I turned to Sasha and nodded toward the stage. "You want to jam with me up there?"

"I'll wait and see how you play. If you're any good, I come up and play."

"That's fair," I replied. "Sort of an audition, huh?"

"Yeah, look at it that way. An audition."

"Are you a professional?"

"Professional what?" he asked, stone-faced, staring at me.

"Musician."

"Oh … no. I like to play. Just for fun of it." The woman beside him watched us both in the mirror.

"Same here. Are you American?" I asked him.

He laughed as the duo launched in to their first song of the set. "No," he said.

We listened to Teo improvise on a pop tune for a while without further conversation.

Sasha Popov appeared to be in his forties. He wore expensive, loose-fitting, cream-colored linen slacks and a red long-sleeved shirt, unbuttoned rakishly at the top, and with sleeves rolled up his muscular forearms. He wore a thick gold chain with a medallion against his bare chest. I noticed he wore a gold wedding band too. His full head of blond hair was cut fashionably, covering his ears. I guessed that he went to an expensive hairdresser, not to a local barber. He had a calculating brashness; when he laughed, it would be at someone else's expense. One might describe him as having Hollywood good looks. And he knew it. Hence the arrogance, the self-possession.

Weeks later Sasha told me that if a jazz musician wore red when he played, an audience would think his playing was hot —even if it wasn't.

By this time, by my count, he had drained no less than three double vodkas, straight. His voice was not in the least slurred. He sat perched on his barstool as comfortably as he had when I first arrived.

When the song was finished, Teo stood up and announced that Terry's had a guest musician in the house. I wasn't sure if he was going to introduce me or Sasha until he looked over and said, "Come on up, Cisco."

I took a final slug of beer and walked over to the small stage in the corner of the room. Three or four people clapped indifferently as I removed the trumpet and Harmon mute from the case. I inserted the mute into the horn's bell as Teo whispered to me, "Do you know 'The Girl from Ipanema'?" I thought to myself, *Only too well*. It was an oft requested song I had tired of playing years ago. I knew the tune backward and forward, and I decided that tonight I would raise it to a new level. I had more at stake than merely going through the motions. I had a certain Russian musician in the house I needed to impress.

"Sure, let's play it." Teo and Boy started out with a medium tempo Bossa nova vamp, and I began playing the theme. After I'd played four bars, some customers clapped when they recognized the familiar melody. I played two choruses of the main theme, and then launched into my improvised solo. The pianist and bass player kept the flame burning behind me with a spirited Brazilian rhythm. And I gave it everything I had—twisting and reinterpreting the melody. Starting low and slow, resolving to a fast arpeggio up to a high C, dropping a funky blue note here and a half-valve lick there. I played a soulful climax after four improvised choruses then turned the song over to Teo.

I walked over to my barstool and sat down to loud applause and whistles. I looked over at Terry, who gave me a grin and a thumbs up. Sasha was nodding his head to the time and eyeing me in the mirror. The woman turned toward me, smiling gaily, clapping her hands. As Teo finished his solo, I walked back to the stage and took the tune home.

During the extended applause, I glanced at the bar and saw Sasha climb off his stool and walk toward me.

"Okay, Teo, move over. My turn." Sasha stood behind the pianist, glass in hand.

"You got it, Sasha." Teo appeared used to the Russian taking over the piano. The Filipino pianist stood up and disappeared into the crowd.

Sasha took a swallow of his drink and placed his empty glass on top of the piano.

"I play boogie-woogie. Can you follow?"

"Yeah, a blues. What key?" I asked.

"We play in F."

I nodded to him. "Start it off."

Sasha began playing a walking boogie-woogie bass with his left hand. Boy, the bass player, followed in lock-step. The Russian played ringing chords with his right hand for two blues choruses. By then everyone in the place was clapping in time to the rhythm. And that's when I came in. I had removed the mute from my horn, now making the trumpet sing for six choruses as Sasha and Boy kept the boogie rhythm going behind me. The crowd's clapping to the beat and shouts increased. I glanced around the room for an instant as I was playing and noted that everybody was rocking and dancing in their seats. Two couples were even on their feet, twisting and grinding their bodies in the tight space between the bar and the tables. Jun had stopped mixing drinks and was standing behind the bar, smiling broadly and clapping in time with everyone else. As we finished the impromptu tune, Sasha and I ad libbed a minor blues riff together along with Boy's rhythmic bass.

The audience let loose with wild shouts and applause. A

joyful Terry trotted up to us and raised Sasha's and my hand up high, as though we'd engaged in a prizefight. I turned to Sasha and smiled. He laughed and clapped me on the shoulder. We'd bonded.

I returned to my seat at the bar. Jun placed a cold bottle of beer in front of me. "On the house," he said.

On the back of my mind, I was conscious that I could never let slip that I knew *anything* about Sasha Popov that night. I couldn't assume that he was Russian. His English was close enough to middle-American. How would I know that he was in the shipping business in Manila? I wouldn't. Other than his talent at the piano, he was a blank slate. He hadn't revealed his family name to me. Nor had I revealed mine to him.

He broke into my thoughts. "Where do you live? It's getting late." The year 1974 had turned to 1975 an hour earlier.

"Oh, I live out in Paranaque," I replied. I looked at my watch. "It's time to go. I better catch a cab." I motioned to Jun to bring me my bill.

Sasha turned and looked at me without saying anything. His half-closed, out-of-focus eyes were showing the effects of his drinks. "That's out of my way or we could drop you off."

He reached into his front pants pocket and removed his wallet. After fumbling through it for a few seconds, he removed a business card.

"Here, this is my card," he said. "We do this again. You play okay."

I looked at the FESCO card in my hand. "Sasha Popov. Sounds Russian."

He continued without replying, "Let me introduce you to my girlfriend." He turned his body toward the woman beside him. "Flora, meet Cisco. Cisco, Flora." I nodded to her and her eyes and lips smiled back. It had been apparent to me all evening that she was not one of the young women who roosted in the sordid bars along M.H. Del Pilar Street. Flora had a chic sophistication. When she smiled at me now, there was a cryptic gleam in her dark slanting eyes. She was indeed the most beautiful woman I had seen in Manila. And she did appear to be infatuated with Sasha Popov.

I removed enough pesos from my own wallet to pay my bill, and before replacing the wallet in my pocket, I removed a Haig & Company business card and handed it to Sasha. He looked at it, then looked over at me before dropping the card into his shirt pocket.

"We stay in touch," he said as he stood up and gave Flora his arm.

"For sure," I replied.

# 2 2

---

JANUARY 1975

I CALLED McCoy's ANSWERING MACHINE EARLY THE next morning.

"Call me back ASAP," I said. "Need to know about that shipment from Jakarta."

Ten minutes later Steve called back.

"How soon can you get to Singapore?" he asked without preamble.

"I'll book a flight for tomorrow."

"Phone me as soon as you get here." He hung up.

I was able to book a business class seat on a Philippine Airlines flight to Singapore that would arrive at noon. I brought only hand carry luggage with me, as I expected to return to Manila after briefing Steve on my meetings with Ernesto Villarreal and Sasha Popov. We met in his office in the embassy forty-five minutes after my plane touched down.

"Talk to me," Steve said as we sat down at the coffee table in his office.

I briefed him on the project with Captain Villarreal, cryptonym: *Seaworth*, and listed the expenses involved in setting up the crewing agency. I wrote up a formal request that funds be remitted to Villarreal's Manila bank account. Steve called in the Marine sergeant, Dubrowski, and asked him to cable Springfield with the request for the money transfer.

I explained how *Seaworth* had referred me to Popov, and how I had met and played jazz with the Russian at Terry's two nights earlier. I believed I had established a rapport with Popov that I could exploit. Steve, the amateur clarinetist, could only shake his head in wonder at the idea of my playing music as a cover.

"About Popov." I could tell by his stern expression that this was going somewhere. I leaned forward. "We've stirred up a beehive in Springfield. It's surprising the brother-in-law didn't pick up on him." "Brother-in-law" was the Institute's informal code word for the CIA.

"Your general manager of the Far Eastern Shipping Company in Manila, also known as FESCO, is a star player of the KGB First Chief Directorate. He was formerly based in the Soviet embassy in Cairo, albeit under a different name. He's been missing from Cairo for over a year, whereabouts unknown. Until now, thanks to you. Congratulations."

"So he's surfaced as an *illegal* in the Philippines?"

"Seems like it. Here's what's interesting. When he was posted in Cairo as Deputy Cultural Attaché in the Soviet embassy, he operated under the cover name Sergei Bordin. He was in Cairo undercover for six years." Steve noted my astonishment. "He departed from Cairo rather unceremoniously. One day he was there, the next he was called back to Moscow, caught the first flight out."

"So Popov and Bordin are one and the same?"

"It appears so. Our sources at Philippines Foreign Affairs have given us copies of his bio and the photo from his visa application. He's the same Sasha Popov, aka Sergei Bordin, who vanished from Cairo in 1973. We have the Egyptian consular visa application. The DOB, POB, and photos are identical. He arrived in Manila six months ago, undercover as the FESCO general manager. His true name, we think, is Popov. As far as we can tell, the CIA never reported his arrival."

Steve continued. "You know, our brother-in-law has become risk-averse these days, what with all the scandals: Watergate, senate hearings, and all that. Add the paranoia of James Angleton, their head of CI, plus the revolving door of CIA directors, and we see a crippled intelligence agency. Anyway, we've checked. They haven't targeted Popov ... *yet*. So we've claimed right-of-first-refusal. That's the word, from General DuPont. And I don't plan to submit a refusal."

"We need to assign him a cryptonym."

"That's right. Any ideas?"

I recalled how Terry had lifted both our arms overhead after we had finished playing. "Let's call him *Slugger*."

"All right." He wrote it down. "Another subject. It's time for you to meet with an Agency spook at the Manila embassy. You're now spending a lot of time in the Philippines. I'll set it up. When you meet the brother-in-law, you brief him, or her, on *Seaworth*. Summarize your crewing op plan."

"Go back, Steve. Can't the Agency just step in now and snatch *Slugger* and say 'fuck you very much'?"

"Unlikely. He's in Manila for a reason: to collect military intelligence at Subic Bay and Clark Air Base. That's our turf. He must be running agents up there. Hiatt suspects they couldn't find a GRU officer soon enough to train as an *illegal*, so they sent *Slugger* to the Philippines. What we do know is that he's a senior KGB operative, and you seem to have slipped your foot in the door. So to answer your question—no, our brother-in-law won't want to tangle with us on this one. They have enough problems on their plate back home. They won't want to pick a fight with the Joint Chiefs over this. And the Chairman listens to Frank DuPont."

"I'll try to remember all that when I meet with the Agency people in Manila."

"You do that. And let me tell you a story that took place a couple years ago. Remember how Nixon ordered that we mine the harbor at Haiphong because he was getting tired of the Russian freighters delivering surface-to-air missiles *carte blanche* to the North Vietnamese?"

"Vaguely."

"An Institute case officer helped make that happen. Our guy debriefed a British ship captain in Hong Kong who had sailed there from Haiphong that same week. He got the ship's logs from the Brit, and from there the navy was able to figure out the depth of the harbor and plant the mines. The Agency had a fit when they learned that our case officer had met and debriefed a British subject. We're not supposed to do that, so they said. They reported their dismay up the chain to the White House. The Chairman of the Joint Chiefs, with the endorsement of the NSC, told the 'brother-in-law' to get stuffed. What works, works. End of story. Let's have lunch and get you back to Manila."

# 23

———

JANUARY 1975

I SPENT THE FIRST PART OF THE WEEK KILLING TIME, planning for the weekend when I would again hit Terry's Bar. In the middle of the week, I made the call to the U.S. Embassy. I asked to speak to Tony Loyola, the Assistant Attaché for Economic Affairs. He was, in fact, the "brother-in-law" McCoy had arranged for me to meet. Loyola was expecting my call and invited me to drop by the embassy at my earliest convenience, as he cagily put it.

Later that day I rode a taxi along Roxas Boulevard to the United States Embassy, where I went through the usual security drill in the embassy lobby. A career secretary named Gloria, a pleasant gray-haired American woman, approached me, introduced herself as Mr. Loyola's assistant, and asked me to follow her to the elevator. On the top floor she led me to a spacious office with a million-dollar view of Manila Bay. I took a seat, and she asked me if I'd like coffee and how I took it. At that moment Tony Loyola entered the office, said hello with brief eye contact, shook hands, and sat down behind his desk. He stared at me for a moment before speaking.

"So, Mr. Mancini, what brings you to Manila?" He leaned back and joined his fingers over his substantial belly. He wore a tailored pink dress shirt and a blue tie with polka dots. The cuffs on his silk shirt were secured with large monogrammed gold cufflinks. He was deeply tanned with a slick head of black hair and a trimmed moustache. One's first impression of him might have been that he was a mid-level South American politician. Or a mafia hit man. I had to assume that he'd been around the block, or he wouldn't have been afforded this grand embassy office with a view. I could only imagine what his actual rank in the Agency was.

Gloria brought coffees on a tray for both of us. I took it black and answered Loyola's question while he stirred cream and sugar into his. It occurred to me that he was unaware I had already been operating out of a safe house in Manila for a month.

"The Institute has me setting up maritime operations in the region. I'll collect intelligence for the navy."

"I see. And Manila?" His dark, alert eyes held mine.

"We plan to recruit agents with access to CHICOM naval ports. They'll observe the Chinese naval order of battle. We believe there are a lot of Filipino seamen sailing there— Shanghai, Qingdao, and Dalian. My aim is to recruit some of those sailors and put them on the Institute's payroll. Get them to report to us and take photographs." I glanced out the bay window at the many cargo ships at anchor.

He stared at me for a few moments, sizing me up, a thin smile on his lips. I had a sense he didn't believe I was leveling with him. He was right, of course, though I doubted he knew of my chance meeting with Sasha Popov at Terry's. At last he said, "Sounds low-level enough. Maritime operations. I used to do that sort of thing in Hamburg when I was your age."

We discussed the security situation in Manila for a few minutes. President, now dictator, Ferdinand Marcos had proclaimed martial law three years earlier in order to perpetuate himself in office. Loyola warned me to be careful, not to trust anyone and so forth. He was aware of my non-official status and reminded me that I wouldn't be able to run to the embassy and ask for diplomatic immunity if I was burned. After pontificating for a while longer about local conditions, he stood up and walked around his desk. I took that as a cue to stand. He reached out and we shook hands.

"Okay, Roy. Let us know if you need any assistance. You've got my number. We're here to help." The cynical smile was back on his lips.

"Thank you, Tony. Nice meeting you." I turned toward the door.

"Gloria will escort you downstairs. Have a good day."

I took an hour and three separate taxis to get back to the house and metamorphose from Roy Mancini back to Louis Francisco. It was late afternoon and I took a swim in the pool as soon as I arrived. As I swam a few laps, I rehearsed my forthcoming phone call to Sasha Popov. I had waited until the middle of the week to make the invitation to meet him appear unrushed, spur of the moment.

"Popov," he stated, answering the phone. I had informed the receptionist who answered the FESCO line who I was after she demanded to know. I gave her my name and told her the call was personal. One sometimes wonders if receptionists pass along that information, or if they merely ask to satisfy their own curiosity.

"Hello, Sasha. This is Louis."

"Who?"

"Louis Francisco. Cisco. We met at Terry's on New Year's Eve."

"Oh … yes. I remember. Cisco." His voice sounded indifferent, tired, and cautious.

"I was wondering if you'd like to get together for a drink."

There was silence while he considered.

"Yeah, why not? We can meet for a drink."

"This weekend? How would that work for you?"

"Let me check my calendar. Give me a minute."

I was beginning to wonder if he had lost the alcohol-induced enthusiasm he'd had at Terry's when we played. He now appeared remote. On the other hand, I now knew what his true undercover role in Manila was. He was a KGB officer with the First Chief Directorate, the foreign espionage department, and the most senior Soviet intelligence officer in the Philippines. Caution would be built into him, especially in his dealings with an American.

"By the way, I'm looking at your name card," he commented in his American English. "What is this Haig & Company in Hong Kong?"

"That's the consulting firm I work for. I can tell you more about it when we meet." I kept my voice upbeat.

"All right. Make it Friday night. We meet at Terry's. Okay?"

"That's fine. Maybe start off a little earlier this time. Say around seven o'clock," I suggested. "We'll have dinner somewhere?"

"Yeah, yeah. Okay. Terry's at seven. See you there," he said, his voice still leaden.

We said goodbye and hung up.

# 24

---

JANUARY 1975

T HE CRAFT OF SPOTTING, ASSESSING, ESTABLISHING
rapport, then pitching, recruiting, and tasking a
clandestine agent to collect secret intelligence, or to
betray his country, is not unlike seducing a beautiful woman.
The process is similar. You spot the woman and find her
attractive, sexy. There's the flirting, the courtship, and the
generous wining and dining. A mutual infatuation and trust
develops; the good-night kiss at her doorstep lingers and is
consummated with either wild or underwhelming sex.

So it is with the development and recruitment of a secret
agent. I had spotted Sasha Popov, by luck, and established
personal contact, if not much of a rapport yet with the Russian.
The challenge ahead was daunting. I had no idea whatsoever
of his weaknesses or vulnerabilities. We knew his impressive
track record of accomplishments, under a different name, in
Cairo. He was cosmopolitan, but they teach that in the KGB
schools outside Moscow. A professional like Popov would, as

an aspect of his deep cover, exhibit a suave sophistication. He too was a seducer—a case officer.

I suspected that he was curious about me and my putative occupation. The difference was that I *knew* what he was doing undercover; he could only guess about me. On the other hand, he had something like a twenty-year lead over me in playing this chess game. And what, I asked myself, was my ultimate objective? Would I eventually breed a new "mole" deep inside the KGB? And how long would it take me?

We met at Terry's. I arrived at a quarter to seven and he walked in at seven o'clock. He was more conservatively dressed than he had been the week before: he was wearing a white, long-sleeved, embroidered *barong Tagalog*—the formal men's attire of the Philippines. No garish jewelry this time. He spotted me at the bar, nodded, and took the empty stool beside me.

"Sasha. Good to see you again."

He twirled a forefinger at Jun signaling for a drink.

"Yeah, good of you to call," he replied, looking at me with steely eyes.

"Is Flora joining us for dinner?"

He drained the double shot of ice-cold vodka in one motion and signaled for another.

"No." He grimaced as he swallowed and shook his head. "My wife insists on dining with us tonight. I told her the story of how you and I met and played jazz together. She found your business card when she was going through my pockets. And she wants to meet you. She likes Americans." He shrugged at this last comment.

There was no enthusiasm in his demeanor. I was struck by his aloofness, carried over from our phone call.

"Does your wife know to meet us at Terry's?"

"No. I never bring her here." He paused. "Be sure you tell Ingrid that we met and played jazz at the Gaucho Bar if she asks. That's what I told her. Anyway, we'll see her later at Casa Verde. I made reservations for eight o'clock."

He sipped his third vodka slowly now. "Tell me about, what is it? Haig & Company? What do you do?"

I was prepared for this next stage of our charade. "Haig is a maritime consulting firm. We want to give Lloyds Shipping Intelligence some competition. We collect information worldwide." I paused to take a long drink from my bottle of San Miguel. "There isn't an area of merchant shipping we don't cover—fleet sizes, port studies, tonnages, new construction, ship scrapping, flags of convenience with their beneficial owners, and recent spot and time chartering details. We have an agent at the Baltic Exchange in London. Name it and we'll include it in our database if it involves shipping." He nodded, seeming to be half listening. "We publish the information, confidentially of course, and offer it to paid-up subscribers."

"You are American," he remarked, looking at me in the mirror. "Why is your company based in Hong Kong?"

"Tax avoidance. We're global. The owners don't have a need for registering the company or paying taxes in, say, New York or London. So they set up offshore. One can make convenient arrangements in Hong Kong."

"So your company is flying a flag of convenience." He snickered.

"I suppose you could look at it that way. We engage free-lance correspondents around the world. Most of these associates want to be kept off the books. So the whole operation is cleaner all round if we operate offshore."

"Do you pay well?" he asked, not looking at me and raising a hand at Jun for a refill.

"That depends," I answered.

There was a prolonged silence as Sasha seemed to ponder my equivocal reply. I finished my beer and ordered another. Sasha continued to look at my reflection in the mirror behind the bar. Was it my imagination, or was his sly expression telling me, "It takes one to know one"?

I broke the silence. "We'd better make a move if we're going to meet your wife in Makati. You said Casa Verde?"

I called for the bill and insisted on paying.

Sasha had parked his car nearby. He drove a black late-model Mercedes Benz.

"Hop in," he said. "I've given my driver the night off, much as I hate the crazy driving in Manila. I'll try to get us there in one piece." I was again aware of Sasha's facile use of American idioms in his spoken English.

He placed a cassette recording of a Miles Davis album, *Kind of Blue*, into the stereo and turned up the volume as we took off. "I know you like Miles. I heard it in your trumpet playing the other night."

"You've got good ears. By the way, where did you learn to play piano like that? It couldn't have been in Russia."

"Why not? Voice of America used to play that jazz program every night. I tuned in to the show when I was a kid." He stopped and seemed to reflect on something in his past. "Of course, when I took piano lessons my parents expected me to play Chopin and Rachmaninov. I wasn't so interested. I would open up our family piano whenever they weren't around and try to copy the jazz I heard on the VOA show." He furiously honked the horn at an errant driver who had cut him off. "Sonofabitch!" He continued. "You could say I'm a self-taught pianist. VOA played a lot of boogie-woogie and swing music in those days, after the war. I used to hear Basie and guys like that." We continued to Makati, listening to the music. Sasha appeared preoccupied.

The Casa Verde was an upscale, dimly lit restaurant in the heart of the affluent, if sterile, suburb of Makati. Sasha mentioned that he lived in one of the exclusive gated enclaves nearby. His wife had her own car and driver and would meet us at the restaurant. I asked him if he had children. He shook his head.

Ingrid was sitting at a table when we arrived, quite late. There was an unopened bottle of wine in an ice bucket. She looked annoyed, fidgeting with a breadstick as we walked in. We spotted her from across the room. Sasha headed toward the table, ignoring the maître'd, and I followed him. Three guitarists were serenading diners with Flamenco music.

Sasha spoke to her in English. "I'm sorry we're late, darling. We were caught in traffic." He motioned to me beside him. "Meet Cisco." The *darling* bit sounded contrived and out of character, like scripted English he'd picked up in a movie.

She offered me her hand and smiled coyly. "Hello. I'm Ingrid." She had a slight accent, that could have been French, could have been Russian.

"Pleased to meet you Ingrid," I said, continuing to stand. "Your husband is a talented pianist. I had the pleasure of hearing him play the other night."

"Yes, he told me you played together." The accent was Russian. She motioned with her hand for me to sit down across from her. Her unblinking green eyes held mine for a long moment. Sasha sat down beside his wife as a waiter uncorked the bottle and filled our wine glasses.

I caught myself staring at the woman longer than I normally would have. I was for a moment speechless. The woman's beauty was, in a word, breathtaking. She had ash-blond hair, fashionably cut and falling down the center of her back. Her face was exquisite, poised and without a blemish. Her full sensuous lips, pornographic. Ingrid could have been taken for a lingerie model ... or a celebrity tennis star. She was the same height as Sasha, five-foot-nine. That night she was dressed expensively, with a beige, knee-length dress suggestively unbuttoned high up her thighs, and likewise unfastened down the neckline, exposing the crest of her firm rising breasts. She wore coordinated gold and diamond jewelry—earrings, bracelets, and a necklace. One had the impression that she did not require makeup, her beauty was so natural. I inhaled her scent as I leaned forward and took my seat at the table.

I averted my eyes from hers, and for some reason pictured Flora in my mind. I looked at Sasha, and smiled knowingly. Here was a man, I concluded, who was performing a complicated juggling act in his personal life. He now had a cold, insouciant expression on his face. I noted that he and Ingrid had not made eye contact since we'd arrived at the table. The innuendo was thick. A waiter approached the table to check on our drinks.

"Give me a Bloody Mary," Sasha scowled. "Make it a double, easy on the tomato juice."

At one point during the meal, there was a lull in the conversation. An awkward silence.

"It must be twenty minutes after the hour or twenty minutes before the hour," I remarked.

The two of them looked at me.

"Why do you say that, Cisco?" Ingrid asked.

"Well, when there's an extended hush in a conversation, like this, you can almost set your watch by it: it's either twenty minutes after or twenty minutes before the hour. One of those mysteries of nature." We each looked at our watches.

"You are right." she exclaimed. "It is 10:22. I will remember that trick, Cisco."

Sasha snorted and signaled to a waiter for another drink.

I've never been one for meaningless small talk. Superficial conversation gets very old very fast. That evening, however, it was my mission to attempt to keep the good cheer alive at the table. Sasha was taciturn one moment and argumentative the next. Ingrid did her best to ignore him and shower me with attention, looking deep into my eyes, pretending, I think, to be a good listener. When she did speak, it was only with me. I wondered if they were putting on an Oscar-winning act.

Could the two of them be working in Manila as a team? It was unheard of for the First Directorate to send a case officer *and* his wife overseas together—unless they worked in tandem: *yin* and *yang*. The KGB routinely kept the wife-as-hostage back in the USSR to prevent defections by their male case officers. And wasn't Ingrid rather too beautiful to be true? Were they indeed even married to each other? If I hadn't met the beguiling and seductive Flora I might have written the evening off as an elaborate play, rehearsed in Moscow. By the end of dinner, I speculated that Sasha and Ingrid Popov were indeed undergoing a crisis of sorts in their marriage, a relationship that seemed to be on the verge of a breaking point. They had nothing to gain by putting on an act for my benefit. I suspected, correctly as it turned out, that the problem involved a triangle that included Flora.

Sasha drove me home after dinner. Ingrid had held my

arm and kissed me on the cheek, brushing my ear with moist lips, before saying good-night and slipping gracefully into the back seat of her chauffeur-driven Mercedes.

We drove in silence with the music, a ballad, playing at low volume on the car stereo.

At last Sasha spoke. "The evening did not go well. Ingrid and I had a big disagreement. I would have cancelled dinner if I had known how to contact you."

"Oh?"

"To tell the truth, Cisco, it was a lot more than a disagreement. I was in the doghouse last night."

"Do you want to tell me about it?"

He gave this some thought. I sensed he was struggling. "I came home late. I'd been with Flora, though of course I tell Ingrid I am out with client, a big copra shipper. I am often able to take a shower as soon as I arrive home from these, how you say in English, *trysts*, if I haven't had time to wash up at the hotel. Ingrid's always in bed. But last night she was waiting for me at the front door when I walk in. Big, big surprise. She wrap her arms around me and kiss me on the lips before I could get to the bathroom."

I could see where this was going.

"My face had been buried between Flora's legs half the night. She loves that. So Ingrid tastes Flora's juices on my face when she kiss me. And hell breaks loose."

There was not a lot I could offer in the way of condolences. I asked him if he would like to come into the house for a drink before he returned home to Ingrid. I had purchased bottles of Polish and Russian vodka earlier that day.

"Yes. I need a drink. We have some time before I have to drive home."

He parked the car in the driveway and I locked the tall cast-iron gate behind us. As we entered the house, I turned on the lights and invited Sasha to have a seat while I went to the kitchen to get the bottle of Russian vodka from the freezer.

"Nice swimming pool," he called out.

The idea hit me as I walked back into the living room with our glasses. "You and Flora might like to come over for a swim sometime. You'd have a lot of privacy. Let me know."

I handed him a cocktail glass filled with the ice-cold vodka. He raised his eyebrows with obvious interest.

"She would like that."

We discussed Sasha's dilemma for the next twenty minutes. He had fallen in love with Flora. This was not a casual fling, he said. Ingrid was now aware of the affair, if not the depth of Sasha's split emotions. And Sasha revealed, over a second drink, that Ingrid's extravagance was costing him a small fortune. "She's making up for the years she was back in Moscow. Now, she sees all these obscenely wealthy women here in Manila, so she wants to compete with Imelda Marcos in her lust for luxuries. I must keep her happy—the jewelry, the car and chauffeur, designer clothes. You saw her tonight." His face was turning a shade of red, from drink or anger. I wasn't sure. Evidently he had taken me on as a confidant.

"Yes, she did look stylish," I commented.

"And Flora, too, wants to be kept in style," he added with a smirk. "She appreciates my gifts and our intimate dinners in fine, dark restaurants. We go to bed, have incredible sex, at the most expensive hotels in Manila. She is now begging me to rent an apartment for the two of us."

I acted as if I needed to think the matter over before I made the suggestion. "Sasha, you and I are friends. We have some things in common—we're musicians, and we're both in the same business: shipping. A coincidence. You and Flora could use my house as your *pied-a-terre*. You wouldn't have to rent an apartment."

He didn't reply. He stared at his drink. Neither one of us believed in coincidences.

"I had better hit the road before I have too much to drink," he said at last, placing his empty glass down on a coaster. "Let's talk about this later next week."

# 25

FEBRUARY 1975

TWO NIGHTS LATER, AT TEN O'CLOCK, THE PHONE IN my bedroom rang three times. The signal. I waited. After ten minutes the phone rang again and I answered it, expecting to hear McCoy's voice.

"This is Mr. Briar speaking. Do you recognize my voice?" This took me by surprise. Mr. Briar was Tom Hiatt's code name. Why would he call the Manila safe house?

"And if so, is it convenient for you to talk to me now? Yes or no is all you need to say."

I answered, "Yes to both questions, Mr. Briar."

"What was I wearing the last day we saw each other?"

We had met during my last day in the office. Hiatt had said goodbye and good hunting. "You wore a dark blue suit, a pinstriped dress shirt, and a blue and white necktie. The pattern of the tie was striped, diagonal. Your black loafers were tasseled."

"Okay. You are to meet me in Malacca in three days.

Travel there directly. Do not, repeat, do not stop anywhere else, as you ordinarily would. I will contact you at the place you're staying. Do you understand me?"

"Yes, understood," I replied. He hung up without another word.

The message was clear enough. I was *not* to stop in Singapore and check in with Steve McCoy. Rather, I was to travel to Malacca and arrive there as soon as possible, and within three days.

Sammy met me at the Kuala Lumpur airport and drove me to Malacca. I arrived at the Majestic Hotel that evening.

There were three messages for me at the front desk. All three had been routed to me via the new Malacca CTI office. Two coffee bean exporters in Indonesia, the one in Makassar and another I'd met in Sumatra, had contacted the office. Both of them confirmed that they would be delighted to supply CTI with Arabica coffee beans and that they looked forward to commencing business with me. During the meetings I'd had with them, they had both broached money-laundering ploys where they would under-invoice CTI for each of their coffee bean shipments. We were to deposit the balance of what we owed to secret personal accounts in Geneva and Hong Kong respectively.

The third message came as a bombshell. It was from my high school tennis partner and old friend, Jack Chapman. We had not seen each other for close to ten years. Jack had gone on to study at Cal Berkeley after graduating from high school, at the same time I had joined the navy. He'd played on the Cal tennis team and had gone on to earn a postgraduate degree. My parents were the only persons, outside of the Institute, who knew I was living in Asia. And CTI in Malacca was the one address they knew regarding my whereabouts. I figured Jack had obtained my contact details from them.

His message said that he was now living and working in Hong Kong. He left his home phone number. The next morning I phoned Jack before he left for work. He told me he had landed a job in Hong Kong and that he worked for a consulting company, the well-known defense contractor, *Cain, Acheson and Carpenter*, known worldwide as CAC. He didn't explain any more than that about his job. I told him that I occasionally traveled to Hong Kong when I wasn't off rustling coffee beans. We agreed to get together during my next visit and renew our friendship.

The following afternoon, on the third day, Tom Hiatt arrived and checked in to the Majestic Hotel. I was jogging on *Bukit China*, Chinese Hill, when he arrived. When I returned to the hotel at six o'clock, I picked up the message that he was in his room. I phoned him and we met in the lobby.

I was rattled by Tom's trip to Malacca. Had I screwed up somewhere? I wondered why he had made a point of not meeting in Singapore, in McCoy's office at the embassy. His insistence on meeting me in Malacca was an enigma, outside the protocol. To put it another way, I couldn't figure out what, if anything, Tom Hiatt needed to conceal from Steve McCoy.

"Hello, Roy." He greeted me in the lobby with a stoic expression. "We need to talk." The inference was that we needed to find a spot where we would have complete privacy. I'd anticipated this earlier and could think of no better place for our *tête-a-tête* than along the jogging paths that wind through Malacca's ancient Chinese cemetery.

"Did you bring along a pair of sneakers?" I asked. An image of the pudgy and stooped Tom Hiatt striding through the cemetery in a pair of sneakers and shorts seemed incongruous.

"No. But if we need to buy a pair, let's go," he replied. "Lead the way."

We walked together down *Jalan Bunga Raya*, through Little India, and along the riverside until we reached the ancient bridge that led to Chinatown on the north side of the river. As we walked he explained why we were not meeting each other in Singapore. He said he didn't want to take a chance that his former CIA colleagues would recognize him, wish to meet with him, and pick his brain about the Institute's operations. He and the Agency's chief of station in Singapore, Hunter Lenihan, were old pals. They had grown up together in the Agency's Department of Plans, the clandestine service. Reason enough for Hiatt to avoid the Singapore embassy.

We fitted Tom with a pair of tennis shoes and some athletic socks at a shop on Jonker Street. I suggested that he also buy a pair of shorts. He declined and said he had a pair of casual slacks that should serve the purpose. Afterward, we had dinner together at a local *Nonya* restaurant where he surprised me with his appetite for chilies and spices. He said he'd acquired the taste during his years operating in the Middle East.

"You're wondering why I'm here," he said as we walked along the riverside back to the hotel. Right then he chuckled and pointed to a large iguana that was floating downstream. "Look, isn't that something?" That was the first time all evening I observed Hiatt do as much as crack a smile.

"In fact, I have been wondering about the purpose of your visit, Tom. The urgency."

He glanced around us. "It's about *Slugger*. We'll discuss it tomorrow. Think of a private spot, outdoors, where we can talk."

"That's why you bought those new shoes."

"Four walls make me nervous, claustrophobic. Especially overseas."

We met the next morning for breakfast in the hotel's aged colonial dining room. We spoke little over coffee, tropical fruit, and croissants. Tom was wearing his new sneakers, a pair of loose trousers, and a polo shirt. He carried a wide-brimmed Panama hat. I wore Bermuda shorts, a fresh blue T-shirt, running shoes, and a baseball cap. I knew the cemetery would be empty in the morning; joggers never populated the hill until late afternoon. The truth is, I felt somewhat intimidated by Hiatt's demeanor since our meeting the day before.

"Well, let's get started," he said after we'd finished breakfast. The Tom Hiatt I'd finally gotten to know at Springfield was not the moody, taciturn person he appeared to be now.

The taxi let us off at the base of the hill. It was eight-thirty, and the air was hot and muggy. Tom and I began our stroll on *Bukit China* at an easy pace. There was not another person on the hill, among the myriad tombstones, as far as I could see.

"Nice graveyard," Tom said and waved an arm at the deserted hillside. He looked rather smart now wearing dark glasses and his Panama hat.

"Roy, you and I never became close back in Springfield. I endorsed your operation plan at the meetings and moved it along, especially the coffee business angle. Other than that, Wright and Pomeroy handled the coordination. You no doubt have heard rumors about my background. So let me fill you in before we launch into the matter of *Slugger*."

"I did hear some of it," I replied. We quickened our pace walking along the path.

Tom Hiatt explained to me how he had been recruited into the Agency soon after it was established in 1947. He had served in World War II as a junior army officer on General Eisenhower's staff in England, and it was there that he made his connections with the OSS officers who recruited him into the new intelligence agency.

The Agency was in its heyday during the '50s and '60s. Hiatt was invited to join the elite corps of officers who spent the greater part of their careers operating covertly overseas, competing head-to-head against the Soviet intelligence services to foster American influence. He specialized in covert operations in the Middle East. He knew Egypt, Lebanon, Syria, Iraq, and Iran intimately. He ran secret agents and venal politicians in each of those countries. The rumor at Springfield was that he had a hand in organizing military *coups* and revolutions throughout the region. As a young man he'd known Nasser and the Shah of Iran personally, and for a brief period he had been a confidant to both of them.

There had been the odd KGB double agent he'd recruited, turning each of them back against their Stalinist homeland. By the late 1960s, as the war in Vietnam took center stage, he had established a larger-than-life reputation in the CIA. He was a friend of the director, Richard Helms, who at the time was a respected counselor to President Lyndon Johnson. After nearly twenty years in the field, it was time for Hiatt to come in from the cold.

As it happened, the CIA's position at the top table in the White House was annulled early in the Nixon/Kissinger reign. Richard Nixon made no secret of his distrust of the CIA, and forthwith all matters of intelligence—foreign and domestic, covert and clandestine—were controlled and coordinated by the National Security Council. Richard Helms and Tom Hiatt were kicked back into the cold, across the Potomac River.

There was one exception. The White House, beginning with the Johnson administration and continuing with Nixon's, tasked the CIA with Operation CHAOS. The Agency was ordered to conduct surveillance and collect intelligence on domestic anti-Vietnam War groups. The justification for the domestic spying by the CIA was that the White House believed the anti-war movements were being set up and funded by foreign intelligence agencies, namely the KGB. Tom Hiatt was put in charge of the operation during the early Nixon years. And Hiatt knew he was breaking the law. The CIA's charter is clear—the collection of *foreign* intelligence. Period. He consulted with the Agency's general counsel staff, and they acknowledged that he might indeed find himself in legal hot water if an issue were ever made of Operation CHAOS. Tom Hiatt resigned from the CIA in 1971 rather than face the prospect of impossibly high legal fees, testimony under oath before congress, or worse, prison.

Hiatt's friend, Richard Helms, who was fired by Richard Nixon more than a year later for refusing to cover up the Watergate scandal, knew about the creation of the Institute within the Defense Department. Helms understood that the Institute had been created as a Unified Command and that it needed an experienced, permanent civilian in its leadership for the sake of continuity. Helms recommended Tom Hiatt to the Joint Chiefs. Tom was hired and awarded the position of deputy director, the number two man at the Institute.

"And that brings us to where we are now, Roy, walking

along a path among these ancient Chinese tombstones in sweaty Malacca, preparing to discuss the recruitment of a Russian mole." Tom removed his Panama hat and wiped his forehead with the back of his hand. I nodded and looked straight ahead as we climbed the hill between the timeworn, four-hundred-year-old gravesites and some of the more contemporary and richly decorated mausoleums.

"I know a thing or two about running double agents, KGB moles. Done it myself over the years. To say that it's dicey is an understatement." Tom was now getting into his stride. He began walking like a man with a purpose. His energy surprised me. "*Slugger*, Sergei Bordin or Sasha Popov, take your pick, is a pro. A consummate professional. We know that as a case officer in Cairo for six years in the 60s and early 70s he recruited a senior British diplomat. He ran an Egyptian deputy in the interior ministry. And let's see, he also corrupted one of our own traitors, an enlisted air force communications specialist who worked deep inside the NSA. Those are three turncoats we know of. My guess is that over a period of six years in a place like Cairo, he added more scalps."

"Why was he moved out of Cairo?"

Tom snickered. "His agent, the elderly Egyptian deputy. Popov was caught, *en flagrante*, having an affair with the minister's sexy half-French wife. In another day he would have been proclaimed *persona non-grata*, or worse. Stupid of him, but there you are. He was called back to Moscow in November '73 where he spent a few months as an instructor at one of the Center's schools outside Moscow. He taught the kiddies there how to behave and speak like Americans. Sound familiar?"

I looked at him and nodded.

Tom continued. "My theory is that the Soviet military—

generals and admirals—needed to have a star intelligence officer in the Philippines to run agents inside Subic and Clark. Those are the two largest American military bases outside the continental United States. The GRU case officer handling that task before him was working undercover as a TASS correspondent. We knew it, and we prevailed on the Filipinos to kick him out of the country. The Soviets needed a replacement, and fast. And because of a supposed Americanized culture in the Philippines, they selected your faux American, Sasha Popov."

"I'm listening."

"You should be. Pay attention. Ordinarily Soviet intelligence targeting our navy at Subic Bay and our air force at Clark would be assigned to the GRU, the intelligence wing of the Soviet Union's military. My guess is they couldn't find a GRU case officer soon enough with the requisite Americanisms. So they sent a KGB operative instead. Sasha Popov."

We reached the top of the hill where we stopped to rest. Tom tried to read the Chinese inscription on one of the faded tombstones. I gazed out at the Malacca Straits and at the islands in the distance.

"You see that large island that looks like a pregnant woman lying on her back?" I pointed in the direction of the Straits. "That's *Pulau Besar*."

"I'm starting to understand why you like Malacca, Roy. Given all the turbulence at home these days." Tom took a deep breath and sighed. "It's so calm here." He removed his dark glasses and wiped them with a handkerchief.

I suggested that we continue to walk and discuss my mission. But Tom remained standing still and gazing out at the Malacca Straits. "You know, when I look at those Straits what I see is a choke point," he remarked as if to himself.

"How so?" I asked.

"They say the traders of Venice in the fifteenth century warned, 'Whoever is the Lord of Malacca has his hand on the throat of Venice.' Now, fast-forward five hundred years." He began walking again.

"Trust me, Mancini—one day China will emerge from this Cultural Revolution nightmare they're living through. Probably have to wait until Mao dies. When they do they will import as much oil from the Middle East as Japan does today. And all of those China-bound supertankers will pass through the Malacca Straits. That's what our navy refers to as a choke point. The maritime intelligence you'll be collecting will be of significant importance. Mark my words. Red China will emerge as a major threat to this region."

I remembered the meeting I'd had at the U.S. Embassy with the CIA officer.

"One thing, Tom, I wanted to ask you," I said as we continued walking down the other side of the hill. "Do you know a CIA officer named Tony Loyola? He's undercover at the embassy in Manila."

"Ha, Loyola. We call him the 'Godfather.' He was one of the gunslingers. What about him?"

"When I met him he made an offhanded remark that maritime operations, the sort of thing I'm involved in, are low-level. He didn't seem to take my mission all that seriously. Is that the Institute's view?"

Tom walked in silence for several seconds. "Yes and no," he said. Further silence as we continued. "The navy brass think it's a big deal. Remember how DuPont ran off to brief the chief of Naval Intelligence about your op plan? They need to know all they can these days about our foes' capabilities—

nuclear submarines, sea-launched ballistic missiles, and so forth. There's nothing low-level about that." He added, "Loyola is full of shit. He was putting you on." And then he paused and looked at me. "And I've explained my choke point theory to you."

"And the flip side?"

Hiatt stopped walking and looked at me. He gave a wry smile. "I look at these maritime ops of yours as sort of a training exercise. An extension of that school you went to in Baltimore, where I recall you graduated with the highest honors. And that's because I see potential in you, Roy. I had no doubt as I observed you in Springfield that you would succeed as a case officer. And that you could, in the future, handle more sensitive, covert operations ... although I never imagined this would occur during your first year in the field." He paused.

"Let me remind you, all the military officers at the Institute—the general, the colonels, the lieutenant commanders, and the lieutenants—they'll put in their three to four years, get promoted, and then move on to the next assignment. They're in-and-out. We civilians provide the continuity, the institu-tional memory. And right now that burden rests on me, alone. One day you might join me at the top table there. *Slugger* in Manila has given you a lift in a lot of people's eyes. We'll see. I want you to succeed, Roy. And I want you to be careful, very careful."

"You must have an opinion about *Slugger*," I remarked as we continued along a flat section of the cemetery.

"That's why I'm here in Malacca. It's why we're meeting one-on-one and not discussing this project in an embassy office."

"Go on."

"The risk is that *Slugger* is an accomplished actor. To put it another way, he could end up exploiting you, rather than the other way around. Over the years the Russians have proven adroit at that sort of thing, nurturing double agents into triple agents, traitors who really aren't, that end up turning around and biting us, gaining more intelligence from us than we ever glean from them. That's the reason the brother-in-law is so averse to taking risks lately. If it were up to their recently retired and unlamented counterintelligence chief, James Jesus Angleton, heaven forbid, you'd be ordered by Mr. Loyola to keep your hands the fuck off of *Slugger*. But I've decided to give you the green light on this. And I want you to listen carefully."

Hiatt's guidance was clear. This operation, the attempt to recruit and run *Slugger* was code-named *Wolverine*. The only persons witting of the operation were General DuPont, Pete Wright, Steve McCoy, and Tom Hiatt. Hiatt, rather than the East Asia desk officer, would coordinate the operation personally at the Springfield headquarters.

McCoy had that week received orders to transfer from Singapore to Manila under a new cover as the Military Sealift Command representative for the Philippines. The CIA would remain unwitting of *Wolverine*, at least until *Slugger* was recruited and being turned back against the Soviet Union.

We had reached the spot where we had begun our slow jog an hour earlier.

"Looks like we'd better make another round," Tom said, taking a deep breath as we continued to walk at a fast pace along the jogging path.

He told me to bide my time and continue to develop a

personal rapport with *Slugger*. I explained to Tom the events of my earlier meetings with him at Terry's, Casa Verde, and at the safe house. Meanwhile Springfield's analysts would continue to dig deeper into his backstory.

My next step would be to recruit Popov as a freelance consultant for Haig & Company. I would offer to pay him $1,500 a month for this innocent consulting work, an amount that would not be suspiciously high, yet would be generous considering the modest effort required of him. We would get him hooked on this steady income and then ratchet the monthly amount up to $2,000 as a bonus for his "good work." The safe house in Paranaque would now be used exclusively for operation *Wolverine*. I would not meet any other agents there.

I had a sudden idea. "There is a Filipino-American woman at our Hong Kong office. Her name is Cynthia Roman. She's working as Davis's personal assistant. Could you send her to Manila to work undercover, perhaps as a housekeeper, at the safe house? I need someone from the Institute living there—someone who speaks Tagalog—especially if I'm traveling. No telling what *Slugger* might try to pull when I'm away. Maybe a black bag job?"

Tom nodded his head in the affirmative. "Consider it done."

"All right. I plan that *Slugger* will spend a lot of time with his paramour at the safe house. I'll offer them one of the bedrooms. So Cynthia would have to be a good actress to play the role."

Tom nodded.

"Leave it to me. She's got the background, former NIS. Father's an American. She grew up in Cebu. I interviewed her before we sent her off to Hong Kong. And she's sharp."

Then he switched gears again. "I'm not going to advise you how to develop and recruit Popov. You figure out the operational details. So far you've been moving it along well. Pace yourself. Use your best method-acting skills. And never ever forget security. In short, *do not* trust Sasha Popov. He's had many years playing at this game. To paraphrase LBJ: 'Never trust a man unless you've got his pecker in your pocket.'"

"When we reach that final plateau, the ultimate recruitment pitch that turns him into a 'mole,' how will we know he's on the level? That he's not gaming us?"

Tom had a quick answer. "He needs to provide us with some intelligence of the highest sensitivity, tell us something really fresh. *Slugger*'s many years in the field and at Moscow Center have provided him with plenty of that. He won't get away with giving us chickenfeed. If he tries, giving us minor league stuff, we'll know soon enough that he's a fraud. You impress that on him when you pitch him. Clear?"

So the plan was to move along with the recruitment of Sasha Popov in stages. When we reached the ultimate stage, inserting a "mole" into the highest level of Soviet intelligence, the value of the information he revealed at the outset would determine whether or not we continued to engage him.

"What's his motivation, Roy?"

"Principal motivation . . . his financial plight. He needs the money we're prepared to pay him. He's made that clear."

"And?"

"A healthy dose of megalomania and derring-do. That too is exploitable."

"You'll need to work up a handle on him as soon as possible."

"Any ideas?" I asked.

"I want you to set up a secret recording device in the safe house. Voice activated. You can connect it to a light switch. I did it that way in Beirut. Start taping all the conversations you have with him. Record all the hanky-panky with the mistress. Bug their bedroom. The steamier the better. Cynthia can help you operate it after she moves into the house. DoD has techs in the Philippines who can do the installation."

Tom continued. "You know, we have an agent sign a receipt every time we pay him. There is then the subtle feature that we can, if we choose, reveal those compromising signed receipts to his superiors if he causes us any trouble. Receipts for payments are a useful handle. The thing is, *Slugger* would be too smart for that. He knows as much as anyone about compromise and blackmail. So the second handle we'll have on him, in addition to the safe house recordings, will be his bank statements showing the deposits. He'll need a secret bank account when we start paying him the real money. And if he fucks us, we'll compromise him with those bank statements and have him shot in the back of the head in Lefortovo prison, the KGB dungeon. He understands that language." Tom's voice was dispassionate, as though speaking from experience.

"On a different subject, Roy, and at the risk of sounding cynical, I'd like to give you some advice regarding your coffee bean business. If you do business in this part of the world, Asia and the Middle East, and you wish to be successful, then drop your good old American sense of business ethics and fair play. Those are mere abstractions out here. Play it the Asian way or suffer the consequence. In this part of the world it's all about making money. The motive to make as much money as possible, any way you can, is paramount. Don't carry the illusion around that anything else counts. I suspect your father and your school teachers in California never taught you that. But there you are. Let's go have a cold drink."

Before we reached the bottom of the hill, I mentioned my suspicion about the person on the plane who had been following me. Hiatt was speechless for two or three minutes.

"That son of a bitch," he finally uttered to himself. And then to me. "There are only two people outside the Institute who knew of your departure date from Dulles—the director of Naval Intelligence and the chief of staff for the President's Foreign Intelligence Advisory Board. And it wouldn't have been the DNI who reported you to the brother-in-law. McCoy needs to report to me if you sense this guy is still tailing you. And that's an order."

# 26

---

I REMAINED IN MY MALACCA HOME FOR FIVE DAYS AFTER
Hiatt left. I savored the respite from the frequent shifts of
identity I was compelled to practice elsewhere in the
region. Here I concentrated on the coffee trading business
from my base at the Majestic Hotel: contacting Arabica bean
exporters in Sumatra, Makassar, Jakarta, and Surabaya and
setting up long-distance relationships with roasters in the U.S.,
Japan, and Europe. Soon, though, I got the itch to return to
the real action. In the Philippines.

Cynthia Roman arrived in Manila on a flight from
Singapore during the first week of March 1975. She entered
the country as Maria Soriano, using a Filipino passport. She
carried documentation establishing that she had been employed
as a housemaid in Singapore, and that her two-year contract
was up. That week she rented a cheap room and contacted an
employment agency in Escolta seeking a job as a maid.

A day later, I visited that office and informed them of my

need to hire a housekeeper. The agency offered me several applicants. I reviewed the profiles and requested that they set up interviews with five candidates, including one with Maria Soriano. I conducted all five interviews, and in the end told the agency I wished to hire Maria. She paid her fee to the agency and moved to the safe house within the week.

During the pretense of interviewing "Maria Soriano," I learned that Cynthia had grown up in Cebu to the age of seventeen. Her American father had been engaged there in the rattan furniture business. Her mother was a Filipino and Cynthia's mother tongue was Cebuano. She also spoke Tagalog fluently. She was the same age as I was, twenty-eight. She'd lived and studied in Seattle after leaving the Philippines and before joining the navy. Most of her career had been with the Naval Investigative Service. She'd been seconded to the Institute a year earlier.

The same week a group of air force techs from Clark Air Base arrived at the safe house in Paranaque. Late at night they installed a sophisticated recording system. They placed mics in every room in the house, in the umbrella in the garden, and in the telephones. The master control was connected to a light switch in Cynthia's bedroom. The tape recorder was secreted beneath the floor in the basement.

The following week I paid a visit to the Manila Yacht Club in search of a crewing position on a racing sailboat. During my high school and college years I had raced sailboats, and I'd won gold medals at regattas up and down the California coast. I'd also skippered the University of Hawaii sailing team for three years. So when I walked into the yacht club, it was with a high degree of confidence that I could offer my sailing prowess to a club member in need of crew.

I walked up to a round dining table and introduced myself, under true name, to a group of sailors who were having breakfast. This was a Saturday morning, early in the racing season.

The Manila Yacht Club had a small fleet of twenty-nine-foot wooden sloops known as Dragons, the World Olympics racing class at that time. The boat raced with three persons—a skipper and two crew.

A fit-looking blonde, blue-eyed Swedish woman in her early thirties welcomed me and asked me to sit down and join the table.

"Can you handle the foredeck, Roy?" she asked with her melodic Scandinavian accent.

"I can, sure." I explained to her something about my years of competitive sailing and how I could indeed handle the foredeck spinnaker operation.

"You're hired," she said with a wide smile. "My name is Monica. Meet our other crew, Cora. Can I offer you a drink?" She introduced me to a Spanish mestiza woman. All of the other Dragon skippers at the table were men. Nine out of ten were expatriates: Brits, Australians, Kiwis, and a German. There was one Filipino skipper in the fleet. We introduced ourselves as white-jacketed Filipino waiters scurried between tables, serving drinks and meals. I ordered a tall calamansi juice.

"The name of my boat is *Jambalaya*," Monica remarked. "You can see her out there at the mooring—the one with the red and white hull. My boat boy, Juanito, is rigging the boat. We'll go out in half an hour."

I looked out at the small harbor and saw the fleet of Dragons. There was also a variety of large and expensive yachts tied up to moorings inside of a rocky breakwater. Further out, beyond the breakwater, were a dozen oceangoing cargo ships at anchor.

We sailed four races that day, each of them around an Olympic course. *Jambalaya* placed first in three of the races and a second in the fourth. I still knew my racing tactics and rules, and I could handle the spinnaker and the foredeck as if it had been only yesterday. Sailboat racing, like riding a bicycle, is a skill one doesn't easily forget. Within a month of racing together, Monica was sharing the skippering of the boat with me. When I had the helm she handled the foredeck, where she enjoyed perfecting the spinnaker operation. Muscular Cora was a strong trimmer with a good sense of timing. We were a prize-winning race team. Within a month I bought a half-share in *Jambalaya*. And I became a member of the Manila Yacht Club.

# 27

---

S OON AFTER I BECAME A PART OWNER OF *JAMBALAYA* AND a member of the yacht club, I began to race the boat on Wednesday nights. This was an informal social event open to all classes of sailboats—from Dragons to luxury yachts. There were no prizes, just a lot of post-race fun and boozing at the bar. I could often find a couple of crew members to join me an hour or so before the race. If not, Juanito and I would race the boat together.

That Wednesday I arrived at the club in the afternoon with the intention of tuning the rigging on the Dragon before the race. I decided to have a beer at the bar with an acquaintance before going out to the boat. I was halfway through my San Miguel when I saw the man from the plane walk in and take a seat at the other end of the bar. He'd grown a full, black beard and was wearing shorts and a new pair of topsiders. The beard explained why I hadn't noticed him following me from a distance during the past few months.

Five months had passed since I had last seen the man at

the consulate lobby in Hong Kong as I was saying farewell to Cynthia. I had indeed forgotten about him. He ordered a drink and kept his eyes focused outward at the bay. I acted as if I didn't recognize him. I would see how this charade played out. I finished my beer and ordered another one as I discussed the previous weekend's race with a fellow Dragon skipper. At last I stood up and walked casually in the direction of the man on the plane. He continued to ignore me.

"Say, would you like to take a sail this afternoon?" I asked as I stood behind him. "I'm going out to tune my boat. I need someone to help me sail it into the bay."

He feigned surprise that I was speaking to him.

"I'm not much of a sailor," he replied. "I only dropped by to inquire about membership."

"Well then, come out and sail with me this afternoon. And I'll sponsor you for a crewing membership. That won't cost you anything. It'll give you a chance to visit the club and sail without having to be a regular member."

I motioned to the bartender. "Tommy. Put this man's drink on my tab. He'll be crewing for me today."

"Yes sir, Mr. Mancini," the bartender answered.

"My name's Roy. What's yours?"

"Roland. I guess I should thank you for the drink," he said with a palpable lack of enthusiasm. There was no eye contact.

I said, "You wouldn't have been able to pay for your drink anyway. They don't accept cash at the bar, and only regular members and crewing members can sign chits. Let's go for a sail. I need to tune my boat before tonight's race."

The man seemed reassured that I had not recognized him from five months earlier when he had been clean shaven. The full beard did serve as an effective disguise. Or so he believed.

He finished his rum and coke. "All right. Let's go," he said. It would have been unnatural for the Agency spook to refuse my invitation.

Juanito had rigged the boat. I told the boat boy I wouldn't need him to sail with me that afternoon.

I had noted from smoke in the distance and from flags flying on the cargo ships in the bay that the wind now was quite strong, blowing about twenty knots. We would have our hands full sailing the Dragon that afternoon with only two people. This was especially so if the man on the plane was as inexperienced as he appeared. A plan was just beginning to form in my mind.

I taught him how to raise the mainsail and to trim the jib as we beat upwind and out of the yacht basin. The boat was heeling at an acute angle and we both sat up on the high side. I could see that Roland was nervous. He was holding on to a winch for dear life with both hands.

"Relax," I told him. "This is what it's all about. Enjoy the ride."

He remained speechless as bay water lapped into the cockpit.

"You know, Roland. Once in San Francisco Bay my mast broke in this kind of wind. Talk about adventure. We were lucky to get back alive."

"Yeah?'

"You didn't know I was from San Francisco, did you? Where are you from?"

He didn't answer me. I saw his knuckles were white from gripping the winch. Water was now pouring into the cockpit. I figured the wind at about twenty-five knots. We were traveling into Manila Bay as fast as a Dragon can sail upwind.

Finally I said, "There's too much wind out here to tune the rigging today. I'll have to do that back at the club's dock. We might as well turn around and sail back. Ready about."

We were now about three miles out into the bay. I tacked the boat and told Roland to trim and then ease the jib sheet until we were on a dead run, heading back to Manila, the wind directly behind us. I let the boom out as far as it would go until it was perpendicular with the boat's hull, then brought the jib around to the windward side so that we were "wing-and-wing." I sat on the leeward side of the cockpit and asked Roland to stand at the windward side and hold on tight to the jib sheet. The boat was balanced, planing and making great speed.

We were now at a risky point of sail in a heavy wind. The boom and mainsail were standing straight out on the port side, perpendicular to the boat so that the strong wind behind us was pushing the Dragon forward. The risk would occur if the wind shifted, even slightly, and crept forward of the mainsail. In that case, if the helmsman didn't adjust his course in time, the sail and boom would violently and without warning thrust across to the opposite side of the boat. And if a crewmember happened to be standing in the way of this violence, he would end up with a terrible headache at best, or a brain concussion at worst, when the flying boom cracked him in the head. And that was precisely my plan from the time we left the bar over an hour earlier.

I pushed the tiller ever so slightly so that the wind crept just forward of the mainsail and forced the "accidental" jibe. As expected, the mainsail and the boom crashed across the cockpit at full force to the starboard side of the boat. The wooden boom smacked Roland in the head and knocked him overboard. I threw him a life vest and shouted "man overboard."

"Roland, are you all right?" I yelled as I hauled in the mainsheet and tacked the boat back to where he was floating. There was no answer. But I saw him struggle to reach for the life vest. I furled the jib so as to reduce speed. "Whatever you do, don't bleed in the water. There are sharks in the bay."

His face was a bloody mess. The boom had hit him square on the nose. I sailed to within five feet of him and luffed the mainsail.

"Now, Roland, since it's just the two of us out here, do you want to explain to me why you've been following me for the past six months?"

"Fuck you. Get me back in the boat, Mancini." The fear in his voice was evident.

I trimmed the mainsail and sailed away from him. "Have it your way. I can leave you out here or I can pick you up. No one else will."

"Come back, come back here. Don't fuck with me like this." He now had the life vest attached to his upper body. He was at last floating effortlessly in the chop.

I sailed back to him. "You think I'm bullshitting about the sharks, Roland? Start explaining everything from start to finish. Don't leave out our flight from Dulles to Singapore. It will be dark before long. They won't be able to find you out here."

"All right. I'll tell you. I'll tell you, damn it. Help me out."

"I'm listening." I was now drifting slowly three feet from him. The mainsail was luffing and snapping wildly.

"We were ordered to follow you, Mancini. Keep you under surveillance after they learned of your mission."

"Who is 'we'? And who gave the order?"

"The White House gave the order. I'm counterintelligence at the Agency. We thought the plan was crazy, okay. But who's to argue with the White House?"

"Sounds like a load of crap, Roland. The White House isn't about to interfere with us. Who gave the order?" I started to sail away again.

"Listen to me, you sonofabitch. It was the chief of staff at the Intelligence Advisory Board. He came to Langley and ordered the new CI director to monitor everything you were doing out here. Said the White House didn't want any more fuck ups. Something about the forthcoming *family jewels* report."

"Can you appreciate the irony, Roland? Someone ordering the Agency to actually *prevent* scandal. That's rich."

"Just let me back on the boat, Roy. I've come clean with you. That's all there is. We didn't come up with this fool's errand. It was the chief of staff at the Advisory Board."

I threw him a line and after considerable effort he was able to hoist himself back onto the boat. I gripped a winch handle as a weapon in the event he wanted to get even with me.

"Roland, when we get back to the yacht club, and after you shower and fix your nosebleed, we're going to find a table with some privacy. And you're going to explain this to me in detail. Everything you know about who ordered whom to do what and why. Don't think for a minute that you can threaten or bullshit me. This matter is going right up the chain of command, if necessary to the CNO and the Joint Chiefs. Trust me, they have my back. I'm operating out here at their behest. But you already know that."

He told me he was just following orders. And he repeated that counterintelligence at the CIA knew the mission was a waste of resources. But what could he do? The Agency was under a cloud, to put it mildly. James Angleton's influence was history. So when the chief of staff of the Board ordered the Agency to jump, the new CI director at the Agency only asked "how high."

Roland Rodrigues and I ended up hitting it off pretty well. He needed to kill the pain, so we got drunk together back at the yacht club. I assured him that if he leveled with me, I would not disparage him in the report I would submit to the Institute about the affair. I was primarily relieved that he had not followed me into Terry's Bar and monitored my relationship with Sasha Popov.

Roland declined my offer for a crewing membership. I believe the burned spook returned to DC later that same week. My report was sent directly to Tom Hiatt.

The chief of staff of the President's Foreign Intelligence Advisory Board was demoted. Years later he was found dead. Suicide or murder? We'll never know. During his lifetime his treachery was never uncovered.

# 28

---

W HEN I PHONED SASHA HE SEEMED PLEASED TO hear from me, in contrast to the last time I'd called him at his office. I asked him if he'd like to get together at Terry's. His enthusiasm now suggested that he had given my proposal some consideration. We agreed to meet there on Friday night.

Steve McCoy had moved from Singapore to Manila in early March. The Institute leadership had agreed that Operation *Wolverine* was critical enough to transfer him permanently to the Philippines. His office in the Port Area was equipped with state-of-the-art shortwave radio equipment, ostensibly to communicate with navy cargo ships at sea. In truth, it was set up to receive the communication from Komang by way of Putu.

Tom Hiatt had suggested to McCoy that he join the prestigious Army and Navy Club, located across the park from the Manila Hotel. This would give us a location to meet each other socially.

CHINA SEA

I arrived at Terry's five minutes early and selected two empty seats at the end of the bar. Sasha arrived at seven o'clock. Spooks are punctual. We learn that in spy school. I ordered two bottles of San Miguel from Jun as Sasha sat down beside me.

"How goes it, Sasha? Everything okay at home?"

He coughed before replying. "Now she wants to join the Manila Polo Club."

"What!"

"This morning at breakfast Ingrid tells me, 'Sasha, dear, I need to be a member of the Polo Club.' Well, I almost choked on my coffee. And I say to her 'what the fuck? When did you take up playing polo?' You see, she meets these rich Filipino women and spoiled Spanish *mestizas* at the spa where she goes to stay in shape. She overhears them saying: 'I'll meet you later at the Polo Club, my dear.' Or 'Little Joselito is taking tennis lessons this afternoon at the Polo Club.' "

"Sounds expensive, polo," I remarked, raising my eyebrows and looking at him in the mirror.

"So I ask her, 'How do you expect me to pay for a membership at the Manila Polo Club?' And she says, 'Tell your company to pay for it. Don't you have to entertain clients somewhere special?' " He shook his head and sipped his beer.

"Change of subject, Sasha. I was thinking of a contest we could have tonight."

"Oh yeah? What contest?" He perked up.

I explained my idea. We would both drink one bottle of beer in each of the bars along M.H. Del Pilar Street. We'd walk south from one bar to the next, crossing to both sides of the street, and have one beer in each joint to see who cried "uncle" first.

My true purpose was so I could discuss my proposals with

221

him and not have to do that in one place, especially not within the confines of Terry's. What's more, this seemed like the kind of hijinks Sasha Popov might enjoy.

"Ha! You don't stand a chance, Cisco. I'll pour you into a taxi before we even reach the blow job bars." Jun looked over at us and I motioned for the bill.

"At least I'm not asking you to eat *balut* in each of those bars." We both laughed. Sasha knew *balut* was the unborn chick that some Filipinos ate out of its shell as an aphrodisiac.

It was in the third or fourth dive that I brought up the subject of Flora and my offer of providing them with a place to meet each other on the sly.

"Yes. I was going to mention that." He sounded sober. "You'd be doing me big favor, Cisco. I'll take you up on that offer. Saves me renting an apartment, which I can't afford anyway."

We agreed then and there that he would bring Flora to the house the next day. I'd alert Cynthia/Maria when I returned that night.

At the next bar along the route, Sasha explained his so-called French formula to me. This was his device where a man can accurately calculate the ideal age for his mistress or girlfriend. A man takes his own age, divides it by two, and then adds seven. And *voila*: he derives the age of the woman with whom he will be most compatible.

"And you know, Flora proves the formula works."

"How so?"

"Okay. I'm forty-four years old. Divide it by two," he commanded.

"Twenty-two."

"Now add seven."

"Twenty-nine."

He grinned at me. "There! Flora's age: twenty-nine last November."

I was intrigued. "And how about Ingrid? How do you apply your formula to her?"

"Listen. When we met in Moscow I was thirty years old. She was twenty-two. An actress. Beautiful. I was captivated. She was intelligent, well educated. Our sex life was . . . through the roof, as you say it. I think it will last forever. And so I ask her to marry me." Before we crossed the street to the next bar he continued with a sneer. "But now she's thirty-six. See what I mean?"

It was while we were seated at the penultimate bar that I popped the question to him. "Have you given any thought to doing some part-time, freelance work for Haig?"

He'd been expecting the question and didn't hesitate. "How much does it pay? And what do I have to do?" The several beers were now having their measured effect on both of us.

I told Sasha I could start him off at $1,000 per month, paid into the bank account of his choice. He would only have to fill in some gaps about Soviet merchant shipping for us. I told him that we didn't have any Russian correspondents yet. He'd be the first. He could start by keeping us informed about developments with his company, FESCO—new trade routes, newly acquired vessels, and so forth. Of course, I told him, his assistance would be held in complete confidence, as would his monthly earnings.

"You have to pay me more than that."

After some halfhearted negotiating on my part, I agreed to pay him $1,500 per month to start. We shook hands on it. I noted Sasha's palms were sweating. I offered to help him open a bank account outside the Philippines, say in Singapore. He said he'd need to receive cash, and could I manage an advance. I told him I could pay him an advance, on account, of a few hundred dollars the next week. At the same time, I requested he give me a list of all of the ships that were currently being operated by FESCO. "No problem," he said.

The next bar we entered was named the White Swallow. It was one of Manila's two notorious blow job joints.

The comely young women employed in those two bars were recruited from the impoverished provinces far to the south of Manila by the sleazy Australian impresario who owned the business. As we entered the bar, a tall, slim, dusky woman attired in a chintzy red bikini called out, "Sasha baby, you're back! You play piano tonight?" I noticed there was an upright piano in a corner.

Sasha gave a sheepish smile in my direction. "Been here before?" he asked. I replied that I hadn't. "The specialty of the house is . . . as they say it in French, *l'art de la pipe.*"

There were no less than fifteen bikini-clad young women milling around the bar, tempting the all-male customers. The jukebox was playing a tune by the Carpenters.

"The private rooms are upstairs," Sasha whispered.

All of a sudden I had a brilliant, if besotted, idea. My aim here was to convince Sasha Popov that if he stuck with me, his anxiety regarding personal finances would be a thing of the past.

As we sat at the bar in the midst of the twittering women and dissipated expatriate customers, I called out to the rat-faced Australian owner at the cash register. "I want to buy this place for the rest of the night. What'll it cost me?"

The man rose to his feet, as if in pain, and walked over to me. "What say, mate?" he asked in his thick accent. I was told later by Sasha that the Aussie had been a garbage collector in

Sydney. He'd won the lottery and the very next day moved to Manila with his earnings and set up this scurrilous business, employing local confederates to prowl the country's southern provinces and entice the prettiest young women there to move to the big city and earn big bucks performing in his two bars.

"I said I want to buy this place for the night. Tell your customers here to leave. And lock the front door. What'll that cost me? Including drinks."

The Australian grabbed a calculator, ran some quick figures on it and said, "Well, mate, since it's after midnight, I can do that for five hundred dollars."

"Done."

The watchful customers, all Caucasians—Australians, Europeans, and the odd American—finished their beers, shook their heads in disbelief at what they had just observed, and departed for the Aussie's bar next door.

Without getting into too graphic a description of the night's orgy in the White Swallow, I do remember Sasha sitting naked at the piano, playing a slow blues tune called *After Hours*, and receiving an equally slow and drawn out "house specialty" by a naked woman, the same one who had greeted him earlier. She was crouched with her hands on Sasha's knees and keeping time with her bobbing head between Sasha's legs, beneath the piano. As her tempo progressed from *andante* to *allegro*, Sasha all of a sudden shrieked and lunged forward on the piano, smashing the keys with his elbows. A fitting climax.

A moment before he fell forward onto the piano in sodden ecstasy, I looked over at him and noticed the tattoo on his chest. It appeared to be a picture of a dagger, a Muslim Kris, pointing south. I would have to ask him sometime what the symbolism was.

\* \* \*

SASHA AND FLORA ARRIVED AT THE SAFE HOUSE LATE THE
following afternoon.

Flora, lovely as ever, wore designer jeans, a sleeveless
white cotton blouse, and leather sandals. The jeans and blouse
did justice to her exquisite figure. As she removed her Gucci
sunglasses, her dark eyes smiled in concert with her lips. We
embraced each other.

Sasha wore a white T-shirt emblazoned with the image of
a large, fierce-looking red rooster perched on top of a beer
bottle. The caption under the bottle in bold letters read:

HAPPINESS IS A RED COCK

Red Cock Brewery Ltd

Bangkok, Thailand

The three of us rested on lounge chairs under an
umbrella, in the garden by the swimming pool. Maria Soriano
served us drinks.

My beverage of choice during my San Francisco period had
been chilled European vodkas—Finnish, Polish, and Russian.

"Sasha, I propose we have a blindfold test."

"Another one of your tricks, Cisco?" he barked, a burst of
laughter escaping at his own furtive hint at the previous night's
escapade along M.H. Del Pilar Street.

"I wonder if you can taste the difference between Polish
vodka and Russian vodka."

"You are kidding, of course? Russian is superior."

I had earlier prepared the two shot glasses and left them in
the freezer to chill, since alcohol doesn't freeze.

"Well, let's see."

I went to the kitchen and returned with the two glasses. The one with Polish vodka was in my left hand, the one with Russian in my right. I placed them both on the table in front of Sasha.

"Tell me, which glass has the Russian vodka and which has the Polish."

"No problem. Easy to do." He reached for the Polish and drained it in one swallow. He paused and then did the same with the Russian. Now there was an extended, somewhat awkward silence.

Flora finally chimed in. "Come on, Sasha, honey. You told Cisco you can tell the difference."

He closed his eyes for another moment and appeared to grind his teeth before calling out loud, "This one is Russian!" He lifted up the glass that had contained the Polish vodka.

I'd sensed that Sasha Popov was not a graceful loser. He had sulked dramatically whenever I'd beaten him in chess, and he'd gloated shamelessly that time he had beaten me. He was first and foremost a proud Russian. His humiliation now at having selected the wrong glass of vodka was profound. He stood up and marched petulantly into the bedroom, ordering Flora to follow him.

The microphone in the room picked up the sound of the shower running fifteen minutes before they left the house at midnight. There were no goodbyes.

# 29

---

MAY 1975

WE RECEIVED THE MESSAGE AT 6:35 IN THE evening. McCoy had recorded the message on a cassette tape, and he handed it to me when we met poolside at the Army and Navy Club. I rushed back to the safe house and played the tape.

Putu, using her call sign *Mas*, spoke in Indonesian as she had been trained. She quoted the series of numbers that she had translated from Komang's Balinese. Those numbers were: 36 4 120 22 22 23 114 6 3 5 3. I searched my world atlas for the coordinates; the codes gave me the locations of the last and the next port of call. *Pacific Star* had been in Qingdao, China, and was en route to Hong Kong. The ship would arrive in Hong Kong on May 3, three days from now. *Clover* considered the information to be *most urgent*. Qingdao, on the Yellow Sea, is the headquarters of the Chinese navy's North Sea fleet where it hosts the country's main submarine base.

The next morning I took the earliest Cathay Pacific flight to Hong Kong and checked in to the Peninsula Hotel.

I had a dilemma with meeting *Clover* in Hong Kong. I planned to ask the Institute's local commander, Geoffrey Davis, if I could use one of his safe houses for the debriefing, but Davis hadn't been available to meet me. So scratch that. I was reluctant to check into a local hotel with my Louis Francisco passport in case a front desk clerk asked to see my Hong Kong entry visa. There was none.

I phoned Jack Chapman at his office. When I got my friend on the phone, I greeted him warmly. "Hey there, Jack. This is Roy. What's happening, man?"

"Roy, you son of gun. Where are you?"

"I'm here, in Hong Kong. How soon can we get together?"

"I was about to take off for a late lunch in Central. Can you join me?"

"Sure. Give me time to catch the Star Ferry. I could meet you in about forty-five minutes."

"Sounds like a plan. Meet me in the Captain's Bar. Mandarin Hotel."

"See you there." We hung up.

I hadn't seen Jack Chapman in ten years. He had changed little—the same suave, fair-haired fit athlete I'd known. He was sitting at the bar finishing an iced tea when I walked in.

"Hey, tennis partner!" He jumped off his barstool.

"Hey, yourself. Good to see you again, Jack." We shook hands. I was indeed happy to meet my old high school pal.

"Yeah. How long has it been? High school graduation? You went and joined the navy on us."

"Right. Joined the navy to see the world."

We left the bar and walked to a popular steakhouse a couple of blocks from the Mandarin. There, in a barely audible voice, Jack explained something about his new job in Hong Kong. CAC was one of the U.S. government's leading contractors and *was* the leading contractor in the fields of security and defense. The company's headquarters were in Alexandria, Virginia, so it could be close to the defense and intelligence agencies that were its clients. Jack informed me that fifty percent of the CAC employees had Top Secret security clearances, or higher, and he was one of them. He specialized in information technology. He'd spent two months training at Fort Meade before he was sent to Hong Kong. I was to learn later that CAC, by coincidence, had set up the Institute's encrypted IT systems worldwide.

The company had established an office in Hong Kong to perform some hush-hush work for the National Security Agency. Jack was a systems administrator, whatever that was. I didn't ask. I could presume that since the location was Hong Kong, the target was China.

Jack mentioned that he had an extra bedroom in his flat, and that I was welcome to stay there if I wanted to save on hotel expenses. He'd learned during a phone call with my mother in California that I was self-employed and that I had set up a coffee trading business in Asia.

Jack was hinting about his association with the NSA without being at all specific. I let him do most of the talking over lunch. At last, I opened up to him.

"Jack, I might have a need for your flat this week," I said, over coffee and dessert.

I told him that I, too, was engaged in classified work and had the same security clearance he did. It wasn't the CIA, but like the NSA, my organization was under DOD. I admitted that I could not reveal any more than that to him. I told him I would appreciate his help. Could I use his flat for a couple of hours sometime within the next two or three days? I'd need to be alone. Jack grinned at me and mouthed the word *spook*. Weeks later he admitted that he assumed then that I was having an affair with a married woman on the island and had needed his extra bedroom for a rendezvous.

"Of course, Roy. Give me a call and let me know when you want me to make myself scarce."

The agent for the *Pacific Star* was Sweeney & Company. I wrote a short note to Komang and sealed it in a plain envelope addressed to the Radio Operator on the ship. My note asked him to meet me for a drink at the Red Lips Bar at six o'clock in the evening. I gave him the address and a map for the bar, which was tucked in a blind alley behind the Hyatt Hotel in Kowloon. I had cased the joint during an earlier trip to Hong Kong and found it to be suitable for my purpose. The place was small and dark and had two entrances, or exits. There were five stools at the bar and four tables. One of the exits was through a thick red curtain that led into the dark, rancid alley.

I was informed at Sweeney that the *Pacific Star* would arrive the next morning and that it would anchor in Victoria harbor for three days to load cargo from barges. This meant that Komang would have to take a service boat from the ship to shore. I assumed the crew would go ashore in Kowloon rather than to the more upscale and expensive Hong Kong Island. Thus my decision to meet at the Red Lips Bar.

I left the envelope with a senior clerk in the Sweeney office. She assured me that it would be delivered to the ship by the company service boat.

Komang and I met at the bar the next evening. Earlier that day I had told Jack I would need his flat later that night, and that I would phone him at home between six and seven o'clock to confirm it. I had earlier located a pay phone half a block from the bar. I used it now to phone Jack after Komang and I left the bar by way of the red-curtained exit.

We drove in a taxi through the Cross Harbor Tunnel to Hong Kong Island and on up to the residential mid-levels until we reached Jack's apartment building on Magazine Gap Road. Jack and I had arranged that he would leave the keys underneath a flower pot. The street was unlit; I found the pot and the keys by the light of the moon and let Komang and myself into the ground floor of the building. We walked up the stairs to the flat on the second floor and entered it with a second key. Jack would spend the time in Central having dinner and drinks in one of his hangouts. Then he'd phone his place at 10:00 to see if I was still there.

Komang had shown a palpable nervousness when we met in the bar. We spoke little during the taxi ride to the island. Now, inside the flat, he was able to relax.

"Whew!" he gasped as he dropped his full weight onto the living room sofa. "We meet again, Cisco. How did Putu's radio code work?" This was the first question he asked.

"It worked like magic, Komang. The two of you have done your jobs well."

He smiled at last. "She and I were able to talk with each other for thirty minutes. Thirty minutes! The reception was clear. This is wonderful."

"But you seem nervous, Komang. You can relax now."

"Yes, I was nervous the past few days. I didn't know if I had been observed on my ship, taking the photos in Qingdao. And earlier in Russia. Two officers on the ship saw me with the camera case. I don't know, Cisco. I am new at this."

"Komang, you are doing your job like a pro. We're safe here. Can you tell me about the photos you took?"

Komang removed three film cartridges from his jacket and explained his activities of the past several weeks, since we had last met in Bitung.

After arriving in Nampo, North Korea, the *Pacific Star* had made three consecutive round-trip voyages to Nahodka, the large port near Vladivostok in the Soviet Union. Vladivostok is off-limits to foreign commercial shipping because it is the headquarters of the Soviet navy's Pacific fleet.

After the third and final trip, as his ship was getting underway and steering south toward the Sea of Japan, Komang looked out the radio room porthole to the west in the direction of Vladivostok. In the far distance he saw what he believed was either a fishing boat or a submarine on the surface, sailing in the same parallel, southerly direction as *Pacific Star*. He had to assume it might be a submarine.

Komang had secreted his camera in his stateroom, which was on the port side of the ship. Now he needed to surreptitiously convey it to the radio room, on the starboard side. He did this with care, making sure none of his shipmates observed him carrying the camera case in the passageway and up a ladder.

There was a close call just after he retrieved the camera from his cabin. He'd had to duck into a storage space when he heard a crew member approaching. The shipmate sauntered past, whistling, unaware that Komang was hiding in the dark behind a closed door. A minute later, the Balinese peeked through the crack. Opening the door wider, and seeing no one in the passageway, he hastened up a ladder to the deck where the radio room was located. He could not avoid being seen there by two Arab officers who, he said, looked at him strangely. He entered the radio room and closed and locked the door behind him.

As quickly as he could, he removed the camera and the zoom lens from the carrying case and assembled the large lens onto the camera. Now, looking out the porthole, he panicked when he did not observe any vessel to the west. At last, looking further to the south through the powerful lens, he saw in the distance that there was indeed a submarine cruising on the surface. Resting the tip of the zoom lens on the edge of the open porthole, and adjusting the lens to full zoom, he focused on the sub and clicked off a series of six photographs in thirty seconds. Almost instantaneously, the sub disappeared beneath the swells as it submerged. Komang's final photograph was of the submarine's superstructure, the "sail", as the long black hull now disappeared beneath the sea.

Komang handed me the cartridge he had labeled "R" (for Russia). I placed it in my backpack.

"I see you have two more cartridges." I picked one up. It was labeled with a "C."

He nodded. "Yes, I took these photos last week from inside my stateroom when we were in Qingdao. Another submarine," he said, pointing at the cartridge in my hand.

His ship had loaded cargo in the northern Chinese port. He was standing on the pier talking with some crew members when he suddenly observed a submarine underway in the distance, across the harbor. Komang excused himself from his shipmates, saying he needed to use the toilet. In this case his stateroom was facing the direction of the harbor. Komang entered his room and locked the door. He assembled the lens onto the camera and pointed it through the porthole at the sub. He clicked off several photos, and continued to do so until the Chinese submarine disappeared beyond a headland and sailed on in the direction of the East China Sea.

I took the "C" cartridge and placed it in the backpack.

The third cartridge contained photographs he had taken from his stateroom while tied to the dock in two North Korean ports: Wonsan and Nampo. He remarked that there were a few small patrol boats in the area. Nothing exciting, or so he thought. I took the cartridge labeled with a "K." As it turned out, he had taken the very first photograph ever of an indigenous North Korean missile patrol boat.

"I'll have these photographs analyzed. You and Putu will be rewarded for your good work."

I called a taxi dispatcher and gave her an address four streets away from Jack's apartment building. Komang and I returned to Kowloon. When Jack phoned his apartment at ten o'clock that night and no one answered, he knew he could return to his empty flat. The keys were back under the pot where he had left them.

I had the taxi drop Komang off at the Star Ferry Terminal. I handed him one thousand Hong Kong dollars in cash for his expenses, and he told me that his ship would leave Hong Kong in two days and sail back to North Korea, to the port of Wonsan on the country's northeast coast. I recalled that Wonsan was the port where the *USS Pueblo* had been taken when it was hijacked by the North Koreans seven years earlier.

The next morning I delivered the three cartridges of film to Major Geoffrey Davis in the consulate. I explained that I didn't want to carry the film with me when I passed through Philippines customs control at the Manila airport. And I requested that he rush the cartridges by diplomatic pouch to the Institute.

McCoy received the analysis on *Clover*'s photos after a week. The shots that Komang had taken of the submarine departing Vladivostok were of especially high worth. They showed a recently commissioned Soviet Yankee Class ballistic missile submarine with sail number K-430. Analysts determined that these photos pictured the sub underway on the surface and then submerging, on its first six month patrol. The submarine's course would take it off the U.S. west coast.

Our navy commanders immediately ordered a nuclear powered hunter-killer submarine, then patrolling submerged in the Sea of Okhotsk, to rush to the Sea of Japan and locate the new Soviet Yankee-class. After it located the Soviet sub, the American attack submarine kept it under close surveillance for the duration of its patrol in the Pacific Ocean. Our sub's recordings of the new Soviet missile submarine's noise emissions, its cavitation, proved invaluable.

The photos that Komang had taken of the submarine departing Qingdao, the Chinese navy's North Fleet headquarters, were likewise A-1. They showed the first Chinese nuclear submarine, the Han class, and the photos identified the number on the sub's "sail": 401. Pentagon analysts believed this newly commissioned Chinese submarine was departing Qingdao for its maiden sea trials.

Another American nuclear hunter-killer submarine, which had been docked in Japan, was ordered to get underway immediately and locate the Chinese sub in the East China Sea, and to follow it. This American attack submarine continuously recorded the Han's peculiar (and noisy) undersea sound signatures.

I arranged a $1,000 bonus deposit to Komang and Putu's Bali bank account following this success.

The same week that I was debriefing *Clover* at Jack's flat, Captain Ernesto Villarreal flew to Hong Kong to negotiate with the managers of Chow Fatt Shipping & Trading Limited. Villarreal signed a one-year contract with the Chinese Communist shipping company to furnish Filipino officers and crew for their Panamanian-flagged ships.

Because of my age, still in my twenties and the youngest case officer in the Institute, expectations I knew were modest. Tom Hiatt had said he considered maritime operations as a good way for me to get some training for better things to come. Now, after these successes with both *Clover* and *Seaworth*, I was starting to perform—not unlike an unseeded tennis player who has just won his first major tournament.

# 30

MAY 1975

HAVING CYNTHIA AT THE HOUSE FULL-TIME satisfied our security concerns when I traveled. And she managed the recording system during Sasha's visits. Cynthia and I were compatible from the outset. After two months, we became lovers.

An hour before sunset, and so I could keep my chops up, I would play my trumpet in the house for thirty minutes. I'd slide open the large glass door that led out to the garden, and a light breeze would blow in.

I'd stand in the middle of the living room and begin playing. Cynthia made it a point to stop whatever she was doing and join me in the room to listen to these practice sessions. She'd sit facing me, cross-legged on the sofa or on a large throw pillow on the hardwood floor. She would often applaud after I played a tune she liked. She had also made it a habit to wear short shorts and sleeveless blouses or tank tops around the house whenever only the two of us were home. The shorts accentuated her striking figure, particularly her exquisitely shaped legs and derriere.

It was inevitable. We became infatuated with each other, sharing that large house as the days turned into weeks.

One evening in early May I played a favorite ballad, "*My Funny Valentine*." I was using a mute to keep the tune soft and sexy. Cynthia, sitting with eyes closed on an overstuffed pillow on the floor, appeared mesmerized by the beautiful tune as I improvised a solo on the theme. As I began my final chorus, bringing the song to a climax, she stood up and swayed her body, trancelike, in front of me. After I played the last note and let it fade, I put the horn down and took her in my arms. We kissed passionately for a long time. It had been ages since I'd felt this kind of hunger for a woman, and she returned the feeling. At last I lifted her lithe body and carried her to her bedroom. She laughed happily and we made love until I lost count. When we tired of the maid's room, we trotted naked to the swimming pool where our passion became so intense that at one moment I feared we might drown.

It was past midnight and right before we fell asleep in each other's arms in the master bedroom when Cynthia asked me, "Cisco, do you ever think about what might have been if you hadn't picked up the newspaper and read that classified ad two years ago in San Francisco?"

"I never look back. I believe we really do make our own good luck."

I TOLD MCCOY AT OUR MEETING THE NEXT DAY THAT I HAD reached the point with *Slugger* where I'd give him the recruitment pitch. I would offer the Russian a substantial pay increase if he would furnish me with secret intelligence.

We knew the ramifications if Popov rejected my offer.

Given the KGB's resources, my cover would be blown in the Philippines, if not throughout Southeast Asia. The so-far successful operation with *Seaworth* and the crewing agency would be placed for the time being on hold. Cynthia and I would be obliged to close the safe house and make hasty exits from the country.

"The brother-in-law will have a fit if your recruitment approach to *Slugger* goes off the tracks," Steve remarked. I had never observed my commander looking this stressed. It was true. Contrary to protocol, the Agency knew nothing of my five-month pursuit of Sasha Popov. "I don't want to think of having to face Tony Loyola and his boss if I have to explain a failed attempt to recruit a KGB operative on their turf."

"Steve, I wouldn't suggest this now if I didn't believe he was ripe."

"It's a gamble, Roy." He looked away, staring far out at Manila Bay, deep in thought. He said at last, "I'll brief Pete Wright on your plans for the *Slugger* recruitment. I'll phone you as soon as I hear something." He stood up to leave. "And give my best to Maria Soriano."

We parted separately. I walked over to watch the tennis players pounding away on the clay courts and wondered if Jack Chapman and I would be allowed to play here. I'd tell him to bring his racket with him to Manila.

During the next two days I focused my thoughts on the impending recruitment pitch to *Slugger*. I wanted the right setting, the right atmosphere. To drink vodka together or to remain cold sober? I decided on the sober option. I would pitch him in the safe house over a game of chess.

When Sasha played chess with me he insisted now on engaging without any alcohol in his system. He hated to lose, and I had whipped him the first time we'd played because he'd had a snootful of vodka in him. He claimed the booze had affected his judgment. He liked to imagine that he was the Russian grandmaster Boris Spassky and I was American Bobby Fischer. And he insisted Spassky would get his revenge. We'd played four or five times and were evenly matched. Win some, lose some, and draw.

I was uncommonly vitalized that month, and I attributed that to my fresh and intense relationship with Cynthia. I now had a powerful feeling of confidence in myself, and of the likelihood of success in whatever I chose to undertake. My energy levels—mental and physical—were at an all-time high. It was no accident that I made the decision to recruit Sasha Popov the day after Cynthia and I had first made love. And, yes, fallen in love.

I briefed Cynthia on the plan a few nights later. The two of us stood together, naked, in the swimming pool with the garden lights turned off. The water was naturally warm after an afternoon of hot bright sunshine. That night, the light of the full moon cast shadows in the trees, and millions of stars formed constellations above a cloudless Manila sky. I held her in my arms.

"We should have no illusions, Maria." Since she had arrived in March, I had made it a habit of calling her by her cover name so as not to slip up in front of Sasha and Flora. She likewise called me Cisco. "If *Slugger* refuses to go along with me when I pitch him, you and I will have to move fast."

"I know. I've thought about it. I knew this day would come."

"If he rejects my pitch, we'll close down the safe house and head to Malacca. We'll figure things out from there."

"Yes, that's the downside of not coordinating this with the Agency," she replied.

"No regrets. The Agency would have stolen *Slugger* from us months ago. Or ordered us to drop him because it was too risky."

We planned that Cynthia would take Flora out under the pretext of buying lunch for all of us while Sasha and I remained at the house playing chess. Cynthia would contrive to stay outside with Flora for at least two hours—window shopping, buying gifts, having drinks in Makati. She would take plenty of cash along with her.

The two women had become good friends over the past two months. As luck would have it, they both came from the Visayan Islands in the central Philippines and both spoke the same local Cebu dialect with each other. This common background enhanced their natural rapport. Flora had questioned why in the world Maria was toiling as a housemaid. She had replied to the effect that it was temporary, and that it had paid well in Singapore.

# 31

---

I PHONED SASHA AT HIS OFFICE. BY NOW THE FESCO
receptionist knew my voice and put me through.

"Hey, Spassky," I said as soon as he came on the line. "I
feel like playing chess. How about you?"

"Let me call you back. I have some things I have to do."
He sounded distracted and hung up without another word.

Soon after I'd started courting *Slugger* early in the year, I
had installed a second phone line in the safe house. That line
was the only number Sasha knew. The phone's recording
device was voice activated, and he would be the only person
who would ever call that number. Whenever it rang, Cynthia
and I knew who to expect.

Sasha phoned an hour later. "You called, Cisco?"

"Yeah. I owe you a chess rematch. Feel like it?"

He thought it over for a moment. "Next Sunday. I'll bring
Flora. What time should we come by?"

"Make it lunchtime. Maria can prepare something for all

of us. Let's say eleven-thirty. We can play a game or two before we eat."

"All right. Eleven-thirty, Sunday."

We hung up. The timing happened to be auspicious. This was the week that I owed Sasha his increased wages, the envelope filled with twenty new $100 bills. I would wait until Flora was out of the house before I handed it to him.

Sasha had gotten rid of his chauffeur. Too dangerous, as he had put it, referring to Ingrid and how she had bribed the Filipino driver to keep her informed of Sasha's dalliances. I hadn't quite figured out how the Russian managed to ration his time: conducting his clandestine activities in Subic Bay and Clark Field while managing the Manila shipping company and entertaining both Flora and Ingrid throughout the week.

Sasha and Flora arrived at the safe house on Sunday right on time. Punctuality had been conditioned into his psyche, as it is for all of us in this game.

He uttered a brief "hello" and went straight to the bedroom that he and Flora used. He changed into his swimming trunks and then darted out of the house, running full tilt through the garden to perform an impressive racing dive into the pool. I was pleased to see him make himself at home. Indeed I had noticed how his spirits and energy soared whenever Flora was with him. I walked over to the edge of the pool and looked down at him.

"Maria and Flora are going out to buy chicken adobo for lunch. Any requests?"

The husky white-skinned Russian shook his head several times, clearing his ears. "Yeah. Have them bring back some cold beer. Last time I was here you ran out."

I walked into the living room and handed Cynthia a wad

of pesos. "Buy what you can. No hurry. Maybe catch a movie," I said. The two women left the house in high spirits, looking forward to spending some time together.

I returned poolside. "I'll set up the board."

"I'll be there in a minute." He dove underwater and swam a lap submerged before getting out of the pool and drying off. I set up the chessboard beneath the umbrella in the garden.

We made our selections and I drew the white pieces. My first move was the queen's pawn to the fourth square. Sasha promptly moved his black queen's pawn forward and up against mine. I moved my queen's bishop's pawn forward, confirming the queen's gambit opening. He took the gambit and captured my pawn with his.

"So you're falling for it?" I commented, staring at the board. He was now one pawn ahead.

"You'll see."

We continued with the opening moves of the "gambit accepted." Fifteen minutes into the game, and after he'd made a smart play with his knight, I looked up. "Oh, before I forget, let me give you your fee before the women return." I went into the house, then returned with a plain white envelope. He removed the bills and counted them. Satisfied, he placed them back inside the envelope.

"Wait for me. I need to put this away." He went inside the house, tucked away the cash, showered, and put on shorts and a T-shirt. He returned fifteen minutes later.

"Sasha. Let's talk business."

"And the game? I'm about to pin you."

"Shall we call it a draw?" I asked.

"You offer a draw so soon? If you see what's coming, you better resign instead."

"You're right. I want to take a break. Let's talk." I tipped my King over onto its side.

He sat back in his chair, baffled by my premature resignation. "Okay. What about?"

"Sasha, my company wants to pay you more money than we're paying you now."

A wry smile appeared on his lips. His eyes bore into mine. "How much more?"

"Far more than I can stuff in that envelope." I motioned with my head in the direction of the house. "More, in fact, than is safe to carry around the streets of Manila in your pocket. You'd have to open a bank account so we can make large deposits."

"How much?"

"We're thinking $290,000 a year for someone with your experience and inside knowledge. That would come to, let's see, just over $24,000 a month."

He was speechless for a long time and seemed to be glued to the back of his chair. He looked skyward for a long moment, debating with himself, perhaps. His eyes never blinked. Then he stared at me hard for several seconds. He glanced down at the chessboard with a scornful laugh. Sasha picked up a white chess piece in his fingers, the queen. I heard him murmur something in Russian as he stared at it.

"I assume you have been recording everything we've said here. How long has it been?" he asked. His eyes were distant, still unblinking. I shrugged.

At last he leaned forward and glared at me. "Round up!"

"Come again?"

"Round it up to three hundred grand and I'll play ball," he exclaimed. Then he clenched his teeth. "Why am I not surprised? You Sonofabitch. I suspected something like this."

"Moscow wasn't going to waste a talented guy like you merely running a shipping line. Am I right, Sasha?"

"You should know," he rejoined. "Okay, let's cut the bullshit. I know what you want. You know my price. And here's the deal. When, as you Americans say, the shit hits the fan, I want protection. A green card. A new identity. These plays never last forever. One day they find out."

"I can agree to that. You have my word. We know how it works." He sat still, a sneer on his lips. It occurred to me he knew this discussion was being recorded, and that there was no turning back.

"Okay. I'm in. What do you need?" he asked, lowering his voice.

"You need to provide us with something we don't already know. You've got to establish your *bona fides* for me," I replied in a hushed voice. I knew the high-performance mic attached to the umbrella would pick it up. "Let's start with your tour in Cairo as Mr. Bordin. We know you recruited the minister and ran him for, what, five or six years? It's got to be better than that."

"Ha. Yes, the old deputy minister. My husband-in-law is what I called him. I suppose you know about my love affair with his French wife."

"We do. And how you were pulled back to Moscow because you got caught. So you can skip that. Give us something major, Sasha. Something that will rattle our cage. That's the condition. Those are *our* terms."

"How much money did you say?"

"We'll pay you $300,000 a year for your full cooperation. Repeat: full, continuous cooperation. Monthly installments. Do I need to find a calculator? It's more than enough for a Polo Club membership." I'd hoped to lighten things up.

"Fuck the Polo Club," he said with unexpected vehemence.

"Then let's get started. What do you have to offer us?"

Sasha smiled without humor. "I will tell you now something that will make you want to dance into that swimming pool of yours and throw up your hands. They'll pin a star on you for this. I ran the meanest sonofabitch in the Arab world. I was his handler. His case officer. The KGB supplies the weapons. You want to take notes?"

"I'm listening." I withdrew a notepad and pen from under my seat cushion, though I knew we were being recorded.

"Yeah? Well, his name is Wadi Haddad. Ring a bell?

"No. Not my area." I wrote it down.

"This guy was kicked out of the PLO by Arafat in the late 1960s because he was too radical for them. Too independent. His stunts embarrassed the old boy. The irony is that Wadi was born a Christian in Palestine."

I nodded.

"We set up the Democratic Front for the Liberation of Palestine with him after he left the PLO. And we supply the weapons, the instructions, and the training. The KGB loves airplane hijackings. Why not? They get a lot of attention. You recall the hijacking of the airliners in 1970 that were flown to Jordan? Dawson Field? And Black September? We were behind it. I planned all of that!"

I leaned back in my chair.

"You want *bona fides*, I can tell you where and when weapons were delivered to Wadi in the Gulf of Aden. We used submarines. He had fishing boats." Sasha sat back and folded his arms. "We keep Wadi Haddad under the radar. Your people, the CIA, believe his partner, Habbash, is the one to watch. Habbash is a decoy. Wadi is our principal, the one we go to."

"And this still goes on today, without you?"

"Of course it does. No case officer is indispensable. Not you. Not me." He gave me a sardonic smile and continued, "When I was sent back to Moscow I trained my successor. He's there today, in Cairo. Name's Filitov. You CIA guys know who he is. But you don't know all he does. Same as you never understood my main mission—Wadi Haddad. You thought I was there to handle that miserable Egyptian deputy minister and fuck his wife, right? That was, how do you say, window dressing."

I never did disabuse Sasha of his illusion that I was working with the Agency.

I debriefed Sasha for over an hour and a half, until Cynthia and Flora returned with the chicken adobo and beer. The KGB's deep connection with Palestinian terrorists led by Wadi Haddad was staggering. The plane hijackings. The suicide bombings. I noted the approximate dates that weapons had been delivered to the DFLP by Soviet submarines late at night in the Gulf of Aden.

Minutes before the women arrived, Sasha told me that he would not pass me intelligence that would harm the USSR—his mother Russia, as he put it. He said he was a patriot. However, he would provide information, and it was substantial, about the KGB's covert affiliations with terrorists and "third-world" governments—those areas that had been his particular specialty. *Slugger* revealed that the KGB currently directed a myriad of terrorist operations throughout the world. He mentioned one terrorist under KGB sponsorship named Carlos the Jackal who was currently committing savage terrorist acts in concert with the DFLP, the most recent being the rocket-propelled grenade attack at Orly Airport near Paris.

Without his putting too fine a point on it, Sasha insinuated that he was cooperating with me because of the money, the $300,000 a year, to support his lifestyle and to pad his retirement. We never discussed the handle we had on him: the compromising safe house recordings. Over time, I was to recognize that Sasha's large ego was also a motive for his betrayal. Playing the role of a conspirator made him feel vital, important, as a player on the world stage. And the challenge for him of being devious played no small part. Having just one of *anything* was not enough for Sasha Popov. Just as he delighted in having a love affair with a beautiful, dark-eyed paramour while remaining married to his stunning ash blond, green-eyed Russian wife. I believe he relished this game of reporting to two competing masters.

Soon enough, and as a part of my deal, he would disclose the identities of the secret agents who were collecting intelligence for him at the American military bases. One of them was an American air force sergeant stationed at Clark Field. The KGB had been paying the sergeant $1,000 a month for his information regarding flight operations.

Sasha also had a cozy, and covert, relationship with a left-wing, anti-American politician in the Philippines. He regularly deposited thousands of U.S. dollars to the senator's personal bank account in Hong Kong. The senator repaid the Soviets with his ardent and eloquent opposition to the stationing of U.S. armed forces in the Philippines.

Sasha was a pro, and he knew better than to spend any of the money he received in the bank account I set up for him in Port Louis, Mauritius. I continued to pay him $2,000 cash in an envelope every month, an amount that in addition to his KGB salary was sufficient to support a stylish wife and a grateful mistress in Manila. "You can deduct the two grand from the big money in Port Louis," he had said.

The reaction in Springfield to my recruitment of *Slugger* was delirious. Dots had been connected. Our intelligence community had until then believed that the terrorist, Habbash, was running the show at the DFLP, and that Habbash was orchestrating the hijackings and most of the violence in the Middle East. As a result, Habbash's whereabouts were being monitored by the NSA and the Agency. The paramount importance, and thus the communications, of the arch-terrorist Wadi Haddad had been a well-kept KGB secret. Clever.

# 32

---

## JULY 1975

URING A MEETING AT THE CLUB ON JULY 1, A waiter approached our table in a hurry. "Mr. McCoy. You have a telephone call at the front desk." The one person who would have known that McCoy was at the club this early in the morning was Sergeant Dubrowski. Steve hastened out of the dining room and to the reception area. I looked at my watch. It was 7:45.

I was observing the tennis players below the clubhouse, a mix of Filipinos, Chinese, and expatriates, when McCoy rushed back to the table.

"Wait here. I'll be back in twenty minutes," he said. "There's a new tape. A message from *Mas* arrived this morning at 0730."

I replied, "Meet me at a table by the pool."

Steve signed the chit for breakfast as the Club didn't accept cash. I walked outside and found a private table beside the swimming pool, three feet from the edge of Manila Bay.

McCoy returned twenty minutes later and made his way

to my table. He removed the cassette from his pocket and handed it to me.

"I'd better get back to the house where I can listen to this," I said. He nodded, and I was off.

I played the tape at the safe house. Cynthia listened to it with me without understanding it. She commented on how the Indonesian and Filipino languages sounded vaguely similar.

I wrote down Putu's message. She had relayed the numbers: 39 15 127 44 22 23 114 6 5 7 3. I looked in the atlas and discovered that *Pacific Star* had recently sailed from the port of Wonsan in North Korea and that the ship's next port of call would be Hong Kong. She was due to arrive in Hong Kong on Saturday, July 5, in four days. And *Clover* considered his information to be *most urgent*.

Komang and I planned to meet each other at the Red Lips Bar in Kowloon whenever his ship anchored in Hong Kong. I would wait for him there every day that the ship was in port at 7:15 and again at 8:30 at night.

The ship arrived Saturday morning and anchored in Victoria Harbor. The weather that day was blustery. A typhoon had whipped across the northern provinces of Luzon in the Philippines. Though the storm was expected to hit China north of Hong Kong, the wind and rain were thrashing the colony on the day of *Pacific Star*'s arrival.

I had no reason to leave the Peninsula Hotel that day. I looked out from my comfortable room at the white caps in the harbor and at the myriad cargo ships tugging against their anchors and skewing with the wind shifts. The Star Ferry struggled across the harbor on its way to and from the island. Nothing for me to do but wait the dismal day out in the hotel lobby and in my room. I did go outside to find a pay phone and call Major Davis to request that he inform the brother-in-law that I was here, hopeful they wouldn't ask me to make a personal appearance at the consulate. They didn't. By now they trusted that I knew my way around.

I left the Pen at 6:30 in the evening. The wind was still too strong to open an umbrella, so I walked the streets and small alleys and tried to stay under cover and dry for half an hour, all the while conducting counter-surveillance. At 7:10 I ducked into the back alley leading to the Red Lips Bar. I stood in the dark for a minute waiting to see if I had been followed. I then entered through the alcove and the thick red curtain.

I sat down at the only empty stool at the bar, a couple of seats from a soused, down-and-out Englishman who introduced himself as Dennis, and who was telling anyone who would listen about his problems with Chinese women and Communists. The dark and decrepit Red Lips was just the place for a character like Dennis to tell tales and stay dry during the storm. And I realized it was fortunate for me that the Englishman was the epicenter of attention.

Komang entered the bar through the front entrance. We saw each other and I motioned with my head that we take a small table in a corner at the back of the room. No one noticed us, with Dennis taking center stage at the bar.

I had decided that because of the storm, a journey across the harbor to mid-levels was ill-advised. The Red Lips would suffice that night. And if it didn't, if we needed to meet privately, we would meet the next day and seek accommodation at Jack's place. I had learned that the *Pacific Star* was scheduled to remain in port for two days.

"Great to see you again, Komang." I thought of the Balinese as not only my agent, but as a friend. This was the second time we had met following his erstwhile Qingdao and Nahodka missions. Our last meeting had been in Kuching. The ham radio set up with Putu as a cutout was working as well as I could have imagined. I had no idea how frequently Komang and Putu spoke with each other off the record, and I never asked. I did trust that Putu was being discrete and that she had taken my warnings about security to heart.

The waitress delivered our bottles of beer and returned to the bar where she could listen to Dennis relate his tales of woe.

"I have film, Cisco," Komang whispered, glancing all the while around the barroom.

I motioned at the backpack lying on the floor between us, obscured from view by the tablecloth. Komang kept his eyes on the few customers and staff in the room as he reached into his jacket pocket and removed a film cartridge. He dropped the film into the open backpack. "Wonsan," he said *sotto voce*. I nodded, understanding. I had placed a small notebook and a pen on the table in front of me. I nudged it over to him, keeping my eyes on the distracted customers at the bar. Dennis was still doing his job.

Komang took up the pen and wrote on the pad in Indonesian: *peti-peti*. I pondered for a few seconds for an exact translation. Then I knew: "crates," or perhaps "boxes." The meaning was clear. He had photographed crates, or boxes, in Wonsan that had been loaded on the *Pacific Star*. I needed to be sure. I asked him, "Loaded on your ship?" He nodded, yes.

"Is there anything else you want to pass to me, Komang?" I asked.

"No, Cisco. That is all. But I think this might be interesting for you. You will see strange writing on the crates after you develop that film. It is not Korean or Chinese. Not English.

I never saw this writing before except when we went ashore in Nahodka. And there it was everywhere."

I thought to myself: *Russian Cyrillic labeling on crates loaded in North Korea.*

"Let's get out of here," I said as I stood up and motioned for the bill at the bar. I would deliver the film to Major Davis the following day and request that he send the cartridge to Springfield.

We parted in the alley behind the Red Lips. I waited until Komang disappeared around a corner. I watched the street until I was confident that he was not being followed. I then turned down a side street in the opposite direction. The wind had decreased and it had stopped raining. I spent an hour walking the side streets of Kowloon, backtracking, stopping at shops and exiting through their back doors.

I delivered the film cartridge to Major Geoffrey Davis at the consulate the next morning, Sunday, after phoning him at home. I had the impression he blamed me for stealing Cynthia Roman, his efficient personal assistant. And I thought to myself: his loss, my gain. Notwithstanding, he assured me that he would send this latest film cartridge by pouch to the Institute that same day—highest priority.

I had a chance to meet Jack Chapman briefly in Central for coffee after leaving the consulate building. We agreed that he should visit Manila for a fun-filled weekend of debauchery as soon as he could get away. I knew when he arrived I would have to explain my dual identities to him. My intuition told me that I would take Jack into my confidence at some point in the future, given his sensitive work for the NSA. I suspected that he might have an even higher security clearance than I did, if that was possible. We'd worked as a winning team ten years earlier on the tennis courts in Central California. I couldn't discount the possibility of future teamwork.

# 33

---

## JULY 1975

I PHONED MCCOY AT HIS HOME AS SOON AS I RETURNED to the safe house. We agreed to meet "for breakfast."
I briefed him about the meeting with *Clover* and asked him to cable Springfield, alerting Gus Pomeroy about the film cartridge that he would soon receive from Hong Kong. Steve should mention in his cable that *Clover* had observed and photographed crates with Russian writing loaded onto his ship in North Korea. My agent didn't know the destination of the crates, nor did he know his ship's next port of call.

"He's done it again," McCoy exclaimed over the phone three days later. "Meet me at the club in an hour."

The labeling on the three large crates was, as I'd suspected, Russian. The analysts at the Pentagon had identified them. Those same crates had been observed two years earlier, in 1973, as they were being off-loaded from a Russian freighter in the Egyptian port of Alexandria. They had contained Soviet SA-6 surface-to-air missiles, and those missiles had had a devastating effect on the Israeli air force during the Yom Kippur War that same year. The missiles had blown something like forty Israeli fighter jets out of the sky.

"Those missiles are lethal," Steve remarked, glancing around to see if he could be overheard in the dining room. "The Institute's priority now is to find out where those SAMs are going to be discharged."

"So we follow the *Pacific Star*."

"That's a beginning. The North Korean angle is troubling. The ship will be stopped somehow before it reaches its destination."

Two days later we learned that the owner, Rolf Beckmann, had changed his ship's name soon after it departed Hong Kong, a ruse to disguise the vessel and make the *Pacific Star* disappear. The ship's new name was MV *Eastern Tribute*. And there was a new radio call sign to go along with it, which Komang relayed to us through Putu as his ship was sailing in the South China Sea.

# 34

---

JULY 1975

OPERATIONS WERE AT A FEVERED PITCH IN JULY 1975. The NSA, a branch of the Defense Department, began its signals intelligence surveillance of Wadi Haddad, monitoring his phone calls. The brother-in-law, with egg on its face, got into the act and shifted its focus from Habbash to Wadi. Operation *Wolverine*, the running of the double-agent *Slugger*, remained in the Institute's hands (and mine) despite grumbling by the Agency.

Five days after my meeting with Komang in Hong Kong, we received a coded message via Putu saying that his ship would arrive in Singapore on July 11. We learned the ship would anchor there for only enough time to take on fuel, and to paint over her old name *Pacific Star* with the new name *Eastern Tribute*. The ship's flag and home port remained Cypriot. Final destination of the ship: still unknown.

I was eager to know the purpose of the missiles and the final destination, and ultimately about the safety of *Clover* onboard the vessel. One way or another, the risk for Komang was now apparent. He was sailing on a ship that would not be allowed to reach its intended destination.

We didn't yet know where the SA-6 missiles were to be off-loaded, and that was causing me anxiety to the point of sleeplessness. Cynthia would wake up in the middle of the night and see me pacing outside in the darkened garden or staring out at Manila Bay. During one of those nocturnal séances, I made the decision to phone Jack.

I called him in the morning before he left for his office.

"Jack. Roy here."

"What's up, man?"

"How soon do you think you can come to Manila?"

He laughed. "You know, I was just thinking about that yesterday. Trying to pencil in a weekend to fly over there. These buddies of mine in Hong Kong, all they can talk about is how much fun they have in the Philippines. One wag, the chief economist here in my office, refers to Manila's RPPI—the Real Price of Pussy Index. He deems it the best value in Asia."

"Well, he may be right. And bring your tennis racquet. Look, I need to talk some business with you too." I gave Jack the phone number for calling me in the safe house.

"Okay, Roy. I'll work on getting away next weekend. Let me clear it with my boss and I'll get back to you."

Jack arrived in Manila Friday night, July 11, on the last Cathay Pacific flight of the day. I met him at the airport. We greeted each other with big smiles. "Hey Pepper, how goes it?" he called out to me, passing through the arrivals gate.

We delighted in the renewal of a friendship that had begun in elementary school in San Luis Obispo. Jack was about 6'2", two inches taller than I. Our high school tennis coach had nicknamed us Salt and Pepper, a reflection of Jack's blond hair and blue-eyed California surfer looks and my black hair, dark brown eyes, and dusky suntanned complexion. We had been doubles partners for three years and had won the Central California tennis championship in our senior year at the tournament in Ojai.

We took a taxi to the safe house where Cynthia had prepared one of the guest rooms.

When Jack saw the size of the four bedroom house, the large lit-up garden, and the swimming pool beside the bay, his first comment was, "I'm in the wrong business. How do you do it, Roy?"

I needed to break it to Jack at some point and decided it might as well be now. "We can thank the American taxpayer for this spread." Cynthia brought us two bottles of San Miguel and joined us in the living room. He looked at me strangely. Soft music was playing in the background.

"So you mean you weren't pulling my leg about that night in Hong Kong? All the while, I thought ... you know." He looked askance at Cynthia.

"Yes, I used your flat for the purpose I told you, though I couldn't explain much about it to you at the time."

"Well, I guess it's time for me to listen to you now," he said as he sat back on the plush sofa. "Tell me, what's the mystery?" He poured beer into his chilled mug.

"First of all, Maria is undercover as a housemaid here. She and I work together. She's privy to everything I'm about to explain to you."

He glanced again at Cynthia.

"You sure you guys want to discuss this with me?" he asked. "I mean, if it's classified maybe you shouldn't." He had a concerned look on his face.

"Yes, it's classified, Jack. Highly. If at the end of the day you want to help us, I would be thankful." I paused. "But first, I'd like to know if you do have access through CAC to help us out."

"You're putting me in a tough spot, Roy. I've signed on to the Espionage Act. I sure as hell can't tell you everything I'm doing." He raised his mug and drank a good half of his beer in one long draw.

"I've signed it too," I replied, "the one that dates back to 1917, right? My clearance is no doubt as high as yours is. And if you were anyone else other than Jack Chapman, we wouldn't be having this conversation. We go back a long way. Would you hear me out?"

"I'm listening."

"I'll summarize the situation for you," I said.

Without mentioning either of my agents—*Clover* or *Slugger* —I explained that we had proof that powerful surface-to-air missiles had been loaded in North Korea on board a Cypriot freighter, now somewhere in the South China Sea, and that we, the Defense Department, did not know where those missiles were going to be off-loaded. I told him that I had become aware of an Arab terrorist named Wadi Haddad based in Lebanon or Syria, and that I was suspicious of a Wadi/ Soviet/North Korean connection. I wanted to know if he, as a systems administrator at CAC, had access to NSA's signals intelligence, and could he monitor that agency's intercepts of Wadi and keep me informed.

After a long pause he asked, "Why me? If the NSA is monitoring this Wadi, then DIA or CIA, the agency that has the need to know, is going to receive those intercepts. Why would you need me as a back door to the NSA?"

"Because I'm not in the loop. And I'm concerned about the life and safe return of my agent—the man who discovered those lethal missiles. My God, Jack, he's the agent who alerted all of us about this shipment in the first place. He's the one I met that night in your flat." I leaned in and looked him in the eye. "It's personal. He's become a loyal friend, and he's not expendable. No agent is. If I knew where those missiles were going to be off-loaded, then just maybe I could have some influence on keeping him safe. Look, I'm not positive Wadi Haddad is involved with this shipment. It's an educated hunch."

"And you think that monitoring phone calls of this Wadi character will help you?"

"He's an Arab terrorist. A KGB agent. Soviet missiles are loaded on a ship in Wonsan. The North Koreans are notorious. There could be a connection. I have good reasons to believe it, Jack." We held eye contact for several seconds.

"Let me sleep on this. I'd have to give thought to how I access the SIGINT. It's complicated. If I didn't know you as well as I do Roy, as you say, we wouldn't be having this discussion. I don't cherish the thought of spending years in a federal prison for violating the Espionage Act. We'll talk again in the morning."

Jack stood up, swallowed the rest of his beer, said good night, and walked to his room. There was a tense silence. Cynthia retired to the maid's room for the night without saying a word. I stayed awake for several hours in the darkened garden, planning my moves and thinking about the risks —for Jack, for Cynthia, and for myself. I went to bed in the early hours of the morning.

When I awoke at nine o'clock, after sleeping for six hours, Jack and Cynthia were already up and about. Jack was sitting under the umbrella at a table in the garden, reading a local newspaper and drinking coffee. Cynthia was swimming laps in the pool. I poured a cup of coffee in the kitchen and joined Jack.

"Sleep well?" I asked him.

"Actually, no. So happens I had a lot on my mind. Just got up an hour ago," he replied, a wistful look on his face.

"Cheer up, Jack. You're here to enjoy Manila. The RPPI and all. I don't want to spoil the weekend. You've brought your racquet. Let's go hit some balls at the Army and Navy Club."

"No, let's talk. I've given this plenty of thought."

"And?" He had my attention.

"Okay. I can access NSA if they're monitoring your target. What's his name, Wadi?" I nodded. "I won't explain to you how I do it. It's complex. You'd need an advanced degree in computer science to understand."

I leaned back and listened.

"Although I'm employed by CAC, I'm a systems administrator for NSA. In a nutshell, I'm one of the persons responsible for keeping the computers up and running and talking with each other. I focus on SIGINT that targets Communist China and East Asia. But I have the capability to link up with other networks in the system, worldwide. I'm designated as a backup in case there's a glitch, anywhere in the world. The global system is failsafe because of this." He paused, reflecting. "It's amazing how much the government, NSA in particular, depends on private contractors to do this kind of work for them."

"I won't pretend to understand that."

"Don't try."

"What have you decided? Regarding my proposal?"

"I've concluded that it's doable, technically. The problem,

the one that could send us to prison, is how do I communicate with you without anyone knowing about it." The worried look had returned to his face.

"We never discuss anything on the phone for one thing," I remarked.

"You've got that right. If I do this for you, my role will be passive. I can monitor the communication and translations in the Middle East as a plausible function of my job. And that's all I'm prepared to do."

"Right. I can't ask for more."

"If you want any of the take, then you'll have to fly to Hong Kong where I can talk with you in absolute privacy. And that conversation won't occur on a telephone or in any building or hotel room where there could be listening devices. And in Hong Kong, being what it is, that means we'll discuss it as we're walking on the beach." I thought of the voice-activated recording device here in the house. Cynthia had unplugged it the day before.

"I didn't know Hong Kong had a beach."

"It does. Leave that to me."

"Does this mean you've decided to help monitor the Wadi Haddad intercepts?"

He nodded his head in the affirmative. "It means if the NSA is tapping his phone calls then I can, through a convoluted process, access that. It also means I'll be taking an insane risk by conspiring with you on this project," he said in a voice that was just above a whisper. "Now since that's decided, let's go play tennis at your club."

I phoned McCoy and told him I had a friend in town, and did he think Jack and I could play tennis at the Army and Navy Club as his guests. He replied that we could indeed, and that he was about to phone me to set up a meeting. Meaning he had some information to pass to me.

I introduced Steve McCoy as the Military Sealift representative, his Manila cover. I told McCoy that Jack was an old pal from California, spending an R&R weekend in Manila, and how once upon a time we had won a high school tennis championship. Steve was eager to watch us play on the club's courts, and he arranged it with the accommodating club manager.

The manager insisted on setting up a doubles match where Jack and I played against the club's teaching pro and one of his hotshot trainers. The match provided some unscheduled entertainment for the fifty or so spectators who sat outside in the shade and in the dining room above—eating, drinking, and watching the game. Jack could be a showboat, hitting winners between his legs and so forth when playing for fun, and he did not disappoint. We won a close match on the slow clay court.

After the match, as Jack was lounging poolside and charming a tanned, bikini-clad Filipino woman named Felicidad—the twenty-year-old daughter of one of the members —I had the opportunity to meet on the sidelines with Steve.

"I wanted to let you know, Roy. NSA has located the *Eastern Tribute*."

"Where is she?"

"She's passed through the Malacca Straits and is steaming northwest of the straits as we speak. The satellite picked up her new call sign and transponder."

"No surprise. The ship is heading into the Indian Ocean," I remarked with a knowing nod. That meant East Africa, the Persian Gulf, or the Suez Canal.

"That's all we know. Until we receive a message from *Mas*, we won't know her next port of call. It's still a mystery."

"*Clover* will let us know as soon as he knows," I said.

"Dubrowski is monitoring the radio at the scheduled times every day."

"Thanks, Steve." He knew I was anxious about Komang's safety and to learn of the ship's course.

The mission tempo against *Eastern Tribute* had now been ratcheted up several notches by the Pentagon and the CIA. And as I had explained to Jack the night before, I was no longer in the loop, as far as the ultimate disposal of the vessel went. My fear was that our navy or special forces would sink the ship one way or another with all hands, including *Clover*, on board. One outcome was certain: the *Eastern Tribute* would not reach its intended destination with those surface-to-air missiles on board.

I was relieved that Jack had made a dinner date with the winsome Felicidad. I would not be obliged to entertain him at one of Manila's dives like the White Swallow, and later on try to explain that to Cynthia. Neither could I introduce him to Terry's Bar in case *Slugger* was holding court there. I did request that Jack not bring Felicidad to the safe house for security reasons. He understood.

He and his new girlfriend spent that night and much of the next day in one of Ermita's pay-by-the-hour motels. By the end of the weekend, Sunday night, as we took a taxi to the airport for his flight back to Hong Kong, Jack claimed he was in love. His glassy-eyed expression betrayed the heartfelt truth in what he said. A weekend in the Philippines had a way of affecting a lot of guys that way.

# 35

TWO DAYS LATER I RECEIVED THE PHONE CALL FROM Jack. We'd agreed on a simple code.

"Hello, Roy," he said, "bring your trumpet with you to Hong Kong on your next trip."

This comment told me that I needed to fly to Hong Kong as soon as I could. Jack had picked up the NSA phone intercepts of Wadi Haddad.

"You can count on it," I replied. I waited to hear if he had anything else to say.

"Okay, then. Goodbye for now," he said and hung up.

McCoy had no knowledge of my arrangement with Jack. I would need to give Steve a reason for dashing off to Hong Kong over the weekend, which was easy enough to do, what with the increased tempo of our Manila crewing agency.

*Seaworth* was now sending more and more crewmen to work on Chow Fatt's ships. And that was providing us with a treasure trove of potential clandestine agents with natural access to not only Communist Chinese ports and naval bases, but to nearly every Communist seaport in the world. I had recruited four Filipino ships' officers, one of them a ship's captain. And I had provided each of them with a state-of-the-art Nikon camera for their missions. My frequent trips that year to Hong Kong, Penang, Singapore, Bangkok, and Surabaya to recruit, brief, and debrief seagoing agents had become routine.

But, to keep it simple, I told Steve I would take a quick trip to Hong Kong that weekend to play in a tennis tournament with Jack.

The morning I left, Cynthia and I played out one of the erotic fantasies that we delighted in. Blame that on my acute sense of the absurd. She would lie in bed in the maid's room, naked. I would prepare breakfast and then surprise her by serving it to her in her room. Playing the role of the callow virgin housemaid, legs spread wide, she would be caressing her *mons Venus* when I entered. Feigning surprise when I opened the door to the bedroom and pulling the sheet up to cover her body, she would call out in alarm, "Sir, what are you doing in here? I'm completely naked!"

"Breakfast in bed for your highness, Maria my dear," I declared as I placed the breakfast tray on a bedside table. And I would proceed to ravage her beautifully toned body, from head to toe, with loving kisses. We only disengaged our bodies that morning when I saw it was time for me to shower and head for the nearby airport. Weeks earlier, Cynthia and I had assented to combine our carnal fantasies with service to country.

Jack and I had decided we would meet each other in Hong Kong on weekends. This allowed us sufficient time to discuss matters privately, away from the Central District. I arrived at noon on Saturday July 19. I called Jack from a pay phone at the airport, and he asked me to meet him at the Repulse Bay Hotel on the opposite side of the island. We would arrive at that hotel separately. I hadn't known that day where Jack intended to hold our meeting. This was his turf, his game plan.

I first checked in to the Peninsula Hotel, and as a returning guest was given a cordial greeting at the front desk by the staff. After unpacking I left through the hotel's side exit and practiced counter-surveillance, along the narrow side streets of Kowloon. At three o'clock in the afternoon, I boarded the Star Ferry for the short, familiar trip across the harbor to the island. I had discovered there was a bus service from Central to Repulse Bay and that the trip would take a little over thirty minutes. I timed my arrival for a few minutes before four o'clock. Jack had already arrived. He was sitting on the colonial-style hotel's outdoor veranda having a drink and gazing out at Repulse Bay. I walked up the steps and sat down beside him.

"I didn't put anything in writing. I don't plan to," he said after a brief greeting.

"My memory's good. I don't plan to write anything down. Trust me," I replied.

We looked out at the deserted beach. It was monsoon season and there were rainclouds overhead. The choppy sea was gray. I called to the waiter and paid for our drinks.

"Let's take a walk on the beach," he suggested.

We crossed the street and stepped onto the hard-packed sand. We took off our shoes and carried them in our hands, walking south along the water's edge toward the far end of the beach.

"I picked up the Wadi Haddad intercept this week. NSA is all over him," Jack commented, sounding cautious and looking down at the yellow sand in front of us.

"I'm not surprised. The intel we provided has stirred up a hornets' nest in Washington."

"Wadi received a phone call from one of his associates. Both of them in Lebanon. Wadi was in Baalbek near the Syrian border. The call to him was from a Beirut suburb. They spoke in Arabic of course. I reviewed the translation."

"Were you able to identify the one who phoned Wadi?" I asked.

"I think the name was Habbash. Sound right?

"Yes. It does."

"Wadi explained to the caller that he is waiting for a cargo of surface-to-air missiles and radar gear. They will arrive in Beirut on a ship that's en route, in about two weeks. The other one, Habbash, asked him something about training. Wadi told him the Egyptian had arrived in Baalbek. There was mention of the Muslim Brotherhood. I think they referred to the Egyptian as 'the Major'."

"That could be a rogue officer in the Egyptian army," I said. "The Arabs used those missiles two years ago against the Israelis. Wadi's people would have to be trained on how to target them."

Jack continued, "The caller asked Wadi if the original plan was still operative. Wadi replied, yes, the target was an American airliner to be shot down soon after it took off from Tel Aviv. He said the planes, according to his informant in Israel, were still flying the Tel Aviv-to-Athens route every Thursday. He gave Habbash the flight number.

"Wadi said it would take seven weeks to surreptitiously

position the missile and radar in southern Lebanon and for the Major to train the crew. He estimates his team would be ready to launch the missile during the week of September eighth."

I was stunned, speechless for half a minute. I removed a calendar from my wallet and studied the month of September. Wadi was planning to fire the missile at the American jumbo jet on Thursday, September eleventh.

"Did Wadi mention the name of the ship, the one the missiles are on?" I finally asked.

"No. I don't believe he did."

I made a quick calculation and estimated that the *Eastern Tribute*, now in the Indian Ocean, would arrive at the recently reopened Suez Canal and the Mediterranean Sea in two weeks.

Jack and I stopped walking. The sea looked cold, bleak. I reflected on how serene it was here at Repulse Bay, how different from Central and Kowloon where the hubbub and bustle were incessant. Jack had chosen well.

At last I started walking back toward the faded old hotel. "One thing for sure," I said in a low voice. "The *Eastern Tribute* will never reach Beirut."

"You can bet on it," Jack replied. "NSA has passed all of this along, up the chain. The president would know about Wadi's plot by now."

I looked at Jack. "Thanks. I owe you."

"I'll collect in Manila. Felicidad says she's waiting for me." He gave me a wry grin.

I told Jack we needed to leave Repulse Bay by separate modes. He took a taxi home and I rode the bus back to Central. That same evening I checked out of the hotel and caught the last flight back to Manila.

# 36

---

JULY 1975

O N SUNDAY NIGHT I RECEIVED THE CALL FROM McCoy. We met the next morning.

"Here it is, Roy." He handed me the cassette tape as soon as I sat down at the table. "Have something quick to eat before you go." I wolfed down a croissant and drank half a cup of coffee.

"I'll phone you as soon as I translate it," I said as I stood up and placed the cassette in my backpack.

I rushed back to the house and played the tape.

"*Mas* calling *Bintang*," Putu called out. "*Mas* calling *Bintang*."

"*Bintang* receiving. Go ahead *Mas*," McCoy replied. He had now become accustomed to the exchange of call signs.

She stated the code in Indonesian: 01 21 103 49 31 15 32 18 28 7 3 before immediately closing the connection.

I knew the first four numbers indicated the latitude and longitude of Singapore, the *Eastern Tribute*'s last port of call. I searched my atlas for the next set of four. There it was: Port Said, Egypt at the northern end of the Suez Canal, with an estimated date of arrival of Monday, July 28. Komang wanted urgently to meet with me. The message inferred that the ship would transit the Suez Canal, which the Egyptians had recently reopened, and sail with those surface-to-air missiles into the Mediterranean Sea.

The next day Tom Hiatt, disguised again as "Mr. Briar," phoned the safe house. He dispensed with any recognition signals. "Meet me in Malacca, and make it fast, like yesterday," he ordered. Hiatt's phone call and the recent report on *Clover*'s position were no coincidence. The United States was about to launch an operation.

Hiatt had checked in at the Majestic Hotel in Malacca. Signals had gotten crossed. No one at Springfield knew where I'd been over the weekend, and Hiatt had speculated that I was in Malacca at the time. When he checked in to the hotel and didn't find me, he'd phoned the Manila safe house.

I booked a flight from Manila to Kuala Lumpur the next day. Sammy met me at the airport.

"Long time, no see," he commented as I climbed into the front seat of his taxi. "What keeps you away?"

"Well, Sammy, the coffee business in Asia is picking up. There's a shortage of Arabica beans because of the weather in Brazil." Which was true.

"Good for you, Roy. I wish you success. Where to? The Majestic?"

"Yes. Take me home."

Tom Hiatt had arrived two days earlier. I phoned him in his room as soon as I settled in. "Let's meet," he said without preamble. I had anticipated that he would be cranky because of my absence when he arrived at the hotel. Instead he appeared indifferent about the matter, and even seemed pleased to have had a couple of days all to himself in Malacca.

It was late in the afternoon and there was still enough light for us to jog a couple of rounds on *Bukit China*. Tom commented that walking on that hill afforded him more healthy exercise than he got all year in Virginia.

There were several men and women—Malays, Chinese, and Indians—jogging along the path when we arrived. Tom and I walked at a brisk pace and discussed *Clover*'s mission.

I began by expressing my foreboding. "I'm really worried they'll sink Komang's ship with all hands on board. We can't let that happen, Tom."

He sighed before answering. "I agree. It would be counter-productive. Our side would hand the Russians a propaganda victory on a silver platter if they order that. In no time Moscow would concoct proof that the Americans had sunk a defenseless civilian cargo ship, drowning who knows how many crew. *Pravda* would have a field day with it. But that's not my decision to make. The decision on how to dispose of *Eastern Tribute* is above my pay grade. It's now up to the president."

"What's the plan?" Never in my life had I felt such anxiety. I may very well have set up a scenario where my agent would lose his life.

"The planning is in the works. Rather advanced, so I'm told. We have a submarine on patrol in the Mediterranean as we speak. I need to talk with you now about *Clover*'s role. I hear we have the ship's next port call."

"Right. Port Said," I replied. "Look, I can't brief my agent if I don't have any idea what he faces out there in the Mediterranean Sea. Help me out here."

When we began our jog along the hill, Tom explained to me what I already knew, thanks to Jack Chapman. He told me that NSA intercepts (he didn't mention Wadi Haddad by name) had discovered that the missiles on the *Eastern Tribute* were to be off-loaded in the port of Beirut, and that they were to be used to shoot down a commercial airliner. I feigned surprise and shock. He was positive that the cargo ship would not be allowed to reach Beirut one way or another. And that *Clover*'s role was critical in identifying the *Eastern Tribute* and pinpointing the ship's position in real-time after it entered the Mediterranean.

"There are two plans." Tom heaved a large sigh this time. "DuPont attended an NSC meeting the night before I left. They had him attend in case Council members needed clarification on the intelligence. The gist of it is that the members debated the matter at some length, and they're divided between a "plan A" and a "plan B." I can't remember which member is for which plan.

"Plan A has our nuclear submarine sinking the ship to send a message to the Swiss ship owner and arms dealer, and to all ship owners who might assist terrorists: this is how we'll deal with you. Beckmann is no doubt complicit in the plot. Why else would he try to hide the ship by changing its name? The plan is to have a small navy ship on patrol nearby so that all of the crew can be rescued after the ship is torpedoed. We don't want anyone in the crew to drown. That navy ship also needs to receive *Clover*'s position reports. Doubtful that Cyprus would declare war on the United States if we sink the vessel."

"And plan B?"

"Yes, plan B." Hiatt continued walking. "The other half of the Council, the doves if you will, they're for having our navy SEALs hijack the ship in the Med, arrest the officers, and impound the vessel. We would gain the propaganda victory instead of the Russians when we display to the world the hidden cargo of Soviet SAMs. Not that the powers-that-be give a shit anymore about what the United Nations thinks. It's the president's call. And that's where we are. Plan A or plan B. The proverbial hawks and doves."

"Fuck! Then I need to arrive in Cairo by Friday," I said, after he had explained my mission to me. It would be tight. I needed to land in Cairo and get to Port Said. Once there, I would case the unfamiliar port city for meeting sites, and learn what I could of *Eastern Tribute*'s arrival date and whether she would tie up to a pier or anchor out. I would have to make contact with Komang on the ship and ask him to come ashore for the briefing.

I thought of calling Sammy to see if his brother at Royal Travel could move heaven and earth to get me on an immediate flight from KL to Cairo. "Let's get back to the hotel. I need to make a call."

I phoned Sammy from my room and explained the urgency of flying to Cairo. I told him there was an East African coffee exporter's convention beginning on Friday, and that I had been invited to be a guest speaker on that day. I had accepted the invitation, and I needed to fly out of Kuala Lumpur the next day, Thursday, July 24. Within one hour Sammy delivered the ticket to me at the hotel. Royal Travel would debit my account for the price of the ticket.

"Pays to have friends in high places," Hiatt commented with a grin when I informed him how the ticket had been expedited.

I told him I'd leave the hotel early the next morning, and so would not see him again before I left. He said he would remain in Malacca to debrief me when I returned the following week.

# 37

---

THE AMERICAN NUCLEAR SUBMARINE *USS NAUTILUS* (SSN-571) was dockside in Rota, Spain, when the urgent message was received from Atlantic submarine fleet headquarters in Norfolk. Commander Rich Mabry, the skipper of the submarine, was puzzled and scratched his grizzled head as he read the decoded orders. He called for his executive officer, Lieutenant Commander Sam Gornnert, to join him.

"Look at this, Sam." Mabry dropped the message on the ward room table in front of his XO "We're due to head home in two days. And now we receive this order from fleet."

The Nautilus had been on patrol for the past six months, most of it submerged. They had spent that period prowling the Mediterranean Sea where they monitored each and every Soviet warship and submarine that entered the Med from the Black Sea. They had followed the Soviet subs into the Atlantic Ocean until they could be picked up and tracked by the newer

U.S. navy attack submarines that roamed the eastern Atlantic. Two days hence, the twenty-year-old *Nautilus* was scheduled to get underway from Rota and make tracks submerged and west across the Atlantic Ocean to her home port, New London, Connecticut. And now—new orders to head east.

"Let me read this again," the XO said fuming, "because I don't believe it. Are we the only boat left in the fleet?"

"No, of course not. Except that each of the boats tied up here in Rota is an FBM. And *Scorpion* has already taken over our patrols."

The captain was pointing out that his boat, the *Nautilus*, was the only attack submarine available. All the other boats at Rota were American ballistic missile submarines, with their nuclear tipped and MIRV missiles, and they had a different mission. And the hunter-killer sub, *USS Scorpion*, had relieved the *Nautilus* in its vital tracking mission.

The XO held the message in front of him and read it aloud. "You are to load conventional torpedoes and get underway ASAP. Proceed at full speed to quadrant ten and wait for further instructions."

"Quadrant ten is in the eastern Med, north of the Suez Canal. It will take us four days to get there at flank speed." Mabry glanced at a wall calendar. "We'd arrive on station around midnight on the 27th. How soon can we get underway?"

"By the time shore patrol rounds up the crew, the ones horsing around now in Rota, I'd estimate we could depart by 1600 hours. We've still got a mix of torpedoes, nukes, and non-nukes on board. A full load."

"All right. Pass the word. Liberty is cancelled. We get underway at 1600 hours. Get the sailors back to the boat ASAP. And draw up a duty roster."

"Aye, Captain." The XO stood up and rushed out of the ward room. Rounding up all the sailors and officers ashore would now be his priority. He knew sailors who were eager to sail home after being away from their families for six months, would not be a happy crew when informed that their home-coming would be indefinitely delayed. Morale was never high after these long patrols. It could only get worse.

At the same time that the *USS Nautilus* was casting off from the pier at Rota, at 15:55 local time on July 23, a twelve-man U.S. navy SEAL team was packing up and preparing to board a navy transport plane in Naples for the long flight to Norfolk, their home base.

"So Lieutenant, it's time to leave our loved ones and return to our dependents," the chief petty officer chuckled.

"Speak for yourself, Chief," the young SEAL team commander replied with a smile. "I'm single and loving every minute of it. Norfolk or Naples. Same, same."

Just then a navy yeoman approached the two men.

"Mr. Sonderstrom, sir." The yeoman walked up to the SEAL commander. "We received this message fifteen minutes ago. We've decoded it. You might want to sit down for this one."

Lieutenant Mike Sonderstrom reached for the message and remained standing. He read it twice.

"Well, guess what, Chief. Looks like you and the men might have a little more time here to spend with your loved ones. We're not going anywhere today. We've been ordered by Norfolk to delay our departure and wait for further orders. *Highest Priority*."

"And that's all it says, sir? No explanation? No mission?"

"Nope. That's all she wrote. Indication is there'll be more to follow. We don't receive this kind of priority message every day," Sonderstrom said. "Tell the men to hold off packing the gear. And stay close to base. I have a feeling we're about to be involved in the kind of thing we're paid to do."

# 38

---

JULY 1975

MY PLANE TOUCHED DOWN AT THE AIRPORT LATE in the hot afternoon. And that was all I ever saw of Cairo. I stood in line for a taxi outside the arrivals gate, and traveling light without check-in baggage, I hopped into the back seat of one with only my backpack and briefcase. The ride to Port Said took four hours. The driver spoke little English, and that gave me far more than ample time to rehearse the modus operandi in my head.

I checked in to the Grand Albatros Hotel after dark. There was a message from Tom Hiatt waiting for me at the reception desk. The message informed me that my consignment of coffee beans would be booked through Al-Mostafa Shipping and Trading Company. Hiatt's sources had identified the agency that *Eastern Tribute* would use during her short stopover in Port Said.

My room at the Grand Albatros was on the highest floor in the hotel. When I woke up the next morning to the sounds of the *muezzin*, the call to prayer from the mosque up the road, I found to my surprise that I had a view of the Mediterranean Sea. Standing on my balcony, I could see the long, wide beach below and the few shuttered kiosks at the edge of the sand. It was well before 7:00 and the beach was deserted. I pondered on the situation before me as I stood on my balcony and watched the sunrise over the Sinai Desert to the east.

I found I could stretch out over the balcony railing and see the Suez Canal to my right where it ended between Port Said and Port Fouad. Cargo ships and oil tankers entered the Canal in single file from the Mediterranean Sea. I noticed a man and woman on the beach far to my left, hauling what looked like tents and lounge chairs from a kiosk onto the beach. I found this activity to be of interest for a reason I couldn't explain. I remained standing and watching them. Sure enough, they were setting up colorful striped tents, enclosures that would offer shelter for families or concealment for lovers. And privacy for the meeting with Komang where I would brief him on his mission in the Med.

I waited until each of the twenty or so tents had been erected. This was Friday, the beginning of the Muslim weekend, and I decided not to waste time. I would go to the beach and rent one of those tents for a week—from that day through Thursday. *Clover*'s ship was due to arrive in Port Said on Monday.

I rented the tent at the far western end from the Egyptian couple, telling them I was here as a tourist and looked forward to a week of relaxation and swimming in the Mediterranean. I paid them in advance for the week. I would live my cover at the beach over the weekend before the ship's arrival.

My next move that Friday morning, before the next call to

prayer and the weekend holiday, was to locate the shipping agency and learn of *Eastern Tribute*'s ETA and docking location. The Al-Mostafa office was located on El-Gomhoreya Street, near the Arabesque-styled Suez Canal Authority building. I took a taxi from the hotel and was dropped off five blocks from the shipping office, on Gamal Abdul El-Nasir Street.

I spent the better part of an hour conducting counter-surveillance on the streets of Port Said—strolling casually among the crowds, watching reflections in shop windows, and admiring the entire circumference of a huge mosque as a typical tourist might do. I carried no identification with me. Satisfied that I was not being followed, I walked on to the shipping agency.

I had written a brief note that I sealed in an envelope addressed to the Radio Operator on the *Eastern Tribute*. In another envelope I placed cash, a gratuity for the clerk who would deliver the note. The message told Komang to meet me at the Al-Shatee Garden at 2:00 in the afternoon. Komang knew this meant that he was to meet me at 1:10, and that he was to try to make the meeting at that time every day his ship was in port. The reality was that the ship would remain in Port Said for only that one day. I carried both sealed envelopes in my backpack.

I had over the past months become accustomed to the modus operandi at the shipping agencies. I would enter the office and stand back near the front door as I perused the list of ships on the arrivals and departures board. If the office had no bulletin board, which was unlikely, I would approach a clerk for the information.

In this case there was a large white board hanging on a rear wall of the office. I could just make out the names of the agency's vessels in Port Said and in Port Fouad on the east side of the Canal. The *Eastern Tribute* was not among them. I could now go up to the desk and inquire about the ship's estimated arrival date from one of the clerks, and possibly engage his or her curiosity to query as to why I needed to know. Instead I chose to make a hasty about-face and left the office without being noticed by any of the busy Egyptian staff.

The rest of that day I lived my tourist cover by swimming in the Mediterranean, and making an effort to read a novel inside my rented tent. One masters the art of waiting in this game. And with a good book, fiction or nonfiction, I am never bored. In this case, I could not keep my mind on the story. My thoughts were on Komang. I envisioned him going down with the sinking ship. And I saw him cursing me right before he sank under the waves for the last time.

There was no notice of arrival for *Clover*'s ship on the agency's arrivals board on either weekend day. Both days I swam far out into the sea, took my meals in the hotel restaurant, and attempted without success to concentrate on my novel inside the tent.

I hit pay dirt on Monday morning. The shipping office's bulletin board listed the *Eastern Tribute*'s arrival in Port Said for that day. I stood back and assessed each of the busy clerks in turn as they conversed with customers or managed their paperwork. At last I selected one. I can't explain why I chose one over another. Intuition at work. This fellow was in his early twenties. I had noticed the past two days that he dressed well, wearing a freshly cleaned and pressed white long-sleeved shirt. I overheard him speaking passable English to someone. His demeanor appeared friendly; he laughed or smiled easily with his customers and with the other staff. He was attending to someone at the counter at the time I was studying the arrivals board. I stood in line, and waited my turn.

"May I help you?" he asked in English, looking up at me from his paperwork.

"Yes, please," I replied. "I'm sorry I don't speak Arabic."

He smiled. "No problem. What can I do for you?"

"I have a friend from home arriving on the *Eastern Tribute*." I glanced up at the board. He turned around to look at it.

"Yes, the ship is due to arrive tonight. She'll be in port for about twenty-four hours," he remarked.

I leaned forward on the counter. "Could I trouble you to deliver a message to the ship for me?" I removed the two envelopes from my backpack and handed him the one addressed to the radio operator.

"I can arrange to have it sent out to the ship," he replied. His English was good in a classroom sense.

"You know, it's important to me that I have this delivered in person. He's a good friend. Could you take the letter to him?" I placed the other envelope, the one with the cash, on the counter between us. "This envelope would be for you, to thank you for your trouble," I said quietly. He took both envelopes in his hands. I had written US$200 in small letters on one of them. He glanced at it and gave a slight nod of his head.

"Sure. I'll meet the ship when it arrives tonight. And I'll look for the radio operator and hand him your letter," he said in a lowered voice as he held on to both envelopes. "My name is Mohammad Aziz. Call me tomorrow morning and I'll confirm if I found your friend."

"I'll do that Mohammad. My name is Cisco. And I appreciate your help. Thank you."

"No problem."

The next morning, Tuesday, July 29, I phoned the agency and asked to speak with Mohammad Aziz. When he came on the line, and after I told him who was calling, he confirmed that he had gone out to the ship the night before and handed the envelope to Komang.

# 3 9

---

JULY 1975

I LEFT THE HOTEL AT NOON AND WALKED TO THE WEST along the hard wet sand on the beach, past my tent. I wore Bermuda shorts, a T-shirt, and sandals. I had left a notebook and pen inside the tent earlier in the morning. I was as certain as I could be that I was not being followed. but one never knows for sure. Abruptly I doubled back along the beach, heading east.

Finally I turned south and entered a grassy park. At 1:08 p.m. I arrived at the Al-Shatee Garden, a cool, green area with pathways that ran through an area of planted flowers and shade trees. Five minutes later I saw Komang emerge from a café inside the park. He saw me at the same time. We walked toward each other and met beneath a large umbrella.

I greeted Komang with a handshake and a pat on the shoulder. He smiled and greeted me cheerfully in return. We walked to the beach adjacent to the park. Komang took off his shoes and socks and rolled up his jeans. We walked together along the water's edge and discussed his recent voyage from Singapore, through the Malacca Straits, across the Indian Ocean, up the Red Sea, and the final transit through the Suez Canal.

"You know, Cisco, the captain asked me why I was leaving the ship. He was not happy, and he reminded me that we would depart Port Said later tonight. I explained I needed to go to a pharmacy and purchase some medicine for my stomach and that I would return to the ship before we got underway. He was about to order me to stay on board. I walked away and repeated that I was sick to my stomach and had to buy some pills. He was angry. A ship can't sail without a radio operator."

"Well done, Komang." I said. "You did the right thing. We have some important things to discuss before you sail into the Mediterranean."

*Clover* knew nothing about the contents of those crates that had been loaded onto his ship in Wonsan. He had delivered the film to me in Hong Kong, and that was the last time we had been in contact. He was unaware of the danger he was in.

"See those colorful striped tents down there? The nearest one is mine. We'll crawl inside and get out of the afternoon sun. We can discuss our plans there."

He lit up one of his clove cigarettes and smoked as we walked and talked. I was not worried about anyone here on the beach in Port Said understanding our conversation in Indonesian. The owner of the tents saw us approach and nodded to me.

When we moved inside the tent I began my briefing. I made a point of keeping any trace of anxiety out of my voice.

"Komang, do you know your next port of call?" I asked.

"No. And that's odd. I should know by now. But this time I don't. All I do know is that we're in Port Said for a very short time. Not working cargo. We're just taking on fuel oil. That work started this morning. And then we leave." He paused. "I did ask the captain where we were going. He only stared at me, shrugged, and turned his back."

"I can tell you what we do know. Your ship's next port is Beirut."

"Oh?"

"Those crates you loaded in Wonsan, with the Russian writing, contain deadly surface-to-air missiles. And we won't allow them to be off-loaded in Beirut. You need to know this— there's a horrific terrorist plot in the works and they involve those missiles you saw loaded onto your ship." There was a long silence as Komang comprehended what I had said.

Finally he asked, "What does that mean, Cisco?"

"It means the U.S. navy is going to arrest the *Eastern Tribute* in the Mediterranean, and we need your cooperation so that no mistakes are made at night, in the middle of the sea. We have to be able to identify your ship. Pinpoint its location."

"What can I do?" He was alarmed. "I'm going to be arrested?"

"You'll be safe, Komang. We've always trusted each other. Trust me now."

He picked up the pen and notepad that had been lying on a beach towel. His stare was intense. "Okay then. Tell me what you want me to do this time."

"All right. We need you to continually transmit your call sign by Morse code after you leave Port Said. Only your call sign. Send it in bursts, three times in a row. Begin by doing that every thirty minutes. Then at midnight tonight, begin sending bursts every fifteen minutes—again, three times in quick succession. And continue doing that, every fifteen minutes, until we stop the ship in the middle of the sea."

I didn't know if the ship would be stopped by a torpedo from a submarine that had homed in on Komang's call sign, or by a team of navy SEALs who would likewise be guided by his radio signals.

"You said missiles?"

"Very dangerous, very powerful missiles, Komang. We cannot allow them to reach the terrorists who expect to receive them in Beirut. You accomplish this mission, and you're a hero in our eyes. My country will be thankful, very thankful. You name it, and it's yours."

He replied with a sly smile, "A green card?"

I clapped him on the shoulder. "A green card, yes. If that's what you and Putu want."

"Just kidding, Cisco. Okay, I'll do my part. Missiles and terrorists—that sounds bad. Just make sure you set me free when the ship is arrested."

I asked Komang to repeat the instructions I had given him. He did so.

"And another thing, Komang. I want you to have a life jacket with you at all times after you depart Port Said. Keep it where you can reach it. You'll be inside your radio room for quite a while after you enter the Mediterranean Sea, until the ship is stopped."

He nodded without expression.

"And, whatever happens, never reveal to anyone that you and I are working together. We can't take a chance that any of your shipmates or the officers on your ship discover our rela-tionship. You cannot trust any of them."

He looked down, an expression of deep worry on his face.

"Komang, my friend, this will be over soon. We need your help. And your silence aboard the ship and afterward. You will soon return to Bali and to Putu. Sooner than you thought you would. This is your last, most important mission."

"All right, Cisco. I'll do this for you."

"Then let's shake on it and agree that we meet each other again in Bali. Soon." I reached out. Komang shook my hand. As friends.

He and I left the tent and parted in separate directions. The last I saw of Komang he had a determined look on his face. I watched him from a distance, where a taxi stopped and he climbed into the front passenger seat.

# 40

---

## JULY 1975

N AVY SEAL LEADER LIEUTENANT MIKE SONDER-
strom called his team together into a small,
soundproof briefing room at the NATO facility in
Naples where they had been training for the past month. They
had been scheduled to return to Norfolk three days earlier.
That plan had been scrapped. And for three days the SEALs
had exercised and waited for further instructions, not from
Norfolk, but from the office of the chief of naval operations.

Sonderstrom held the decoded cable. "Here it is, men," he
said looking down at the sheet in his hand. "We depart Naples
at 1900 hours, by chopper, loaded for bear, including rubber
boats. Says we rendezvous with the submarine *USS Nautilus* in
the eastern Med. I've got the coordinates. And we wait for
further instructions." He hesitated and looked at his men.
"We've done this drill many times. Though I suspect this time
it's not a drill. Any questions?"

There's nothing navy SEALs delight in more than the

eventuality of action, the chance to put all of their unequaled physical, mental, and high-intensity combat training into practice. There were unanimous happy fist pumps at the news and expressions of relief. The wait was over.

Sonderstrom informed his men that a U.S. navy helicopter would take them to the Greek island of Crete, where the chopper would refuel. They would then be flown to the precise latitude and longitude coordinates in quadrant ten that were listed in the Top Secret cable. At the very moment the chopper arrived on station, at 0530 hours local time on Monday, July 28, they would see the *USS Nautilus* identified by 571 on its superstructure rise to the surface. The forward escape hatch on the sub would be thrown open, and the twelve navy SEALs with all their equipment would repel from the helicopter to the submarine's deck. That operation would be accomplished in seconds rather than minutes. After the men and equipment were inside the sub and the hatch closed, the *Nautilus* would submerge back into the depths of the dark Mediterranean Sea. The submarine's captain would await further orders—from the president of the United States by way of the chief of naval operations.

# 41

---

## JULY 1975

THE M.V. *EASTERN TRIBUTE* CAST OFF FROM THE PIER at 10:15 p.m. on Tuesday, July 29, 1975. She made a turn, headed north, and picked up speed as she entered the Mediterranean Sea. Thirty minutes later the Turkish first mate informed Komang that their next port of call would be Beirut. The radio operator nodded with a shrug and without comment.

At 10:30 p.m. the radio operator sent his first burst by Morse code. As usual, he was alone in the radio room. He transmitted again at 11:00. At midnight he repeated it, and from then on he continued to drink coffee to stay awake and transmit the ship's call sign every fifteen minutes, throughout the small hours of the morning of Wednesday, July 30.

The *USS Nautilus* was cruising slowly in quadrant ten at periscope depth after midnight. She had been on station, circling submerged, with a team of navy SEALs on board since Monday, July 28. In addition to having her periscope up, she had her radio antenna raised just above the surface of the sea. The radioman on the sub had picked up the call sign, P5Z4T, when it was first transmitted at 10:30 at night on Tuesday. The sub then located the navigation lights on the cargo ship and followed 1,000 yards behind it. The summer night was clear and the *Nautilus'* captain, squinting through the periscope, focused on the Cypriot freighter dead ahead of him as they both proceeded northeast at twelve knots. The submarine's sonar operators likewise had the cargo ship in their sights. Each of the torpedo tubes was loaded with conventional Mark-48s, the navy's latest and the most lethal of the non-nuclear fish. Captain Mabry commented to an officer in the conn that this mission was bordering on the ridiculous. To shoot a sitting duck at point-blank range. What was going on? He waited for orders now from the CNO, which was unheard of: orders *direct* from that high up the chain of command, bypassing Atlantic Fleet Submarine HQ in Norfolk. He'd earlier asked the lieutenant in command of the SEALs if he knew what the hell was going on. He hadn't a clue.

# 42

***

## July 1975

THE PRESIDENT OF THE UNITED STATES STEPPED into the situation room at the White House at 7:30 p.m. on July 29 and asked the men and women around the table, the members of the National Security Council, to take their seats.

"Hello, everyone." The president gave a thin smile. "I've been briefed by Roger. Seems we have a decision that needs to be made right away. Is that correct, Roger?"

"Yes, Mr. President, that is correct," replied the national security advisor. "We have a window that is closing fast. I'd say two hours max."

"Well, then, let's get a move on. Who wants to make their case? Plan A or plan B, as you refer to it." The president looked at his secretary of defense. "William?"

"Sir, the *USS Nautilus* is on station and following close behind the target, the Cypriot cargo ship, *Eastern Tribute*. The name of that ship when she loaded the Soviet missiles in North Korea was *Pacific Star*. The fact that the ship's owner changed its name means he wants to disguise its mission. This proves beyond doubt that the owner, a Swiss millionaire named Rolf Beckmann, is part of a conspiracy to deliver the weapons to the terrorists who we learned plan to shoot down an American passenger airliner. Plan A is for the submarine *Nautilus* to fire a single torpedo at the freighter and sink it."

"Why sink it?" asked the president.

"The United States needs to send a message to this ship owner and arms dealer," the Secretary replied, "that he or anyone else who conspires in such a heinous plot will pay the price. This plot, this connivance involving the Soviets, the North Koreans, the DFLP, *and* Beckmann to shoot down an American airliner amounts to a declaration of war. Imagine if we had not received that intelligence in North Korea." The secretary of defense paused for a moment. "And one more thing. The NSA director informed me one hour ago that someone on the *Eastern Tribute* switched off the ship's transponder soon after it entered the Med."

"Meaning what?" asked the president.

"Meaning, Mr. President, that someone on board is trying to hide the location of that ship. Without an active transponder, no one can monitor its course and position. This is more proof of a four-way conspiracy in motion."

Everyone at the table looked at the president, waiting for a signal.

The secretary of defense continued. "Sinking that accursed ship would serve as a deterrent like none other, Mr. President. It's the least we can do to bring those culprits to justice."

"And what about the crew aboard the ship?" asked the president. "Do you believe they should be sacrificed, William?"

"Not at all, Mr. President. We have a navy intelligence

ship, an AGTR, nearby. She's underway two miles from the cargo ship. The AGTR has been monitoring the ship's radio transmissions from the beginning. By the way, for some unknown reason, the freighter sends its call sign out every fifteen minutes so that we know her exact position. The plan is for the AGTR, and perhaps the *Nautilus*, to rescue the crew as soon as *Eastern Tribute* is hit and begins to sink."

There was silence in the room. The council members at the table and the officials sitting behind them along the wall continued to look at the president for a decision. The president appeared in deep thought. At last he nodded twice and turned toward his secretary of state.

"Megan, what have you to say about this?" he asked.

"Mr. President, sinking that ship would cause a public relations disaster. In no time, the Soviets would broadcast to the world, proof or no proof, that the evil Americans had sunk an innocent civilian cargo ship in the Mediterranean Sea. They'd haul us before the United Nations. And they'd wring every ounce of propaganda they could out of the incident. We'd be the ones made to look like villains instead of them." The secretary of defense stared with a look of disapproval at the secretary of state as she made her case. "On the other hand, if we arrest the ship, bring it to an allied port, and expose those Soviet missiles for the world to see, then we win the battle of public opinion. Plan B is for our special forces, navy SEALs, to take over the ship and guide it to a nearby port. We then call in the international press to observe the cargo of missiles with the Russian writing. It's a win-win. The weapons are prevented from arriving in Lebanon. And we roast the Russians."

The president looked over at the director of Central

Intelligence. "Matthew, don't you have an asset on the ship? Didn't I hear that?"

The DCI looked down at the notes in front of him, then shrugged and glanced at General Frank DuPont who was sitting on a chair against the wall. "General?"

General DuPont stood up. "Yes, indeed, Mr. President. Our agent on board that ship is the same man who discovered and photographed those surface-to-air missiles in the North Korean port of Wonsan. *Clover*, that's the agent's code name, is the radio operator on the ship. He's the one sending out his call sign every fifteen minutes—because our case officer instructed him to do that when they met in Port Said one day ago."

The secretary of defense looked sideways at the DCI. The director of Central Intelligence could only roll his eyes and shrug. Neither had been briefed about the Institute's case officer, Roy Mancini, meeting *Clover* in Port Said.

Those at the table could see the president squint and furrow his brow. "You mean to tell me that if we sink that ship, our agent, the guy who told us about those missiles in the first place, might end up in the drink? And he's also the one pinpointing the target for the *Nautilus* right now?"

The chairman of the Joint Chiefs replied, "Yes, sir, that is correct. He's on board the ship."

"Well, ladies and gentlemen, that isn't going to happen," the president said with emphasis. "Our country doesn't pay back the people who help us by drowning them. I've made up my mind." He turned to the secretary of defense. "William, I am ordering that this matter be handled by the navy SEALs." He turned to the chairman of the Joint Chiefs. "That's plan B, right?"

The four-star general answered, "Yes, sir."

"All right, then." The president turned to the secretary of state. "Which port will the freighter be taken to, Megan? Didn't you mention a friendly country?"

"Sir, I will contact the Israeli Ambassador as soon as this meeting is finished. I'll brief him about the threat and the mission, and request that we bring the ship into one of their ports. After all, the terrorists' target, the airliner, was to take off from Tel Aviv."

"That would be Haifa," the chief of naval operations, stated.

The DCI glanced at the president and said, "We should arrest all the officers on that ship and interrogate them as soon as they arrive in Haifa. I'll interface with Mossad. They can haul the officers off to one of their facilities. The captain of the ship, at the very least, must have known of the plot. Get him to confess and we parade him before the press."

General DuPont cleared his throat and raised a hand. "If I may suggest something about that, Mr. President. Bring the officers, and that must include our agent the radio operator, off the ship and lock them away in prison *before* you call in the international press. We cannot have *Clover* photographed or identified. Wait until they're all behind bars before you summon the press corp."

"That makes good sense, General," the president said. "Matthew, make that happen. The agent's safety is important. Keep *Clover* out of sight."

"Yes, sir." The DCI made a note.

The president stood up. "To reiterate, my order is that the SEALs will arrest the ship and steer it to Haifa. The rest of you can coordinate on how we get the most PR out of it. Let's not waste any more time talking about this. Do what you need to do, and do it now." The president left the room accompanied by his national security advisor.

The chief of naval operations rushed out of the room to the communications center next door. He had an urgent message to encode and transmit to the *USS Nautilus*.

# 43

JULY 1975

THE *NAUTILUS* WAS AT PERISCOPE DEPTH IN THE CALM eastern Mediterranean Sea at 0430 hours local time, forty-five minutes after the president had made his decision. The submarine was 2,000 yards behind the *Eastern Tribute*. Both vessels continued on a northeasterly course.

Twelve navy SEALs loaded weapons, gear, and two rubber boats into the forward escape hatch, the same spot where they had entered the boat two days earlier. One by one the SEALs emerged from the hatch and swam upward to the surface. The sky was dark, and there was no time to lose before daybreak in less than two hours.

The SEALs sped up to the starboard side of the *Eastern Tribute* two and a half minutes after departing from the *Nautilus*. A SEAL aimed and fired a grappling hook. It attached to the ship's rail a short distance behind the ship's superstructure. In seconds two SEALs climbed hand over hand up the hull and landed on the deck of the freighter, M-16s at the ready. Seeing that they were safe, one of the SEALs attached a rope ladder to the ship's railing and let it drop down the side. Within one minute the other ten SEALs were on the deck of the *Eastern Tribute*, covering every direction with their M-16s.

"Go," Lieutenant Sonderstrom said to his men beside him.

At the debriefing in Haifa later that day, Sonderstrom would describe what happened next. "Like taking candy from a baby." The lieutenant was notorious among his men for his tongue-in-cheek utterances of wise guy aphorisms.

The team rushed inside the ship's superstructure where they split up. Three of them went to the wheelhouse where they arrested the ship's duty officer and relieved the helmsman of the wheel. The SEAL who took the helm altered the ship's course to 90 degrees, due east.

"Who are you?" screamed the enraged Arab second mate as he was handcuffed with plastic strips and a hood was placed over his head.

"We're pirates," a black-clad SEAL calmly replied from behind his ski mask. "And we're hijacking your ship and cargo."

Lieutenant Sonderstrom had a diagram outlining the ship's staterooms and offices. As he jogged down a passageway toward the captain's stateroom, he ordered another SEAL to go to the radio room and arrest the radio operator. When he arrived at the captain's quarters, he rapped on the door with the butt of his trench knife.

A tired, heavily accented voice called out, "What do you want? I'm sleeping."

"I want you to open your door within five seconds or I'll open it," Sonderstrom replied. He pointed his M-16 at the lock. The door was yanked open from inside. At first glance the captain appeared furious. His fury changed to wide-eyed fear as he saw the man, clad entirely in black, aiming a semi-automatic rifle at his chest. "Step back inside, shut your mouth, and put your hands behind your back." The Greek captain did as he was told and was soon gagged, handcuffed and tied tightly to his bed.

And so it went. The "pirates" repeated this with all four officers and the radio operator in their staterooms. The SEALs had not received any indication that the Indonesian radio operator was to be treated any differently from the others. Orders were that he too should be arrested along with the captain and deck officers. Most of the ship's crew remained asleep, unaware of the abrupt change of the ship's course. Those who were on watch only knew that their ship had been taken over by pirates, and that cooperation with the heavily armed attackers was the best policy. One of the SEALs re-entered the radio room and signaled on the shortwave set, in a prearranged code, that the *Eastern Tribute* was under U.S. navy control and on its way to Israel: ETA Haifa was 1200 hours. Noontime. The president was informed just before bedtime.

A month and a half later, one morning in mid-September, the *International Herald Tribune,* Paris Edition, reported that a Swiss millionaire ship owner and alleged arms dealer, Rolf Beckmann, had met with a fatal automobile accident while driving on a dark road near his Italian villa on Lake Como. Foul play was suspected.

# 44

---

AUGUST 1975

I LEFT PORT SAID AND FLEW FROM CAIRO TO KUALA
Lumpur without having a clue as to the destiny of
Komang and the *Eastern Tribute*. I had located a television
set in the Cairo airport that was tuned in to the news. There
was no report concerning any unusual activity in the Mediterranean Sea.

Tom Hiatt had told me that he would wait for me in
Malacca. I was anxious to learn if the president had decided
to proceed as, Hiatt had suggested he should—capture each of
the ship's officers and display the missiles on board the ship for
the world to see. Or had the hawks in the NSC prevailed? I
agonized over Komang's fate during that long flight from
Cairo to Malaysia. I had to trust that he'd not ignored my
instruction to keep a life vest close at hand in the event the
ship had been sunk.

As soon as I entered the Majestic Hotel lobby, I smelled
the piquant aroma of Balkan Sobrani tobacco. Tom Hiatt was
sitting alone at a table, smoking his briar pipe and having a

drink. He waved to me when I entered. The smile on his face told me that things had gone our way. I rushed over and sat down beside him. A waiter took my order for a very cold Tiger Beer.

As soon as the waiter walked away, Tom said, "The president did the right thing. I spoke with DuPont earlier today and he informed me that plan B was executed like clockwork. That's all Frank said. All he needed to say."

I was speechless for several moments. I breathed deeply. "Thank God," I exclaimed out loud.

We left the lobby after we had finished our drinks and strolled along the riverside, toward the town center. I was walking on a cloud.

"I don't know any of the details. *Clover* should be in an Israeli prison somewhere. I suspect our Agency people handling the interrogations have been briefed on his innocence."

"How long before he's released?"

"Anyone's guess. We need to protect his identity. Put on a good act. It will have to be handled discretely. We don't want the Greek captain of the ship, or anyone else, to suspect *Clover*'s involvement."

I thought it over. "That captain was in cahoots with the terrorists. He would have collected a lot of money if they'd pulled this off."

"I'd say so. The chief mate would also have known about the cargo loaded in Wonsan. That's his job. And he'd know the destination. *Clover* could be in danger if the bad guys suspect he's the one who foiled their plot."

The two of us walked silently past the old red Dutch buildings, looking to our right for iguanas in the river.

"And, Roy, job well done. A lot of people, the 200 or so

passengers on flight TA310, owe you their lives. That route, Tel Aviv to Athens, is flown by a 747. Let me buy you dinner."

AFTER DINNER IN CHINATOWN, WE STROLLED BACK TO THE hotel.

"Let's talk about *Slugger*," Tom said as we walked back along the river to the hotel. "You're going to have to come up with an escape plan for Popov. An emergency exfiltration."

"Yes. I've been thinking about that. I'm planning to work one out when I get back to Manila."

"You have a 'hello' telephone, right?"

"Yes, of course. *Slugger*'s the only person who knows the number."

"So you don't receive calls on that phone from anyone else?"

"Correct. Not on that second line."

"Then use it for your exfil plan. Come up with a code. When you answer 'hello,' and he states the code words, it means one thing: he knows he's in danger and he needs to get out of town on the double. It means he's been compromised. It happens."

"I'll set it up the next time I see him."

"The second thing you need to know. We're going to run a disinformation ploy through *Slugger*. He'll send fictitious intel back to KGB Center." Tom filled his pipe as we walked. We stopped at the riverside so he could strike a match and light up. "Nothing like a good smoke after a so-so Chinese dinner." We continued our stroll. "Where was I? About disinformation. The Pentagon gurus are planning to concoct information that appears credible. Except that it will be false. You'll feed that to Moscow through *Slugger*."

"Give me an example," I asked, intrigued by the idea and of my participation in the plan.

"I can't be specific. Except that it has to be believable. It will pertain to our navy and air force operations in the Philippines. Intelligence that he would normally obtain from his assets at Subic and Clark."

"Then those agents have to remain in place. We can't allow the Filipinos or our CI people to arrest them."

"You catch on fast." He grinned. "*Slugger* continues to run those agents through the dead drops. We'll doctor the intelligence. There are specialists in the Pentagon who do that kind of thing for a living. We'll send the disinformation back to you, and you pass it on to *Slugger*. He reports it to Moscow Center as if nothing has happened. They swallow the hook, and he gets the praise. And we benefit by sending the Soviets off on the odd wild goose chase."

Hiatt and I did an inventory of *Slugger*'s assets in the Philippines before we reached the hotel. Sasha Popov ran two Filipino agents in Subic Bay who worked in the shipyard overhauling U.S. navy warships. Neither one knew the other. They both submitted reports to *Slugger* twice a month that detailed ship maintenance schedules and general readiness of the fleet. Popov had traveled to Olongapo, the sleazy town beside the base, in a disguise where he assumed the cover of a western beachcomber. He used dead drops—for collection of the Filipinos' information reports and for making his payments to the agents. Both agents were paid $500 a month. Pentagon analysts had determined that the information they provided *Slugger* appeared to be accurate for the most part with minor embellishments. The Institute had allowed those two agents to continue their espionage for the time being—so as not to show our hand.

After recruiting Popov, I had serviced those drops—issued instructions, picked up the agents' reports, and left the payments in their place. And McCoy sanitized *Slugger*'s reports prior to the Russian's transmissions to Moscow Center. Sasha Popov no longer saw his agents' original intelligence reports.

"That sergeant at Clark is a problem, though. The air force generals want him arrested right now. DuPont has so far persuaded the chiefs to let it play out a little longer. We need the disinformation ruse to appear seamless," Hiatt explained, referring to the American at Clark Air Force Base who was selling secrets to the Soviets through *Slugger*.

Sasha, in this case, had traveled to Angeles City, the city outside the huge base, and posed as a western tourist. As he had done in Olongapo, he used dead drops to receive the sergeant's intelligence reports, send him instructions, and pay the venal sergeant $1,000 per month.

And just as in Olongapo, I now serviced the dead drops in Angeles City. McCoy would expunge sensitive intelligence from the reports before they were turned over to *Slugger*, who would forward them on to Moscow.

The American agent was supplying information about U.S. air force flight rotations and planes' maintenance schedules. And the agent had access to copies of top secret air force communications that he had also been passing to *Slugger*. Pulling all that together, the Soviets had known for the past three years how many combat aircraft—jet fighters and bombers—were deployed and combat ready at Clark Air Force Base. The generals were understandably losing patience with the Institute's plan to keep the turncoat in place.

"It's pretty obvious, Tom. If we arrest his assets, there's a good chance *Slugger* will be compromised. That would raise suspicion. His supervisors in Moscow will question him."

"That's true. It's smarter, strategically, that we feed disinformation through *Slugger* rather than arrest the traitors. That's how it works. And we can control his agents, keep them under surveillance, and isolate them. The value of their reports has already been neutralized since we're servicing the drops and sanitizing the reports we give to *Slugger* to forward to Moscow. I can tell you from personal experience, we can string this disinformation game out for a long time."

# 45

APRIL 1976

THE INEVITABLE HAPPENED IN FEBRUARY 1976, SOME seven months after the *Eastern Tribute* heist. The air force generals prevailed. That month the American sergeant who had been providing the Soviets with sensitive, top secret information was quietly transferred to an air force base in Texas. The disinformation campaign had begun soon after my last meeting in Malacca with Tom Hiatt, in August 1975.

The sergeant's bimonthly reports were filed for future legal action, and *Slugger* would transmit reports to the KGB in Moscow that had been manufactured by specialists in the Pentagon. This was a subtle ploy. Enough accurate information was included in those bogus reports so that they would not raise doubt at the KGB or GRU, yet there was enough false intelligence included to deceive the Soviets where it counted. The scam had run smoothly for six months.

We were mistaken in our belief that the KGB, or GRU, would not learn that their agent had been surreptitiously transferred back to the U.S. and secretly charged with treason under the Espionage Act. The Soviets had an asset, a "mole," planted somewhere in the American national security bureaucracy. We suspected that Moscow became witting of the air force sergeant's fate soon after he was arrested, charged, speedily convicted, and imprisoned. Our disinformation became implausible sometime after February. As *Slugger* had predicted on the day I recruited him, twelve months earlier, "the shit had hit the fan."

The "hello" phone rang seven times that day in April before I answered it. The precise number of rings was set to change every day so *Slugger* could be sure it was I answering the phone. There were never fewer than six rings, never more than thirteen.

"Hello," I said after the seventh ring.

"Surf is up in Marinduque." His voice was calm, no sense of duress or panic.

I had set up the emergency exfiltration protocol with Sasha eight months earlier, in August, soon after my Port Said mission, and the same month he had begun sending the disinformation reports to Moscow.

I had devised two levels of urgency. His comment after I answered the phone would indicate Sasha's sense of danger and how quickly and by which method he needed to flee the Philippines. At level one, exfiltration through the Manila airport on a commercial airliner was still feasible. The second level, the one where he states, "Surf is up in Marinduque," meant matters had come to the point of no return, an exit through the airport was no longer an option.

"Copy," I replied and hung up the phone.

I called Sergeant Dubrowski.

"Military Sealift Command. May I help you?"

"Ski, Roy. I need to speak with the boss. Urgent."

Steve McCoy came on the line. I glanced at my watch. It was 4:20 in the afternoon.

"Hello, Roy. What's up?"

"*Wolverine* level two. Repeat. *Wolverine* level two," I said.

He paused for a second. "Copy that." We hung up. The code indicated that we had a critical situation on our hands. *Slugger* needed to exfiltrate the Philippines through the back door. Popov and McCoy had never met each other. They soon would. But first Steve McCoy would make a phone call to the U.S. navy Commander at Subic Bay.

At around the same time I phoned McCoy, Sasha Popov was making his escape through a second story window at the FESCO office in the Port Area. While the Russian escort sat in his office, he excused himself, claiming he needed to go to the toilet. Once inside the bathroom, he locked the door with a deadbolt. He then fastened the loop end of a one-inch thick, 20' length of Manila rope to a makeshift cleat he had secured to the wall behind the toilet. He tossed the length of rope out the open window. The opening was just large enough for him to squeeze through. He shimmied down the wall, hand over hand, until he was able to drop to the ground. From there he ran through a garbage-strewn back alley and cut between buildings. Once out of the Port Area, he hailed one of the many taxicabs passing along Bonifacio Drive.

THE GAUCHO BAR WAS TWO BLOCKS FROM THE MANILA Yacht Club, on Roxas Boulevard. It was a nightclub, and as I expected there were few customers there in the afternoon. McCoy arrived first, carrying a small roller suitcase. Two minutes later Popov entered the bar. Neither one knew or recognized the other, so they sat at separate tables and waited for me. I arrived five minutes later and motioned to them to join me at a back table. Steve was wearing civilian clothes. I introduced him to Sasha as "Billy" from the embassy.

The reason I'd arrived later than the other two was because of the preparations I'd needed to make. I had first phoned the yacht club and asked the manager to page our boat boy, Juanito. After an anxious ten-minute wait, Juanito came on the line. I asked him to rig *Jambalaya* for me because I was going sailing that evening with friends. He would attach the mainsail and the jib, and he'd be sure the spinnaker was inside the boat. I'd packed two warm jackets and two pairs of topsider sailing shoes in a bag. I had determined Sasha's shoe size weeks earlier.

I looked inside McCoy's case and saw that he had brought the marine radio, a battery pack, and a powerful flashlight. Popov had only the clothes he was wearing.

"Have you ever been sailing, Sasha?" I asked. I gave him a reassuring smile.

"Once or twice when I was a kid in Leningrad. Why?" A sullen expression marked his face.

"Because you're about to crew for me on a very fast racing sloop."

He'd assumed I had a plan for this contingency, though he had never known what it involved. He'd had no need to know until now.

"Oh yeah, who are we racing against?"

"Time," I answered. "You can explain to me what's caused us to go to panic stations when we're on the boat. Are you positive no one followed you here?"

"I'm sure. There were two of them in the snatch team. I left one in my office when I made my getaway. The other one's at my home, keeping an eye on Ingrid." His brow creased at the thought.

"Will Ingrid be okay with this? Your departure?" I asked, not yet knowing exactly what was happening and why Sasha and possibly Ingrid were at risk. He glanced at McCoy and shrugged without answering.

I asked Sasha to remain seated, motioning to Steve to follow me to another table at the opposite end of the room. We needed to talk.

"Were you able to contact Subic?" I knew he had a closely held, unlisted phone number at the naval base for just this occasion.

"I did. And with luck you're set to go. The USS Ranger has a couple of its escorts docked up there. The base commander had to refer to an encoded message he'd received from the CNO's office a few months ago. He got back to me and confirmed that a destroyer will get underway before midnight. I told him they should look for you tomorrow morning west of Lubang Island. It'll be dark out there. There's no moon. You'd better make a move."

I stood up, signaled for Sasha to join us, and grabbed hold of the suitcase Steve had brought with him. "Well then, wish us luck," I said. Popov and McCoy nodded to each other without speaking. Steve left first so that he could watch our backs. A minute later Sasha and I left the bar and crossed Roxas Boulevard for the short two-block jog to the Manila Yacht Club.

# 46

---

THE BARROOM AT THE YACHT CLUB WAS FILLING UP with an early after-work crowd. I greeted a couple of rum-drinking Dragon skippers with a wave. Juanito was standing at the small landing below the clubhouse, waiting for me. The club's outboard motor boat was tied at the dock. It would bring us out to *Jambalaya* at the mooring. Juanito took the suitcase from me, and the three of us hopped into the boat. "Will I sail with you, Roy?" the Filipino asked me. Sasha maintained a poker face at the mention of my name ... Roy.

"Not today, Juanito. We might be out late tonight. You can go home after you take us to the boat. I'll put away the sails when I return. And thanks for getting the boat rigged and ready."

"No problem, sir. I'll see you on Saturday." Juanito delivered us to *Jambalaya*, and Sasha and I stepped aboard the sloop. Juanito waved and drove the motorboat back to the dock.

Sasha sat in the cockpit and looked at me. He gave me an ironic chuckle. "And now what?"

"Now we leave Manila behind us. Go up to the mast and raise the mainsail." I pointed to the halyard that ran down from the top of the mast. Sasha moved quickly, raised the sail, and then cleated the halyard as I pointed the boat into the wind.

"Cast off." I pointed to the lines attached to a cleat at the bow. Sasha leaped forward and threw the lines off the boat and onto the round mooring.

"Nicely done, sailor. Care to crew for me someday after you get to California?" As I unfurled the jib, I grinned at him in an effort to make light of the perilous situation he was in. This was the first time any mention had been made of a future in America.

"Now, Sasha, you'd better explain to me why we're here in a forty-seven-year-old wooden sailboat on Manila Bay making a dash for the South China Sea."

"The two guys in the snatch team arrived undercover as diplomatic couriers at 6:30 this morning. Ingrid was in bed. I was sitting on the toilet, you know. The maid, damn fool, let them in. They did a quick search downstairs and upstairs, and when they got to our bedroom they ordered Ingrid to get up and get dressed. I listened to these two thugs from the bathroom. It was no mystery what was going on. The game was up."

I trimmed the sails and we heeled on a fresh southwest breeze, racing out of the anchorage and past the breakwater. I asked Sasha to sit up on the high side of the boat.

He continued. "When I entered the bedroom, they ordered me to sit down on the bed. They had Ingrid sitting on a chair at her dressing table, wearing a negligee. No need to frisk me. I was wearing briefs. Funny thing is, I knew one of the thugs. We'd worked together on body snatches years ago in Hungary. The asshole laughed at me now."

"Why were you burned?" I asked, keeping my eyes on the jib telltales to make sure we were making maximum speed toward the setting sun.

"Because you nincompoops arrested my agent at Clark. Here I am sending bullshit reports to Moscow Center that are supposed to be coming from that fucking sergeant. And he's not there anymore. What do you think? You can fool some of the people all of the time ... how does it go?" I ignored his reference to Abraham Lincoln's aphorism.

I said in a barely audible voice, "His transfer was top secret. How could they know?"

"We have assets. Someone inside tipped off his arrest. As you Americans like to say, the rest is history. And here we are." He looked out at the bay and at the last of the ships at anchor. "What are we going to do?"

I ignored his question. "How did you get away? Escape?"

"They told me they were going to escort me to Moscow on a flight this afternoon. Some nonsense about a summons to a high-level meeting back home that I needed to attend. God only knows what will happen to Ingrid," he said with a worried frown. "One of them, the one I recognized, rode with me to my office so that I could collect material in my safe. I told them those documents would compromise the KGB if they were found by the Americans. They were reluctant, but I was persuasive. Ingrid, she sat and glared at me the whole time, not knowing what was going on. One of them stayed with her. And this guy took me to my office and never let me out of his sight, so I said I had to go to the toilet, take a poop.

He tells me to leave the bathroom door wide open. I told him to get fucked and locked myself in before he could stop me. I'd installed a private phone inside the bathroom soon after I started working with you. So I called you with that code about surfing in Marinduque, then made my escape down a rope. I started planning for this two months ago when you fools arrested my agent at Clark." His eyes continued to bore into mine. "You know, I didn't just fall off the turnip truck. I've been in this game a long, long time, Cisco. Or is it Roy?"

The sun would set soon. I was sailing west, almost directly at the large red ball just above the horizon. The sky ahead was changing from a dark blue to a chiaroscuro of reds, blues, oranges, and yellows. The wind continued to blow hard enough so we could beat upwind without having to tack. The island of Corregidor was ahead of us, some fifteen miles distant. We watched as inbound passenger ships from the southern islands sailed past us.

In less than thirty minutes it would be dark. Our Dragons had no running lights since we only raced them during the day. So I had brought along the powerful flashlight Steve had packed. We would have to use that to signal to any large ships or craft that approached too close.

"Now you tell me what you have planned for us tonight. The curiosity is going to kill me," Sasha said loud enough to be heard above the wind.

There was no point in keeping it secret any longer. "A U.S. navy ship will meet us in the middle of the ocean."

There was a long silence as Sasha stared at me with an anxious look. "And?"

"And we transfer you to the ship and to safety. I've promised you, remember, a new identity, a ticket to the States.

That's how the game is played, right? They'll want to interview you."

"You mean interrogate me, don't you?"

"Just cooperate with them, Sasha, and you'll be fine."

"All about *bona fides,* isn't it?"

"I suppose it is."

Sasha hesitated for a long time before speaking. The sun was now dropping below the horizon, behind Corregidor Island. Soon it would be pitch-dark with only the lights on the island and on the occasional passing ship to guide me. I had not brought a compass. The course was a straight shot to the west before falling off slightly somewhere beyond Lubang Island. If all went as planned, we would rendezvous with a navy ship southwest of Lubang.

"Well, I want to tell you something, then, before we part. Because we'll never meet each other again. And I think you ought to know."

"I'm listening, Sasha."

"Ingrid and I are not married to each other."

I looked at him sharply. "Why am I only hearing this now?" I asked. I recalled the awkward dinner at Casa Verde. And about my doubts then.

"She's KGB. The First Directorate believed that my cover would be more convincing to your people if I appeared to live in Manila with a wife. Ingrid and I have known each other for fifteen years. We've been lovers off and on, whenever I've been posted back in Moscow. Most of her career has been at the Center." He paused for a second. "Her jealousy over Flora was no act, though. She hated me for that. Beyond that, it was all a masquerade."

"That's all she did there? She's along for the ride to

pretend to be your wife, to enhance your shipping manager cover?"

Sasha gave a sharp laugh and slapped a hand on his leg. "Ingrid's a honey-trap. She's having regular sex with two assets. One of them is the military attaché at your embassy. Don't tell his wife." He chuckled at my surprise. "The other one is a Filipino playboy, a deputy in Marcos's defense department. She targeted him because he's the liaison with the American military. She meets them at a safe house in Makati. An apartment. They both think she's French. Neither one knows *yet* that their sex scenes are being filmed. Both are ripe for compromise."

"What will happen now? To Ingrid?"

"She'll be a suspect. They'll take her back to Moscow. Probably on their way now. And they'll interrogate her. It won't be pleasant. She'll suffer. You see, they'll believe that she and I were *both* working for the Americans. I could tell by the way those two gorillas treated her this morning. I feel bad about this. I love Ingrid."

We were abeam of Corregidor Island and the Dragon was in perfect trim. The wind had lightened somewhat, reducing the heel of the boat. As we cut through the darkness, leaving Manila Bay behind and entering the South China Sea, the boat seemed to be sailing itself with only slight adjustments. Sasha was silent and appeared content in his own private reverie. It gave me time to think. And my mind turned to my friends, Komang and Putu, and to their home in Bali.

THE OFFICERS ON THE *EASTERN TRIBUTE*, INCLUDING Komang, had been arrested by the navy SEALs when the ship was in the Mediterranean Sea. A SEAL took the helm and steered the vessel to the port of Haifa. The Israeli Mossad, along with a CIA contingent, were waiting for the ship in Haifa. The Agency spooks were informed beforehand about *Clover*'s role in the heist. To maintain Komang's cover in the operation, he was to accompany the rest of the ship's officers to the secret facility, located somewhere in the Negev desert. As far as I knew, which wasn't much at this point, the Greek captain and his junior officers were still incarcerated and incommunicado, some nine months after their arrest. The captain and chief mate, motivated by greed, had been accomplices in the shipment of those Soviet surface-to-air missiles to the DFLP.

Komang had acted out the charade of being interrogated along with the others. An Agency case officer informed him quietly at the beginning of the ordeal that it was all for show, so that he would not be a suspect in the eyes of the DFLP terrorists or their Soviet KGB sponsors. At the time, the DFLP was a wholly owned subsidiary of the KGB. It would not pay for either organization to become suspicious of Komang. They both had a long reach.

Komang had been released in October, after spending over two months of his life in the rat- and scorpion-infested prison.

I traveled to Bali, and to Amed in November. By then, Komang and Putu had gone to Denpasar to withdraw money from their bank account. They were shocked when they found that in addition to the regular payments of $2,000 a month they had been receiving from the Institute, and which had remained untouched, there was a one-time deposit of $100,000 from Haig & Company of Hong Kong—a bonus for the couples' critical role in averting the disaster over the Mediterranean Sea.

I had been apprehensive about this rendezvous in Amed. I wasn't sure that Komang would not hold me responsible for the foul treatment he had received those two months in that wretched desert prison. He could rightly blame me for not being on the level with him when we met on the beach in Port Said. I had only warned him that he must keep a life vest close by. He had not known of plan A. And he never would.

They greeted me in Amed like an old friend, with their warm smiles. Putu looked as lovely and juvenescent as ever, and Komang had a fresh appearance due to his happiness at being home at last. The large, unexpected sum of money in their account had salved his wounds. And the experience over the past months had given him a story, as he explained it to me, to tell his children one day. I recommended he keep the tale secret for a while longer.

I asked Komang if he had been serious about obtaining a Green Card and moving to the United States. I told him I could arrange that if he wanted me to.

He and Putu looked at each other for a moment after I asked the question. "No, Cisco, we don't think so. I'm happy to be back in Bali." He pointed in the direction of the beach and the calm sea. "This is home and it's where we belong, and where we want to stay. Because of our money in the bank, I can build some boats now and own a small fishing fleet."

"Who could blame you, Komang? You and Putu live in paradise."

They both nodded their agreement. "You know, I've seen a lot of the world over the past two years," Komang continued. "There's no place like this." They were holding hands.

I said in English, "No place like home." They understood.

I suggested they apply for a license for the shortwave set. Komang said he would do that. He would tell the authorities that he bought the radio to keep in contact with his planned fleet of fishing boats.

The three of us spent four days snorkeling over the coral beds in the clear warm blue-green sea off Amed and dining in the evenings on fresh tuna steaks and bottles of *Bintang* beer. I even joined Komang once on Nyoman's fishing boat. We spent the night far out at sea, catching tuna and barracuda. Beneath the stars I listened to the two men speak to each other in their unintelligible Balinese language.

# 47

---

SASHA POPOV BROKE INTO MY THOUGHTS. "YOU know," he said. "I've been thinking about something."

I glanced up at him. He'd been sitting on the windward side of the boat. I sat on the lower, leeward side, a habit of mine from racing the Dragon. We were now well into the South China Sea. Before long I would fall off onto a reach when I saw lights on Lubang Island.

"What's on your mind, Sasha?"

"I should mention something I learned during my months in Moscow, when I taught at our American language and culture school."

I nodded and kept my eyes on the mainsail and the wind indicator at the top of the mast.

"When the Center was briefing me for my mission, targeting your navy with the agents at Subic Bay, I heard a rumor. Maybe you call it gossip, right?"

"Yeah, rumors. Gossip. What was it about?"

"Well, I was taking a break from a briefing session when I ran into an old friend, one of our senior case officers who had recently returned to Moscow from Washington. He was on holiday. And he was curious about my mission because it involved the United States navy. He said a colleague of his in America was running a high-level secret agent there. Then he tells me this is far too sensitive for him to discuss and he changes the subject. Of course, that made me curious. I badger him a little bit, take him out for a drink or two . . . or three. A lot of drinks actually.

"Finally he opens up and tells me that one of our case officers has been running an American, a navy chief warrant officer, for the past five years. He is a communications specialist at the Atlantic submarine headquarters in Norfolk. The American is passing our embassy the U.S. navy's *crown jewels*, as he put it. This guy is selling your navy's most secret codes to us. The thing is, he tells me, having those encrypted codes without the machines was only half good enough. So the Kremlin ordered the North Koreans to capture your intelligence ship, remember the *USS Pueblo*, in 1968. That is the same year your American sailor started selling us the codes."

I leaned in closer.

"The North Koreans arrested the *Pueblo* and hauled it into Wonsan. As soon as the ship arrived, the Koreans removed the encryption machines and delivered them to Moscow. The puzzle is now complete. He tells me that we have everything we need to read your navy's top secret communications. You better hope we never launch World War III. Amazing, huh?"

"You *must* bring that up when they interview you, Sasha. Don't forget." I stared at him for several seconds.

"Interrogate me."

"Look, we're working together. There will be someone on the ship who wants to have a chat with you. Same when you arrive in the States. You're one of us now. You made that choice yesterday." I had my doubts whether Sasha believed that.

MY CONTACT REPORT LATER THAT WEEK INCLUDED Sasha's stories about Ingrid's "honey-trap" role and the navy traitor. I didn't hear anything about either case and assumed my report had been lost in the shuffle. Much later I learned the Institute's analysts suspected that Popov's tale of a *USS Pueblo*/navy spy connection was apocryphal. And an issue was never made of Ingrid. She had departed the Philippines with her Russian escorts the same day as Sasha.

We can assume that Ingrid's paramour, the military attaché at the embassy, was transferred to a place like Alaska, if he was lucky. And we now know that Chief Warrant Officer John Walker continued to spy for the KGB for another eight years, until his arrest in 1984.

"I want Flora to join me in America," Sasha said a minute later. "That's the main thing now. I'll be happy then."

"I'll see what I can do. Maria knows how to contact her."

"Yeah. It means a lot to me. See if you can arrange it."

"Right. That's a promise. I'll run it through my people."

"Thanks, friend."

Two hours after sunrise we approached the small island off the western tip of Lubang Island. I sailed clear of the islands and continued southwest, further into the South China Sea.

Soon I began transmitting on the battery-powered radio. The prearranged plan was for me to broadcast on channel 13. I spoke the word "*Jambalaya*" over and over into the mic, and I asked Sasha to keep his eyes peeled for a warship on the horizon as I began my calls.

At 9:10, sixteen hours after we had hoisted our mainsail at the yacht club, the guided missile destroyer *USS Goldsborough* DDG-20, twenty miles west of Lubang Island, responded by radio to *Jambalaya*.

"I think I see it," Sasha shouted. He had been standing at the mast, searching for a ship.

I stood up and stretched forward. "That looks like the one. Hand me the flashlight. It's down below." He jumped down into the cabin and handed me the light. "Here goes." I pointed the light at the navy ship and sent the code for *Jambalaya*. The destroyer signaled back: *Goldsborough*. And now for the first time, I tacked the boat and sailed straight for the warship, as if she were a racing mark. The distance between us closed quickly.

"We might as well say goodbye now, Sasha. You're going to be real busy in a few minutes. Can you swim?" I tried to make light of our farewell.

"Wish me luck, Cisco, or whatever your name is." He smirked. "Don't forget about Flora."

"You got it. I'll keep track of your whereabouts, if I can."

"You won't be able to do that. It's not the way the game is played. I'm going to disappear." A weary smile creased his face. "Keep swinging. It's been fun." With his fingers he pantomimed playing a few notes on a trumpet before turning his back.

Navy sailors dropped a rubber boat into the sea between the ship and the Dragon. Sasha hopped into the boat, gave me a brief wave, and was hauled over to the *Goldsborough*. I tacked the Dragon around 180 degrees, raised the spinnaker, and sailed downwind to Manila Bay. I arrived back at the yacht club just before 3:00 a.m. the next day. May Day. I never saw Sasha Popov again.

# ACKNOWLEDGMENTS

---

A great big thank you to my editor *extraordinaire*, Jean Jenkins. Her eagle eye and sage advice have been invaluable. I am lucky to have met her at the Southern California Writers Conference.

You would not be holding this book in your hands if it were not for Stacey Aaronson. Stacey did the work required to get this novel published in a form that rivals the quality of a conventionally published book. She is an independent author's best friend.

You can tell a book by its cover. And I have Bespoke Book Covers in the U.K. to thank. Peter has been great to work with.

And many thanks to my lifelong friend, Dorothy Ingebretsen, for her sharp-eyed proofreading.

My mother, Meri Swafford, read my complete manuscript twice. She provided valuable critique when it counted. Just one more reason among so many where I owe her my heartfelt thanks.

And my wife, Des, has been my guide regarding the ins and outs of social media, and all things Indonesia.

# ABOUT THE AUTHOR

STANTON SWAFFORD was born in Los Angeles and grew up along the beaches of Southern California. He attended the University of Colorado and the University of the Philippines, where he majored in economics and Asian Studies. He speaks Indonesian, Tagalog, and Mandarin Chinese.

Stanton served aboard submarines in the United States Navy during the Cold War era, one of which was the *USS Nautilus*, the world's first nuclear submarine. During his period living, working, and playing in Southeast Asia—in the Philippines, Singapore, Malacca, Malaysia, and Bali, Indonesia—he operated undercover as an intelligence officer, ran a timber export company, and performed throughout the region as a jazz musician. His debut novel, *China Sea*, portrays a plot and settings derived from that experience.

Stanton is an avid tennis player and sailor, as well as a self-taught musician who continues to play piano and lead his jazz band, the Blue Notes. He lives in Southern California with his wife and son, Louie.

www.asianaffairsblog.com
www.Facebook.com/SASwafford

www.ingramcontent.com/pod-product-compliance
Lightning Source LLC
Chambersburg PA
CBHW032140190626
46814CB00005BA/1774